"I used to die, back when it was illegal."

Stone grunted. "An ar-teest." Then his eyes grew wide with recognition. "You're Lydia Melmuth!"

"Mel*moth*," Frankly corrected.

"Wow!" Stone said. "I never saw you die but my brother did, in DC. Claims you were the best. Used to carry a Polaroid of your corpse in his butt pocket."

What I feel is a rush, a thrill. I don't *want* to like fame, but I do.

Dear Reader:

Just a moment of your time could earn you $1,000! We're working hard to bring you the best books, and to continue to do that we need your help. Simply turn to the back of this book, and let us know what you think by answering seven important questions.

Return the completed survey with your name and address filled in, and you will automatically be entered in a drawing to win $1,000, subject to the official rules.

Good luck!

Geoff Hannell

Geoff Hannell
Publisher

VIRTUAL
DEATH

VIRTUAL
DEATH

SHALE AARON

HarperPrism
An Imprint of HarperPaperbacks

This is a work of fiction. The characters, incidents, and
dialogues are products of the author's imagination and are
not to be construed as real. Any resemblance to actual
events or persons, living or dead, is entirely coincidental.

HarperPaperbacks *A Division of* HarperCollins*Publishers*
                         10 East 53rd Street, New York, N.Y. 10022

Cover illustration by Peter Gudynas

First printing: August 1995

Printed in the United States of America

HarperPrism is an imprint of HarperPaperbacks.
HarperPaperbacks, HarperPrism, and colophon are
trademarks of HarperCollins*Publishers*

❖ 10 9 8 7 6 5 4 3 2 1

For T. J. & N.

PART

1

Above the buildings that lined the tracks, a narrow throat of purple sky held a discontinuous string of clouds, which shone pink in the dying light, like sutures in a bruise. I touched my own throat, goose-pimpled from the cold, a single vein throbbing against my fingertips, then I shoved my fists in the slender pockets of my skirt and leaned against a light pole on the concrete platform. The pole held an umbrella of fluorescent lamps whose light turned my skin a pale green.

Frankly Adams, my best friend and roommate, lingered on the station's open deck beside me. We had no destination ourselves, but waited for the arrival of my brother, who had fallen into some kind of trouble, the kind of trouble that could not be discussed over the phone. The delay had me worried.

"Lydia," Frankly said, turning from the digital train schedule, "you're out of your mind." He said this as if it were listed on the schedule: *4:15 Lydia Melmoth wigs out.*

"Hush," I said.

"It's your chance to be somebody again," Frankly went on. "Everything important you do happens a long time ago." Frankly was a Nowist and refused to speak in the past tense. "I sell my mother for a chance like this."

"They don't want your mother," I told him.

Earlier, the crowd at the station had boiled in readiness, 1 head and then another bubbling up, peering into the vacant distance. But now, the train 2 hours late, Frankly and I stood alone on the expanse of lacquered concrete, looking alternately at the darkening sky and the long stretch of tracks. Each held the future, I thought, the tracks vibrating with the remote promise of train, the sky coloring with inevitable darkness. I had reached that point where worry turned to boredom.

Beneath my feet, polished pebbles embedded in the lacquer sparkled in the light. I imagined this as the past—shiny particles glued together, which, under a spray of artificial light, possessed a certain kind of beauty.

What, then, of the present? I wondered. Where was the present?

Vending machines, crowded together in a row, provided a windbreak. They dispensed candy, condoms, combs, and disposable guns. A cold blow whistled through the gaps, sending a swell of greasy pistol wrappers tumbling past my boots.

Frankly hugged himself and began hopping. Fully erect, in his bare feet, he reached the height of a 3rd grader. He hopped to be taller—a leftover trait from an old act. For 3 years he worked as a stand-up depressionist, his last stint more than a year past. The routines slept within him, waking occasionally to anoint the ears of strangers with his professional misery, or to send him hopping around a train station. "Plus they pay you a thousand bills," he said, poking my arm at the crest of a hop. "How can you sneeze at a thousand bucks?"

"Blackout," I said. "I'm not going."

Among the dedicated, the dying addicts, the serious Morbids, I still reigned—the Living Angel, the Mistress of Death, the Queen of Dying. By my 18th birthday, I had died 7 times—a record that still stood, almost 20 years later. My display in the Hall of Dying Fame proclaimed me "Lydia Melmoth, the Original Genius of Dying." The buzzbox beneath my photo announced my accomplishments: "7 verifiables. All zer0-beat/zer0-hums. No discernible gray rot." In the photo I'm a teenager smiling the old lowers-only snarl—the big fad back then, stupid-looking now. I had visited the Hall only once, disguised and alone, both thrilled and embarrassed at the celebration of my past.

This weekend a boy named Qigley would attempt to surpass my record—*our* record; he had tied me last August before thousands of spectators and a national television audience. Qigley had the half-mouth most dying artists got, which caused the stutter the kids imitated; otherwise, his head held together well—no obvious gray rot, 7 deaths and counting.

As for me, I had only an eye-twitch now and again. No neurological business. I had excelled at the craft of dying. A professor at Emory University wanted to study me, to isolate a biological factor that let me come and go easily. "I don't want to be known as a dying queen anymore," I'd told him when I turned him down. "And I don't ever want to be known as a lab rat."

Quintessential Broadcasting Network had requested I attend the record-breaking die in Filadelfia to do an interview. "Just yak about the old-timey days," the QBN girl had said over the phone. "Nothing major. Little lip service 'bout Cops, danger. We'll pay you a grand, plus tickets to the show."

I died before it was legal—in illicit bars, at the homes of patrons, once in the middle of the night in a public park. No 1 had ever paid me to die—to take money for it amounted to selling out. All of us felt that way back then.

I last died the year men were growing Grizzlies, those grotesque on-the-neck-only beards. The cartoon adventures of Fuffy the Slipper had the kids temporarily enthralled, and Velma rOOst had just debuted her now world-celebrated bosom. My dying belonged to that time, that part of history, while my current self, I hoped, belonged to the present.

Frankly had once had some fame himself. He had played several of the stand-up depression clubs in Manhattan. But his misery revolved around his height. When the country elected as President J. S. "Stumpy" Gallion, Frankly found himself out of a job. Short no longer sold.

Afternoon turned to evening. A layer of clouds moved in, making the sky close, turning it the gray of pencil smudge, like a bad erasure. The distant pop of neighborhood gunfire punctuated the constant whoosh of wind, a tuneless melody like Arbitrary Real Rhapsody, the antiArt music that had briefly dominated the radio. I hated artistic pretension—although not enough to dress unfashionably. I had on an angle-cut houndstooth print jacket and matching skirt, a zebra-stripe leotard beneath it. The skirt barely reached midthigh, and my legs nubbled and ached from the cold. I took consolation in reminding myself that I looked good, that Frankly had told me I could pass for late 20s. But why would I want to appear anything but my real age? Whenever I tried to worry through my relationship to the prevailing culture, I got lost, could not tell what existed outside my head and what originated in my own skull. Even my considering it all seemed fashionable.

"Your brother doesn't remember me whenever we meet," Frankly said now, sounding almost sad about it.

"He remembers you," I said. "He just doesn't like you."

"Same thing," Frankly insisted. "He forgets me from the very start. Like you forget what it is to be successful, so you aren't going to this die."

"Oh, give it up, will you?"

What I couldn't make Frankly understand was how much dying disrupted my life. It appeared simple. The dying artist was given Ater—1 whiff caused instant death—then the rescue crew fit the Accu Shock/Retrieval unit over the artist's chest. The Accu was shaped like a huge gray butterfly, with levers like wings that ignited the shock. Early on, the crew also administered mouth-to-mouth, but the practice was abandoned; people wanted to see the artist's face the whole time she was dead. It looked simple, but dying worked strange tricks on daily life. It made me weirdly distracted, made me forget things—not where I put my keys or how to program my refrigerator, but how to go about having a romance, or what it was I had planned to do with my life. Things like that.

The digital marquee started flashing: sniper alert downtown/air quality sub-ephemeral/train 3 minutes from station. Snow began to fall, brown and fluffy, spiderlike.

"I should have worn hose," I told Frankly, but he was examining the "1-Shot" disposable gun machines. The company sold condoms under the same name. "Tacky," I said.

"This is good material for a routine," Frankly said, fingering the change slots, "but it doesn't depress me." He shook his big head at his unfortunate contentment. In 1 of his routines he had measured heads in the audience to prove his own normal in size. "I have the cranium of a man 6 feet tall," he would say, then produce a curved mirror that made him look that height, his head perfectly proportioned in the reflection.

"Smoke," Frankly said suddenly, turning from the machines, pointing. The dark exhaust of the train appeared over the tops of the nearest buildings.

"Finally," I said, thinking, *The future is a train*. I could almost see it coming.

The train arrived with the piercing screech of brakes, a black haze of smoke, and a corrosive odor. Now and then I felt nostalgic for the technoPast, the way things had been before the InfoTechno Collapse, and never more so than when smelling a stinking new train. The Collapse had happened 20 years ago, long enough past that I didn't think much about it. A temporary pause, most people had predicted back then, a technological respite—which had now lasted 2 decades. Except for a few aging Rads, people hardly considered it at all anymore. A fact of life, like television, taxes, IT.

The sliding doors opened as the train shrugged to a halt, a torrent of people pouring out. Several carried guns. Frankly offered the traditional hands-over-head gesture, but I merely smiled and hoped they weren't lunatics. Hundreds of people flooded past, but my brother Stamen did not appear.

"Son of a prick," Frankly said.

While I searched the faces of the people remaining on the landing, the conductor, a black man with hamburger sideburns, grabbed my elbow. "Lidya Melmouth?"

"Moth," Frankly said. "Mel*moth*."

The conductor ignored him. "I got a package for you from your brother." He waved a fat manila envelope and puckered his lips dramatically. "He said you'd give me a 20 tip."

"Nobody gets a 20 tip," Frankly said. "Stamen doesn't say this."

The conductor pulled a folded scrap of paper from the vest pocket of his uniform and handed it to me. The note looked authentic. My brother had the magisterial penmanship of a life-long bureaucrat.

Lydia,
Give him a 20 if the envelope's seal is intact.
Patience,
Stamen

The conductor clutched the package firmly as he displayed it, his face changing expression, as if each corner of the envelope caused a new emotion.

"You have any money?" I asked Frankly, who hopped fiercely beside me, pretending not to hear. "Stop it," I said. "He's not that tall."

Frankly glared at me. I wasn't supposed to reveal the secrets of his personality. "You are paying me back tonight," he said, and shoved a bill at the conductor.

"Nowists are cheap," the conductor said, handing over the package. "They think the past is gonna cost 'em a few bucks." His whole face smuckered at this, as if to underline its wisdom.

"Did my brother give you this personally?" I asked him.

"If he's a 10-foot light pole, not a ounce of meat on him, gray as concrete."

"That's him," Frankly said.

"He's a little pale," I said, "but he's only 6-6."

"Fellow who gave me this was at least 8 feet tall. Weighed 'bout a pound. Pinhead."

"That's him," Frankly said.

"Did he say why he couldn't come himself?" I asked.

The conductor's eyes squeezed shut, his whole face squished together. "All he said was if I wanted a 20 tip I should take this envelope to Lidya Melmouth."

"Moth!" Frankly said. "Mel*moth*."

"Did he look all right? My brother?" I asked.

"I already told you he looked like the sort of thing you stick a fuse in and light."

"He doesn't say that," Frankly said.

"You mean I *didn't* say that, you little bulb."

"The past tense is a lie," Frankly said.

"*Dim* bulb," the conductor said. "Watt and a half."

"Thanks," I said.

The conductor frowned happily. "For a 20, I'da brought you a coffin."

A few people now loitered on the platform, standing in line to use the new bank of pay phones. I led

VIRTUAL DEATH   1 1

Frankly into the men's room. Although relatively clean—only the soles of our shoes became soaked—Frankly held his nose and tucked his head under his arm to inhale his deodorant. He could not stand the smell of natural odors. A single rose could make him puke. The condition carried a popular psychological label, but I simply thought Frankly a ploW, a wimp, a washrag. I liked that he had this weakness. Strong people made me nervous.

The package held a book, an actual paper-n-print book, *I Am A Big Man Not* by Iglesia Smith, and another note.

Lydia,
Danger everywhere. Take care. Have patience.
Something's up. Real danger. I mean it.
Sincerely Yours,
Stamen.

My stomach tensed and swooped. "Read this," I said, giving the note to Frankly as I sloshed across the room. My distorted image in the bathroom's metal mirror reflected they way I felt—gray, scarred, and slightly warped. My brother, whatever his faults, was not an alarmist. I took a deep breath and held it to calm myself.

"You want to watch me pee?" Frankly asked.

"Pass," I said. "Stamen's in real trouble, I think."

"Hey," Frankly said, "look at this." Paging through the book, his nose still aimed toward his pit, he discovered a 20-dollar bill, which he shoved into his pocket. "This is serious," he said. "Otherwise, he doesn't include the 20."

We headed for our subway stop. Snow turned our

hair a ratty brown. My calves grew numb, which made me think again about the stupidity of fashion, the stupidity of my own life. By the time my mother had reached 37, she had already made a real life for herself, already given birth to 2 children, already lost a husband. Now, Mother had gone dual, a secret so deep I had told no 1 but Frankly. She still rambled around Cleveland like always, but she had a 2nd identity in the Banjo Society. I couldn't help but think that Stamen's trouble was connected to Mother's alter ego.

I carefully followed Frankly down the icy stairs that led to the bowels of Pummel Street. The subterranean station held a garish crowd of people, many of them only pretending to wait for the train, hoping to spend the night out of the snow in the relative warmth of the underground. The subway arrived with the same screech as the other train, carried the same retro smell.

"What *is* that stink?" I said.

Frankly breathed in deeply and smiled. "That's the odor of love," he said. He wasn't kidding. He liked it.

My apartment, a single room in the Lockview Building, I had decorated in cotton, an expensive act of self-expression I had undertaken during a fleeting period of gainful employment. Cotton walls had become passé, but nobody came to see me anyway. I had imagined a certain kind of life for myself, 1 involving dinner parties, swank bars, occasional overpriced hotel rooms, and trips to dry cleaners. Instead, I had muddled along, constantly busy, continually bored, a harried, uneventful life.

Eventually my employers fired me—not for my miserable social skills, but it might as well have been.

I had created a life for myself—an imaginative project much like the ones I had created in school—but then I failed my own exams.

The cotton wallpaper I still liked, a houndstooth print identical to my outfit. Frankly cringed the 1st time he saw it. "That's just what the inside of my head looks like," he had said.

The 16th floor apartment had a view of the barges on the river, the freeway shootings out on I–892, and on a clear night, the magnificent tear-drop fires of Triple Flame Towers. Frankly slept on top of the TV— a little demeaning, but it was a console model. We ran it with the sound off for warmth. The sheet we draped over the tube created a glow like a nightlight.

I had a bed, big enough for Frankly to join me, but I didn't share it. Every night he asked to sex; every night I turned him down. I wasn't a prude, but a romantic, which, so far, had kept me single for 37 years.

"Yestermonth or so I hear about this guy." Frankly waved the book at me. "He is never famous during his lifetime. Just as his ActiveCube is coming out, the InfoTechno Collapse hits. The megaVirus fries everything. Finally he reconceives the whole thing in words, writes it all out in longhand. He finishes it just before he dies, and now it's a bestseller." Frankly shook his big head in smug awe. He loved whatever was stinG, and the stinGest thing right now was reading. Libraries that had lost whole collections to the megaVirus had built shelves, begun purchasing old-fashioned paper-n-print books. *Book Hop* had become the rage on TV. Every dink on the street was writing a novel—including Frankly. He hadn't told me what it was about, and I didn't ask.

The phone started bleeping. Frankly rushed to it.

"Frankly Jefferson Adams and friend," he said, although it was *my* apartment, and *I* gave blood every month in order to keep the phone on line. Then he said, "Why aren't you on the train?"

I wrenched the receiver from his hand. "Stamen?"

"What's that little turd doing there?" Stamen said.

Frankly, who had switched on the speaker, began furiously hopping.

"Where are you?" I said. Static filled the line, and in the background a mechanical *oom-pah-pah*, like a polka machine.

"Nearby. I need to talk, but I'm afraid of implicating you. We have to meet in secret. Go outside and wander around. When it's safe, I'll appear." *Oom-pah-pah, oom-pah-pah*. "And don't let that runt come with you," he added.

As soon as I dropped the receiver, Frankly said, "Pay phone at the waste treatment plant. The big wheel makes that noise, that *who-papa-papa*."

Who-papa-papa sounded like rock and roll, while *oom-pah-pah* sounded like a polka, and that summed up the difference between Frankly and me.

I rushed to the window to check out the treatment plant, a squat, square building with a bowl top. Yellow steam billowed up from the lip of the bowl, turning the snow on the roof to a brown stream that rained on the streets.

Frankly dragged a chair to the window. "Why does Stamen hate me?"

"There he is," I said. A man emerged from the yellow haze, hunching forward, taking enormous strides. He walked as if each step cost him money.

"He's even taller than I remember," Frankly said, standing on the chair.

"I guess I should go meet him." Down below, Stamen crossed the street, then slinked behind the corner of an ammunition shop, eyeing the front door of the Lockview Building.

"You go," Frankly said. "He follows you, then I follow him." He hopped once, which almost sent him flying through the window. "Whoa," he said, "I forget I am on a chair." He peeked again out the window at the sludgy street below.

I walked in the snow and cold, waiting for Stamen to make his appearance. I knew he was following me, but I pretended not to know. This seemed like the story of my life.

The story of Stamen's life was as different from mine as blood was from Mint Tea. His life had been consistent, a song with 1 long chorus, like that song on the radio a couple of years back:

> *I* love my baby so I'm eating her up.
> I *love* my baby so I'm eating her up.
> I love *my* baby so I'm eating her up.

And so on, to the point where normal people screamed. Stamen's life had a slight shift in emphasis from year to year, but it was the same ditty always. He had held the same job since finishing college—the official spellChecker for several congresspeople. Of course, he did more than just check spelling. He had clearance to operate a government computer, which made him a member of an increasingly exclusive population. The computer did the actual spellChecking, but Stamen read and corrected, edited and formatted, looked for malfunctions. "Punctuation is a lost art," he had told me more than once. "Proper capitalization has gone the way of the whales."

Before the Collapse, big technoFirms had solicited him. Even now, he could make more money working for private industry, but Stamen did not like change. He had never been good in social situations and had been self-sexual for years. He lived in Cleveland, where 50 thousand died from IT last year, so who could blame him? Half the people in his office had become moles. "The operation is simple," he had told me. "No pain to speak of."

"You lose your balls," I pointed out. "Among other things."

"Testes," he said, "and I wouldn't lose them. They'd be redefined."

Moles had their genitals moved to other parts of their bodies. Where they wound up depended on the person's job. A traffic cop had them implanted at the elbow, so waving cars on became pleasurable. Most moles moved their sweet parts to their armpits. They orgasmed while they mopped, while they swept, while they rowed their stationary boats. A pathetic deal, but more and more people did it. Support groups had started up all over the country. The going joke was that the group counselors had theirs in the cheeks and talking got them off.

After 13 blocks of frigid meandering, Stamen called my name. He stood in front of a dingy bar, waving for me, a flickering halo of red neon above him. Dressed in black with a black pullover hat, he called to mind an enormous ballpoint pen.

Frankly secretly waved at me, too, from behind a

StinkBus—1 of those ancient runs-on-garbage things.
He waved for an instant, then dropped his hands to
his knees and leaned heavily against them, catching
his breath. Somebody shot off a rifle up the street,
and Frankly ducked beneath the StinkBus drip pan,
still huffing.

I guided my brother inside. "This is the 1st time
I've ever seen you in a bar," I said.

"It's the last place they would think to look," he
said. The place was dimly lit, but Stamen had the
beady eyes of a bat and ushered me to a booth. He sat
across from me and leaned low over the table. Brown
bits of snow rimmed his eyebrows. "It's Mother," he
whispered. "She's no longer dual. She had to go
under. She's completely under."

"Oh, my god," I said.

"I've been implicated," he added. "I was at her
apartment when they came to arrest her. I had gone
to tell her she had to quit the Banjo Society. I was on
their side, but the Cops emphatically do not see it
that way." He pressed 1 of his long fingers to his lips;
the waitress approached.

Heavyset, wearing a black leather Yankees cap and
matching halter top, the waitress walked with the
laconic stride of the perpetually bored. Her short
skirt was held up by a black cowboy belt and gun holster. "4 and 4," she said. "Divvy."

Stamen laced his fingers together, eyeing me des-
perately.

"Give her 8 dollars," I said.

Stamen nodded, smiled weakly. From the thin
wallet he kept in his shirt pocket, he removed 2 bills.
The waitress quickly rolled them into little tubes,
then shoved the tubes into the part of the holster that

should have held bullets—the law permitted her to keep her pistol loaded but no extra bullets.

"All we sell is draft beer," she said. "3 and 3."

"Give her 6 dollars," I said.

Stamen complied and the waitress idled off.

"4 and 4 was the cover charge," I said. "That means there's music or some kind of show. We should talk before it gets loud. What happened when the Cops came?"

Stamen again leaned close. "They found Banjo literature stashed in 1 of Mother's drawers. I told them I was just her son and didn't know a thing about her dual life."

"That was brave of you."

"You would have done the same thing," he insisted. "I thought they believed me, but when I left, 1 of them followed. He was so obvious that I asked him why he was tailing me. He denied it, even denied that he was 1 of the men who had searched Mother's apartment, although he'd taken 1 of her antique combs and used it on his hair while he talked to me.

"I went to work. The Cops can't get into my building. It takes a Silk-Level pass, and believe me, those are hard to come by." He stopped and put his fingers to his forehead. "All of that's gone now. A man works all his life to get Silk-Level clearance, and in the flick of an eyelash, it turns to dust."

"Is Mother all right?"

"I don't know. The Cops haven't arrested her, but is she all right? I don't know."

The waitress reappeared carrying 2 shoes of beer. "1 for flagpole," she said, setting a tall boot in front of Stamen. "And 1 for Miss Priss." She slapped her bare belly loudly.

"I don't see why people go to bars," Stamen said.

"They're not all like this," I said. My eyes had finally adjusted. A crudely built counter squatted against 1 wall, while a row of crude booths huddled on the other side. The bare concrete floor had been painted black. Graffiti scarred the tables. Scrawled into ours was the message, "Don't button your lip, lip my button." Folk poetry, I guessed. Each table held a pile of peanuts, and empty shells littered the seats and floor. 2 men and a woman hunched over the bar. The woman, her halter top identical to the waitress's, spoke to a short man with an enormous head who was completely out of breath. Frankly's legs didn't even reach the rungs of the bar stool. The guy next to him wore a cut-off T-shirt.

"Oh, Stamen," I said, "I think this is a navel bar."

"Sailors?" he said.

"Belly button sex. That's why the big cover charge. There are cubicles in the back for sex. Navel sex."

"We don't *have* to, do we?"

I shook my head. "It's just weird being here." Tonguing peanut shells was a come-on for Navelists. I had read an article about them in *NewsMinute*.

"3 of my representatives voted to approve it as a form of safe sex," Stamen said, craning his head to stare, "but I never pictured anything like this." He whipped back around to face me. "I told you not to bring that little turd."

"He's my best friend. He was worried. He almost killed himself trying to keep up with you."

"You still don't understand the gravity of the situation. 1 of my congressmen heads the committee on the Banjo Society. I went to Mother because her name appeared on the pinklist. They keep 3: the yellowlist, which is 'may be a Banjo,' and has about a million

names. She'd been on that 1 a long time. I warned her
about that a year ago. Last week she appeared on the
pinklist—'definite Banjo sympathizer, arrest on sight.'
I went to her house, and I've told you the rest."

"What's the 3rd list?"

"The graylist. 'Exterminate.' You understand, this
is top secret information. I could lose my job for
telling you about the existence of the lists—if I hadn't
already lost it. When I got back to my desk and called
up the file, Mother's name was off the pink and onto
the graylist, while her spot on the pink had already
been filled by another name."

"Yours?"

He nodded. "The thing is . . . I'm guilty. Having
warned Mother, that moves me to the graylist. I suspect they let me go hoping I would lead them to her."

"How'd you escape?"

"I crawled into an air duct. Big Boys with a court-
ordered Silk-Level pass searched for me, but
assumed I'd gotten out. I hid 3 more days before
leaving through the front door."

Frankly suddenly appeared in the booth behind my
brother, waving at me and making faces. "He already
knows you're here," I said. "You may as well join us."

Frankly scrambled over the seat. "This is a navel
bar," he whispered. "We are going, please?
Survivalists creep me out."

"I can't go with you," Stamen said. "It's too dangerous. If they found you with me, you'd be arrested."

"Do you think they tap her phone already?"
Frankly asked.

"Not yet." Stamen straightened and looked shyly at
me. "I removed your name from the yellowlist before
I disappeared."

I took his thin hand, still cold from the walk over, and patted it gently. "That's so sweet of you," I said. Then I added, "I didn't know you had that kind of power."

"The computer won't accept big changes without higher approval, but I altered the spelling. That was my job, after all. If anyone is getting her phone tapped, it's a woman somewhere in America named Lidya Melmouth."

"Uh-oh," Frankly said.

2

The Cheaper-Than-Home Hotel, a rendezvous pit for lovers who craved seediness, had carpet the color of rat hair in the lobby, the only furniture a greasy wicker couch wedged between flaking beanbag chairs. A blinking red EXIT sign, the 1st 2 letters dead, flashed IT IT IT, like a warning from the Surgeon General about hotels like this 1.

Stamen hadn't sent a package by the conductor. "I should have realized it wasn't like you to send a package," I said, shivering in the doorway, stomping snow from my shoes.

"Especially with a 20 inside," Frankly added.

We had walked the dark streets for an hour, turning randomly, veering away when we heard shots or shouts, wondering whether it was safe to go back to my apartment. The snow had thickened, the night turning as black as octopus squirm. I led us to the Cheaper-Than-Home. "Better to get fleas than freeze," I had said. No 1 had laughed.

The cashier, a girl maybe 17, had a Dalmatian haircut that had grown out and looked awful, like she just had brain surgery. She blew glow-in-the-dark bubbles with her gum while we registered under phony names. Without luggage, we had to pay by the hour. "Sorry about that," the girl said gaily, her head bouncing from side to side. "Cheaper-Than rules." She popped her gum and smiled—a volunteer lobotomy, I suspected.

While Stamen counted out the money, Frankly said, "You think they implicate me in all this?" He had an odd half-smile, which reminded me of Qigley, the boy planning to break my dying record.

Stamen turned his back to the cashier and whispered, "If they know you've met me surreptitiously, then they'll implicate you. I'm sorry. I asked Lydia to keep you out of this."

"You call me a turd," Frankly said.

"Eavesdropper." Stamen handed me a roll of bills. "Turd."

"I am paying for the room," Frankly said cheerfully, which made us stare. "If I'm in trouble with the law, I have a new reason for depression. I'm back in business!"

Stamen snatched back his money. I headed across the carpet to the elevator. I had spent a few nights in the Cheaper-Than during a degrading affair with a newsChannel reporter. He'd had a collection of actionCondoms, and every time we sexed was like a trip to an amusement park. He had no inkling that I had ever been a dying queen, but otherwise he was a zer0.

In the elevator, Frankly said, "I am forgetting my receipt. Everything is material now. Tax deductible."

Stamen said, "Nowism, to a US Government Silk-Level spellChecker, is a slap in the face."

"I never slap moles in the face," Frankly said. "They may get off on it."

I didn't mean to laugh, but the expression "slapped him silly" popped into my head, and I couldn't help myself.

"I decided not to become a mole," Stamen said seriously as the elevator rocked to a halt. "Partly because of the prejudice still prevalent among people such as yourselves."

The room had 2 beds the width of ladders and an enormous TV. Frankly shoved aside an ashtray and a scorpion paperweight, then hopped up on the set. Complimentary condoms filled the ashtray, and he sifted through them for his size. The room's gray wallpaper resembled badly weathered wood, marked by long rusty water stains. I hadn't liked the reporter who took me here, but I had liked the Cheaper-Than. I often required a little seediness. Flicking a dead roach off the bedspread, I decided the place had become too authentic.

"This bunk is designed for dwarfs," Stamen said mournfully, eyeing the other bed. "I rushed out here to see you so I could beat the Big Boys, but it looks like I've ruined your life."

I had a problem with his word choice. "Don't say *ruined*. We can straighten this out, don't you think?"

"Would I run away from my job if I thought it could all be straightened out?"

Frankly, from the TV, said, "Why do you need to see Lyddie?"

Stamen settled his head on the thick foam pillow. He would have to sleep with his knees draped over the end, his feet on the floor. His thighs brushed against leather stirrups tied to the metal frame. I hoped he didn't notice them. I hated explaining sexual stuff to him. "I need your help, Lydia," he said. "I have to go underground, and I don't know how to do it." He turned to look at me, a lapdog sadness in his face. "I didn't mean to drag you into this. I just needed advice. How does 1 go about it? How do you go underground?"

"I haven't been under in 20 years," I reminded him. "What makes you think anything I know would still apply?"

"Who else could I turn to? I didn't know where to find Mother. I was afraid I'd lead the Cops to her, who would then shoot her. Imagine having that little picture in your head."

I settled down on my bed. Frankly leaned back against the console. We lay quietly in the shabby room: dim bulb on the TV, flagpole with his feet on the ground, former dying artist on a mattress narrower than her narrow shoulders. Things might have been worse, but no weirder.

Mother joined the Banjos after the assassination of Senator BFD. She hadn't liked BFD. She had been much more attached to Walt Wadkins, the shortstop for the Indians shot while fielding a grounder deep in the hole. The assassination of BFD was merely the final nudge.

BFD had been running for her 3rd term as senator from Pennsylvania, traveling around the state, claiming to have support in Congress for her "Prosthetic Loan" plan, which was going to erase the national debt over a 10-year period. She proposed selling government loans to fake banks; when the real banks tried to track them down, they'd find the impossible-to-track paper chase that BFD was long familiar with having been a lawyer for a pharmaceutical company before becoming a senator.

Most people believed the sniper who killed her had been hired by Mega-Metro International Bank of Feenix, but it could have been any of the big internationals.

BFD was mowed down in a nursing home where she had been registering mentally incompetents to vote. Earlier that week, 2 actors had been assassinated by a loony fan, 4 rock and roll lipsynkers had been shot during a concert, and a ballerina had been gunned down on her yacht by a woman who then shot herself, leaving no note of explanation. That was not counting the usual political pops—a half-dozen abortion advocates snipered, a handful of free-speechers perforated with rat-a-tats, the usual.

Mother called me the night of BFD's assassination. "More people are killed by guns in this country than any other single thing," she said. "Except IT, of course."

"Hi, Mom," I said.

"Guns are the number 1 cause of death among children."

"I heard about that woman senator," I said. "Did she die?"

"Yes," my mother said, "and I'm going to do something about it."

I thought she would write her congressman. Instead, she joined the Banjos. She made a trip to NeYork to tell me about it. "Not even Frankly can know this. It's too dangerous." She used her most motherly tones, and I was helpless to do anything but

agree. "There's only 1 thing these people understand," she explained. "This is the only option left."

The Banjo Society started a decade ago with a
group of women in Denver. They took the name from
a mildly famous woman banjo picker who lost her husband to a high school hold-up boy who shot 6
bystanders during a grocery robbery. She went out the
next day, bought a gun, then promptly shot the man
who sold it to her. She killed the owners of 9 gun shops
before being caught. During her trial, she claimed that
by killing 9 gun shop owners, she'd saved hundreds of
lives; therefore, she was mathematically innocent.
Her official plea: self-defense in the abstract.

Assassinated before the trial was completed, she
became a martyr to the cause. People all over the
country started killing gun salesmen and members of
the National Rifle Association, leading President J. S.
"Stumpy" Gallion to make the extinction of the
Banjos his top priority.

"We fight fire with fire," Mother said to me. She
was a lanky women on whom clothes inevitably
looked a size too large, draping over her shoulders
like bad upholstery—nothing looked particularly
good on her, but always it seemed the clothing's fault
and not the body's. The worse she dressed, the better
she looked. When she was young, her hair had been a
soapy blond, a natural bubble-do, but gray had
invaded, creating a rippling effect of color, like a
mildly polluted rushing stream.

"Let me show you something," she said and pulled
from her purse a pistol with a 6-inch barrel.

I tried making a joke, doing my best Freud. "Dat
ist not a peestol, dat ist a penis."

Mother smiled. "Now you understand us," she

said. "We've tried everything else. This is the only thing they respect." She looked over the black barrel carefully. "A gun's a terrible thing," she said, "but this 1's a beauty, isn't she?"

"Let me see the note," Stamen said.

I'd almost nodded off. Frankly sat up on the TV, his feet dangling before the screen, looking groggy himself. "It's your handwriting," I said, handing Stamen the message.

He held the paper under the lamp, a brass replica of the Raising of the Flag at Iwo Jima, the slanting flagpole serving as the lamp stem. Maybe the original lampshade had been red, white, and blue, but the 1 on it now was covered with Disney characters.

"How could you possibly have thought I wrote this?" Stamen asked indignantly. "There's a fragment."

"The handwriting—" I began.

"Where is the book that came with this?" Stamen asked.

"My apartment," I told him.

"We should go there now." Stamen stood to emphasize his resolve. "This is the handwriting of Mother. It's almost identical to mine, but she doesn't close the loops of her gs. Have you ever known me not to close a loop?"

Frankly immediately eyed his watch. "Why aren't you thinking of this 10 minutes ago and saving me an hour's rent?"

Before I turned on my light, I knew somebody was in my apartment. Of course, I always felt this way and usually I was wrong, but this time I was right and felt pride along with the terror.

"Greetings," said the black train conductor, although he no longer wore a uniform and his big sideburns had vanished. He sat up in my bed, rubbing his eyes. "Your mother gave me a key."

"Thank god," Stamen said, closing the door. He rushed over to grab the conductor's hand. "This is Ananias Long, a friend of Mother's." Stamen suddenly jumped away from him. "You're not a Banjo, are you?"

"Guilty," he said, still blinking sleepily, "although I'm not in the kind of hot water you are." Without his disguise, he looked exceedingly normal: a middle-aged black man, modestly dressed, modestly handsome.

"Why do you deceive us at the train station?" Frankly demanded.

"I had to be sure it was safe—for me—to contact you. I had to pretend to be a messenger until I was sure you weren't being followed yet."

"Yet?" I said.

"Just a matter of time until your brother's computer deception is noticed," Ananias explained. He threw his arms out wide and stretched. "We'd been monitoring his screen for the past couple of months. That's why your mother was already out of the house when the Cops came. When we saw you change Lydia's name, we figured you'd be coming here."

Stamen became angry. "How were you monitoring my screen?"

"Your mother gave you a set of ties for your birthday and threw away the old 1s?"

"That's typical behavior for Mother," Stamen said.

"The ties have miniature receptor dishes in them. Plastic babies that pass metal detectors. The characters on the computer screen burn their images onto microscopic film."

"StinG," Frankly said. "Where are you getting these ties?"

"Garage sales," Ananias said. "They're illegal now, but before the InfoTechno Collapse they were everywhere."

Stamen said, "You made me a Banjo spy."

"You'd already passed Silk-Level information," Ananias pointed out. "All water under the bridge now, anyway. I'm here to help you folks. Stamen will be put on the graylist. Could be on it already. As for you," he turned to me, his eyes zer0ing in on mine, "you may not be moved to the pinklist. They don't automatically pinklist relatives. But Stamen's altering of your name could make it look like you have something to hide."

"But I haven't *done* anything," I protested.

"You're affiliating with a Banjo as we speak," he said. "You've been out most the night with a self-described Banjo spy."

"I can't believe this."

"Our business right now has to be undergrounding Stamen, which is no simple task." Ananias reclined again in the bed, staring up at my houndstooth wall. "No ordinary disguise will work on a person who literally stands head and shoulders above others. Can't do a sex-change disguise for the same reason."

"You don't move your face like you do at the train station," Frankly said.

"That's my disguise," Ananias said. He touched the cotton wallpaper incredulously. "Don't see this much anymore," he said, running his fingers over the design. Suddenly he sat up. "I play the down-home-out-for-a-buck-black stereotype. You know of any bone-thin-tall-as-a-tower stereotypes?" He looked us all over, but his gaze came to rest on me, as if I were withholding the answer.

"We should all think," I said. "We should put our heads together and think." I hated when people said the absolutely obvious, but I said it anyway. "Think, think, think." I tapped my finger to my head to be totally redundant.

The windows, black now, reflected our images—another kind of redundancy. The future is the night sky, I thought, staring at the frightened woman in the dark glass.

I 1st died when I was 14 years old. I'd seen a couple of boys do it months earlier. Everyone else was obsessed with watching them die, watching the heart monitor go silent, watching their bodies quake and then stop—followed by the revival effort, the rapid work of the crew, the amazing tension of life and death. What got to me was how those boys seemed changed after dying, how they seemed calmer, older. That's why I decided to die. Oh, I liked the attention, although most of it was focused on you while you were dead, but more than anything else, I wanted to feel that change, have the knowledge of death sink into my bones.

The party where I died was at a big house with wooden floors and large, elegant windows, whose owner, a grown-up with gray hair, liked to watch kids die. The survival rate was about 90 percent, and only a third of the survivors had noticeable gray rot—if they did it once. The figures quickly changed for the worse the more you tried it. A person had only so many deaths.

2 dies were scheduled for the party—teenage boys—and both came off without a hitch. I volunteered as soon as the 2nd boy was revived. No 1 had seen a girl do it. People became edgy, excited. Several of the boys insisted on kissing me before I died, all those lips pressing against mine.

I took to death the way a parent takes to a newborn—without judgment. The Ater put me down quickly. Oh, I fought it, that suffocating pressure—like having the air knocked out of you—and then the stripping away of life—like the peeling off of wet clothes. But even the 1st time I let go pretty fast, sinking under the black wave, a startling final surge of shake and rattle, and then it was just like everyone said: peace.

A gray light, like a cloudy sky at dusk, shown in the distance—though to think of it in terms of measurable space is misleading—and there was my father, smiling kindly at me as he had when I was a child.

"Lydia, my lovely girl," he said. I recognized his voice, although it was a voice I didn't know—he'd died when I was 2. I had no memory of him but photographs of a tall, kind-looking man with large, pink ears.

"I'm so pleased to see you again," he said. "You'll like it here. The exquisite thing about death is that it is the perfection of life." He held me, then, a sweet, fatherly embrace. "Your hair smells like apricots," he told me.

"Daddy," I said, "I've missed you all my life. I didn't know it was you I was missing until just now."

He smiled at me. "There are 7 labors of death, my angel, and you've just accomplished the 1st—the recognition of someone who loved you."

"Really?" I said. A wash of emotion made me waver on my feet, as if I might fall. "It was easy." I reached for his hands. The rough knuckles and smooth palm moved me—how many boys had I loved because I'd felt in their hands these hands?

"The labors are easy if you can give up the pride of the living." He looked about us in the misty gray. "I want you to meet a friend," he said, taking a step away and then shaking my hand as if he were a stranger. He said, "1st there was chaos, the vast immeasurable abyss, outrageous as a sea—dark, wasteful, wild." He touched my cheek suddenly. "You look like you're breathing." His face blanched. "Listen to me, life and death are like 2 floors in the same building, only what's furniture in 1—"

My hand yanked itself from his as the Accu jerked me back into life. The last thing I saw were his fingers turning, opening, losing me.

Suddenly I was back to the hard coffee table beneath a circle of young faces, their cheeks wet with tears. Even the boys who'd gone before me openly wept. I knew right then that I was good at this, that I had a knack for death. I also knew that what I had suspected was true: the die had changed me, made me older, different.

My 1st death had been like every story I'd ever heard about dying—see your loved ones, feel full of warm and fuzzy.

The deaths to come would be startlingly different.

———

My brother and I shared my bed. He was so thin and unmannish, I hardly noticed him. His body gave off no heat, and I grew cold. Ananias had the extra blankets wrapped around him on the floor. Frankly snoozed on the tube.

Dying screwed up your ability to sleep. Everyone who had died said this. I often wondered whether insomniacs had died without realizing it, or maybe they lived closer to death than the rest of us.

Ananias thought I was holding out on him. What did I know about the underground anymore? After my 3rd die, I'd been arrested at school, charged with illegal death. I skipped out before the trial and went underground. I stole an Accu and traveled around the country. I had 6 different IDs, a colorwheel of hair dye, several makeup tricks, even a stat-flattener so I could pass for a boy.

I didn't mind sexing for a place to stay. A lot of the bars where I hung out had once been sex bars, drug bars, or some strange thing. I spent a week sleeping over a joint in Seattle that once had been a beastie bar. People still came in carrying elaborately dressed chickens or lambs. Later on, dying itself got bad. The dying artist had to strip. Some of the boys came at death, and all of them got hard. Sex with the dead became a big fad, although I only did this once as a dead person and once with a dead boy. The boy didn't make it back. I remember thinking that I shouldn't take my pill in the morning, that I should have the child, who would grow up and have children, and maybe they'd all be dying artists to honor their ancestors. I thought how I was the vessel for generations of dead.

That was the kind of logic you got into when you were dying all the time.

I had a lot of connections, but when I gave up dying, I purposely lost track of people. I worked as a maid for a while in Chicago, then I moved to Madison, Wisconsin, and hustled drinks in a restaurant. I'd been back in Cleveland 6 months, living within a block of my mother, going to college under the name Eliza Small, when dying became legal.

I turned myself in. A fuss of media attention followed. *The Day After Tomorrow Show* wanted me to do a Major Minute Interview, but I said no. I wanted to let my past, well, die. After 9 months of community service, I was once again free. I had come to like the weekend work, helping at the IT hospice, taking retarded children on field trips. Mother said I should get a degree in counseling, but I saw the people who did the work everyday. They were worn down and blackened like old erasers.

"You're awake." Ananias spoke softly but his voice startled me nonetheless.

"Insomnia," I whispered.

He nodded, his face wrinkling up as it had at the station. I took it as a sign he was preparing to manipulate me. "Your brother's a freak," he said.

"That's an insulting way to put it."

"Too weird looking to hide, too wishy-washy about the Cause to live as 1 of us. He certainly doesn't have the charisma to mooch his way through the underground."

"I'm not even wishy-washy about the Cause. I don't like the Banjo Society. I wish my mother had never joined it."

"I know that." He raised his brows and stared off at the into the semi-dark of the room. "Your brother has piss for blood, but I like him. And I love your mother. She's inspirational. I'd die for her." His face flattened out entirely, which added weight to his words. "But Stamen is a problem. He's acquainted with more of us than he thinks. The Cops, if they catch him, will make a list of every person he knows, which would include several duals. Duals are extremely important to us." He grimaced, his yellow teeth showing crookedly. He was 50, I guessed. "Your mother's already had to go under, which was a big loss. We're spending a lot of energy and money to keep her low. Now with Stamen, the more we try to help him, the more of us he knows. We need someone outside the Society to take care of him. Someone who cares about him. Someone who knows a little about the underground already. Someone who could call in old debts."

"I catch your drift, but I have a life of my own, and I haven't had anything to do with the underground for ages."

"That life of your own, tell me about it. That watt and a half over there, he your husband?"

"Friend."

"No spouses?"

"That doesn't mean I don't have a life of my—"

"Tell me about your career, your present job."

"I'm sure you already know that I lost my job, which makes this method of questioning a bit coy, doesn't it?"

"How was it you lost that job? I don't know this part, honestly."

"What difference does it make? I was fired, all right?"

"For what reason?"

"For being lousy at my job."

"Which was?"

"Ragaccountant."

"Whew! Big bucks in that, ain't there?" His face was alive again with mock astonishment.

"That's a lousy act you've got."

"Ragaccountants *do* make good money. Am I right?"

"I was a Junior Rag. You don't make the money until you've been around for a while."

"You got this apartment."

"And it'll take all of my savings to keep it."

"So this life of yours includes the humiliation of being incompetent at the very thing you spent 4 years studying in college. It includes no love life of any sort. It includes living with a washed-up depressionist no taller than a fire hydrant, who hops around like a kangaroo on speed. I can see why you'd want to hang on to what you got."

"Fuck you very much."

"Most of the people underground are underground for good. You might be surprised how many familiar faces you're going to see."

"*I'm* going to see? It's my brother who needs to disappear."

"Don't be so sure."

"Because he changed the spelling of my name?"

Ananias rocked his head and stared off at nothing. "That might do it. Or it might need a little push. We might have to pass some information on you to insure that you go down."

"You wouldn't do that. That's . . . that's shitty."

"Look at it from our point of view. We've got a big problem in your brother, and nobody is better suited to take care of it than you. If you're thinking about abandoning your family responsibilities to us, then we have to find a way to make you live up to your responsibilities." He paused, then added, "It was your mother's idea."

"You're lying."

"She wrote the note I gave you, sent me down here to locate you—for your protection, but also for you to help Stamen. He's in trouble because he tried to save his mother. Seems only fair that you should be willing to give up a little to help them both out." He patted my arm, looked me straight in the eyes. "Think about what I've said. Sleep on it." He settled back on the floor.

My heart was racing, a familiar feeling. When the Accu brought you back, your overstimulated heart zoomed. I lay in the dark, remembering, wondering, worrying.

From the TV, Frankly whispered, "I am *not* washed-up."

3

The heart-shaped viewing deck at the top of Triple Flame Towers quickly filled with tourists gawking at the view of the mammoth city below and the brilliant flames above. Frankly and Stamen sat on either side of me and stared out, pretending to be absorbed in the sight of the big dirty city. 1 of the keys to the underground was moving in crowds—ballparks, tourist spots, national historic sites. We were safe here. The bellows above exhaled their flames loudly, 30 feet of fire. Most of the heat flew off into the atmosphere, but we stayed comfortably warm.

"We need a plan," Frankly announced.

"I know that. Why don't *you* come up with something?"

Stamen said, "Do you realize how stupid it is to ask a Nowist to make a plan?"

Frankly grunted his response—presumably in present tense.

By the time we woke this morning, Ananias was already gone. An unsigned message lying on his pillow said, *Don't spend another night here. Destroy this note. Good Luck.*

"He's right," Stamen had said. "The Big Boys are very efficient. They could be here as early as this afternoon."

I began packing a bag.

"Could we hide at your apartment?" Stamen asked Frankly.

Frankly flinched. He had lost his apartment a year ago when he quit doing depression. "I am staying here," he said.

"You can't stay here," Stamen said. "The Cops will arrest you."

"Adjust, Stamen," I said. "He Nows. Get with it."

To live underground meant traveling light, but it might also demand changing your appearance often. I tried to prepare for everything, even packing long pants. A woman wearing slacks had been shot in the thigh just last week in Dallas, but Protest Wounds were only legal in a few of the Plebeian Substates, and you could never tell what might be demanded of you.

Frankly packed, too. "I come with you. This is the break I am waiting for."

"1 small bag," I had told him, which he now held on his lap. Stamen had nothing, wearing the same black clothes he'd had on yesterday. He whispered, "When do we go underground?" Frankly leaned in to catch my answer. A flurry of car horns sounded beneath us while the bellows above continued their roar.

"We *are* underground," I said, staring at the city 12-hundred feet below us. "We're safe here for the day. We went under by coming up here."

"We're underground just sitting here?" Stamen said.

"It's less glamorous than it sounds," I said. "The hardest part is dealing with the combination of tension about being discovered and the boredom from remaining anonymous."

"There has to be something more to it," Frankly said. "This depresses me, but it doesn't play well on stage."

I shrugged. I kept thinking my brain would come around, but I'd spent so many years trying to forget the bad old days that I couldn't get any cooperation from upstairs. We watched the city fall into cloudy shadow, and then watched snow fall into the falling city. The huge bellows above us kept us dry and fairly warm. I tried to think, but I wound up mainly thinking about thinking, like, *why can't I concentrate*?

Triple Flame Tower was 1 of the 1st buildings erected after the InfoTechno Collapse, a monument to the postTech grunt-n-bear-it school. The project had employed 10 thousand workers for 3 years, according to the official pamphlet distributed in the elevator. An unofficial RadMimeo handed out by a pair of razor-heads argued that the 10 thou had been badly *under*employed, getting about 75% of the ever-downwardly revised minimum wage. According to the faint print on the mimeo, the whole Collapse was a management conspiracy, a scam to wrest back control given up to labor during the techno days.

I showed the mimeo to Frankly, but he told me mass-depressive items didn't interest him. Stamen wouldn't distinguish their argument with a comment.

We grew bored, but at times the view overpowered the boredom. The city looked symmetrical from up here, as if designed by a master planner whose hands, even now, were clean. In truth, the city had grown from crisis to crisis without a clue, and existed despite its readiness to collapse. But the surface beauty of it was astounding. A phalanx of solar panels pivoted suddenly in response to the sun's own imperceptible movement. All across the city, panels shifted, sunlight glinting off them, sparking in unison, as if choreographed.

My 2nd death took place in a city park, Hayden Public Lawn, in Cleveland. During the day, parents brought children to swing and slide, dogs chased balls, kids tossed phramax and bellowed out scores. At night it became a dangerous place—drugs, muggings, rapes, gangs. Dying there took some courage but set no precedent.

About 20 people showed up. The Accu I had stolen earlier in the week was fully charged. I wore a pink taffeta dress, a cloying girly-girly thing, but not a bad outfit to die in. I lay on the grass and everyone gathered around. Each bent down to hold my hand and say good-bye—a circle of familiar shadowy faces. Then I took the Ater.

The physical sensation of giving up life: like surfacing to air after having held your breath too long, a gasping intake of death. I expected to see my father as I had the 1st time, but my expectations died with my body. I entered the new world blindly.

There was pink. Pink above, pink below, pink newspapers beneath my feet, covering a pink floor. Even the lettering in the newsprint was pink. The same pink as my dress. I walked over the paper, my skin not pink but luminously yellow. Out of the pink came voices saying strange things: "I get no kick from Charlemagne . . ." and "Limber bones live alone . . ." and "Hickory lickory letch . . ." and "She's a professional personality . . . "

Then the dogs showed up, real dogs with human heads, like something out of the Greek Boys. The 1st 1, a Labrador with a man's face—a flushed middle-aged, lecherous man, whose lips curled like old shoes. "Say, High and Mighty," he addressed me, "you gotta lotta legs on yew."

A full-sized poodle with the puffed black face of a jazz musician trotted up beside the Lab. "Scrabble the oyster quick and lick my fur," he said. A German Shepherd lurched past them and started humping against me with a dog's typical lousy aim. I slapped him down. His tiny, furious human face turned rocket red. "I slip my slide with your backside and not hear nothing like it from you," he cried.

"Bad dog," I said.

A dachshund with the alcoholic face of an English professor said, "Here is your 2nd exam: felicity, fidelity, and the fat man who holds the cards—shoes in the cracker box standing guard."

"Shoes in the cracker box standing guard?" The Labrador was incredulous, speaking as he tried to mount my face.

I slapped him down and grabbed newspaper from the floor, quickly rolling it into the classic dog-weapon. They backed away, the professorial mutt saying, "You're in the pink, but still a long ways to go before you find the gift."

"What gift?" I said. Behind them, in the dim light of the distance, another dog watched, a huge dog standing with a strange sort of dignity—a dog with 3 heads on 3 long necks.

"Yikes," I said, and in the next moment I was alive, in the park, rain falling on my pink taffeta dress, a man's mouth pressed against mine, pushing in the saving breath.

We departed Triple Flame Towers at midnight—closing time—the biggest rush to the elevators. Stamen had never left his seat the whole day long except to pee. "Crouch," I told him. "Hunch like an ostrich." We'd brought him food from the Triple Flame Tower Firepit: barbecued ribs and beer. He had kept track of the shootings and traffic accidents he could hear, giving us a running total every few minutes.

When we emerged from the building, I let the crowd carry us along. Buses from the big hotels waited outside the huge doors. I led us onto the Wonway Inn Shuttle.

"Why?" Stamen asked, once the bus began moving.

"This hotel is way out on the west side. Take us an hour. We'll be safe another hour," I said, twisting to get away from somebody's knee that poked me in the butt. The bus was crowded, and we were standing.

"And then?" Stamen asked.

"And then we'll be across town from my apartment and close to the edge of the city." I looked for Frankly but couldn't spot him. "What happened to Frankly?" I slapped at the knee.

"Ow." I'd slapped Frankly's head. Kneeling, he had the back of his head against me. "I can't get up," he said. "I'm paralyzed with fear."

"Practice your routines on your own time," I said.

"Your bottom is a heavenly pillow," he told me.

"Shh." I glared at him and then my brother. "Make yourselves invisible," I whispered.

An hour later, we were on the freeway in a stolen GMC van, rolling west through snow and darkness, passing convertibles and coupes, station wagons, compacts, limos, waddles, sports cars, and luxury editions. In the bad old days, I had stolen cars all the time. It was 1 of the 1st things you learned when you went under. I had searched the parking lot for cars dating back to my time under—the new models were a mystery to me. Frankly complained, though, because the driver's seat was too high for him to reach the pedals. "I always hate vans," he said, sitting beside me in the passenger bucket, his legs dangling down, feet inches above the worn carpeting. "And sport-utility vehicles," he added. He bounced in lieu of hopping and huffed into his hands. Stamen slept in the back. A high, thin snore, like a dying siren, wafted into the front.

Where we were heading was a mystery even to me, behind the wheel and ostensibly in charge. But we were making good time. Bad weather made for good driving because the Cops were less likely to set up Road Checks, and the Roadies were less likely to lower their windows and take potshots. Freeway shootings dropped 65 percent in foul weather.

I found something comforting about this dark van with a defective heater, a gaping hole where the television belonged, light from the dash turning our faces greenish white, speakers buzzing with bad music.

Frankly kept checking the radio, scanning for a Nowist station; he hated to hear the same song twice. A lot of roadkill marked the snowy shoulders, mostly DropOffs—old people and household pets—but also a raccoon and something that might once have been a deer.

"Filadelfia," Frankly said, abruptly switching the radio off. "We're going to Filadelfia. I just realize this." He smiled at me, like he was on to my plan, but I didn't have 1. "We're going to the die."

"Forget it," I said.

"How else are we finding your mother?" He began bouncing wildly in the seat now. "She is there meeting us, I bet you."

"You think?"

"Where's that book she sends us? I think she sends us a clue in the book." He started searching the glove compartment, although we had put nothing anywhere, and the bags still rested on the floor in the back. The glove box held a wadded up tie-dye T-shirt and rolling papers. "Hippies!" he said, holding the shirt with the tips of his fingers. "We steal a hippie van!" There was nothing worse to a Nowist than a hippie.

"Get the book," I said. "It's in my bag."

Frankly lowered his window, tossed the shirt and rolling papers into traffic, then climbed into the rear.

The wipers streaked snow back and forth, making the wintry freeway a blur of dreamy colors. I didn't like the idea of going to the die, but it did make sense. How else would we find Mother? How else would she find us? Besides, an interview on network TV would make me temporarily invulnerable. Even the Big Boys respected national exposure.

Frankly returned to the front seat, his big head bobbing over the pages of the book. "I like the title," he said. "*I Am A Big Man Not.* Says it all, doesn't it?"

He read for clues by the light of the glove box. I drove, aware now that we were going to Filadelfia. I even knew people there we could stay with—not friends, no 1 the Big Boys would know about—Blib and Joanna Towson. I'd met them at a special exhibit at the Manhattan Cathedral of Fashion and Art about a year ago.

The artist, a woman who called herself Slit, had lined the museum's walls with glass boxes. In each, you could see the lower half of a naked person, while the upper half remained behind a black curtain. The models kept shifting their positions, completely exposing their lower selves. As the models turned, little slits in the black sheet permitted patrons of the arts to get a peek of the model's faces or their upper bodies, which were clothed. The slits in the sheets opened and closed quickly, providing only a second to see her eyes, or his neck, the cut of her shirt. The power of the work was the reversal of the ordinary, how the private part of the body was exposed while the public part was hidden, burlesque in reverse, being thrilled by a momentary bit of jaw, a fleeting view of the bridge of a nose.

I had been in line behind Blib and Joanna, who had loved the exhibit, giggling, shifting their heads to get a better glimpse of the model. "We think we know this 1," Blib explained to me, and pretty soon I was ducking and bouncing my head around, trying to see. Joanna and Blib were certain she was the Kitty Grub woman, the 1 you see in the commercial sitting in her tub, covered with purring cats.

So began our courtship. We wandered through the Fashion and Art Cathedral, then had dinner together. They told me about their life in Filadelfia (she dealt cards at the casino; he owned a pet store), their wedding (Joanna had bled all over her white dress during the ear stapling), and their apartment (3 rooms!). The next night I took them to a Chinese place I knew, and the night after, we ate Ethiopian. That same night they proposed. There were candles, they brought their health certificates—all quite romantic.

I turned them down. Why was hard to explain. Not, as Frankly suggested, because I wanted to marry him but couldn't admit it. Blib and Joanna were nice people, but how far could nice take you, when you got right down to it? Besides, Blib had this habit of clearing his throat before every utterance, and Joanna plucked her eyebrows down to a weenie thread of hair.

The truth: I was a holdout for love. I'd had probably 15 couples propose, 4 or 5 individual men, and 1 woman, but I was still waiting for the real thing.

"Listen to this," Frankly said, holding the book up as if I was supposed to read along with him. "'Cruz mistook his automobile for the woman he loved, taking off his clothes before slipping inside through the open passenger window.'"

"How is that a clue from Mother?" I demanded.

"It's not. I just like it."

Stamen's voice suddenly came from nowhere. "You read in the past tense."

"I'm a Nowist," Frankly said proudly, "not a censor."

At the freeway McDonald's, we ordered lambSnacks and ate while we rode, Stamen still lying down, out of sight, but telling us a long story about some snook in his building who collected his own urine. "He stored it in bottles at work, which he would take home and empty into an aquarium. He was determined to find a species of fish that could survive in his urine."

"Thank god the government's in such good hands," Frankly said. "Is this guy a mole, too?"

Stamen was silent only a moment. "My friend found a South American fish that thrives in his urine. He wanted me to fill a tank with my urine so that he could see whether the fish could live in any urine or only specific people's urine. He thought there might be a new way of categorizing people, according to their urine and what kinds of fish—or amphibians— could survive in it."

"Your tax dollars at work," Frankly said.

"This was on his own time," Stamen said, his voice rising.

I cut him off, addressing Frankly. "It's no stranger than some of the stuff you used to do on stage."

Frankly closed the book, a finger marking the spot. "I am proud of all I do back then. I am a 1st-rate depressionist at the time."

"He used to grease his hair, then slip his head into a fish bowl," I told Stamen. "He used to flatten his face against the fish bowl and pretend to be deformed."

"It is a very moving thing to see," Frankly insisted, bouncing again. "I work in the great tradition of Shakespeare, the Greek Boys, Lenny Bruce, Jenna Ft, Velma rOOst." He glared at me and bounced accusingly. "You never like my work. From the very beginning, you think I'm only a mild downer. You never respect my talent."

"Oh, come on. I was your biggest fan. I saw every routine about a million times."

"What?" Stamen said, his too-little head appearing between us on that bamboo body. "A Nowist who repeats routines?"

The van became utterly silent, except for the blowing heater, the slaps of the wipers. The great contradiction in Frankly's life suddenly seemed to take up all the air, and I cracked open my window. But I didn't say a word, just stared ahead at the brown snow, the rutted asphalt.

Stamen's head rose serpentlike in the rearview. "Get down," I said. "Be invisible."

"I give them a new twist each night," Frankly said. "I switch the order of things. Nightly depression is a big challenge to the Here and Now."

"Do they have support groups for the Temporally Challenged?" Stamen asked. "You could be depressed about repeating yourself."

A long, uncomfortable silence followed.

"I am fuming," Frankly said softly. We rode those fumes all the way to Filadelfia.

We spent the night in the van, parked in the crowded lot of a 24-hour liquor store. I slept in the driver's seat, waking periodically from the cold, running the engine just long enough to warm us up. Frost patterned the windows when we woke, intricate geometric designs that I studied for a long time while Frankly and Stamen slept, thinking that the molecular makeup of these flimsy crystals must be identical to this pattern, so that the outward expression of the frost matched its inner composition. An altogether philosophical morning, until I spotted a Cop car navigating the other side of the parking lot, and I realized that the frost was a dead giveaway that we had spent the night in the van. Such are the dangers of philosophy.

I started up the engine and cruised out of the parking lot, lowering my window and sticking my head into the frigid morning air in order to better see the icy street. I drove us on in to Filly. We ditched the van in front of a water store just within the city limits.

"We should get bottles to take with us," Stamen said. "Filadelfia tap water is toxic."

"Oh, shut up," I said, realizing as I spoke that I was in a bad mood. "Water is too heavy to lug around." I noticed that Stamen carried a bag, too; a huge denim thing with patches.

"It was in the van," he explained. "I decided I might as well take it."

We followed the signs to the nearest train stop, walking together, keeping to the back streets, the No-Traffic Zones. Filly was gray, grimy, and desolate—not much different from NeYork, but NeYork was *my* gray, grimy, desolate town, while this place seemed cold and malevolent. "Hunch," I reminded my brother.

He hunkered his head down, cranelike. We hiked through the frozen muck. While Filadelfia had the official title of "The City of Women Horses," it was the dogs you had to worry about. Filly had become a free/dog city, 1 of a handful around the country. The law forbade neutering, spaying, or killing dogs. They roamed the streets in packs—especially at night. The idea was to keep people from sleeping on the side-walks, and it worked. As soon as a few folks napping on the curb got their ears chewed off, the other homeless ("Freedom People," Stumpy Gallion called them, "Let them be free!") tended to leave town. Filly was known for innovative solutions to civic problems.

"Lyd," Stamen said softly, my old nickname, "what happened to your job? I didn't know you'd been fired."

"Oh," I said, losing my footing for a second on a slick of black ice. "Well," I said, and pointed to a huddle of sleeping mutts. "Umm," I said, and Frankly, good friend that he was, jumped in to explain.

"She is caught greasing her palms," Frankly said, "soaking her wick, padding her pockets, stuffing her bra, cramming her—"

"He gets the idea," I said.

"You were stealing?" Stamen asked, his voice a familiar reedy mixture of shock and dismay.

"That was the official reason." I kept the explanation short. Ragaccountants kept track of hidden money for the wealthy who wished to avoid excessive taxation, divorce settlements, custody payments, and so on. We kept the paper trails long, confusing, and *active*, but we still earned the consumer a nice monthly dividend. We had an ugly reputation before FAS (Familial Assassination Syndrome) hit the news—children gunning down their parents to get their inheritances early, staging the deaths to look like Freeway Shootings, Neighborhood Pops, Gang Kills, Drive-Bys, or Random Blow-Aways. It started to seem fair for the wealthy to conceal their money in order to protect their hides.

It turned out that most of the early FAS activity had been sponsored by an advertising company trying to help a big Ragaccounting firm with its image. The ad company had to pay a big fine, but the scheme worked; my esteem in the community soared.

Standard operating procedure encouraged the Junior Rag to accept kickbacks, extort small bribes, and kiss ass for tips. The covert ActiveCube, which sold for $29.95 at Kmart, featured a full kickback etiquette. We all knew that the bosses would use payola against us if they ever wanted to fire us, but why would they want to do that?

I screwed up 3 accounts. I let 1 slip into a bank that folded 3 days later. Another I put into city bonds for just a week—an emergency move—only to see the bonds' value slide into the abyss before I could cash out. The final 1, well, just disappeared. I made the trail so elusive, I finally couldn't keep track of it myself.

I got axed. "Improper Monetary Customer Conduct" was the official reason, but really it was just incompetence.

I finished explaining on an ancient train platform that had been a museum piece before the InfoTechno Collapse. Stamen looked relieved that I suffered from stupidity rather than dishonesty. "I think I understand," he said, nodding flamingolike.

"It's all that dying catching up with her," Frankly said, hopping madly. Tall people really caused him grief.

"No." My brother shook his head. "This all happened right about the time Mother went dual, didn't it?" He tried to look at me with compassion, but the best Stamen could do was a dog-caught-chewing-the-furniture look. "She turns Banjo, and we all suffer."

"Don't blame Mother," I insisted, but the elevated train was pulling near and my words were lost in the hiss and roar, the painful squeal of the brakes, the pungent smell.

My 3rd death happened in StLouis at a grown-up's house, a woman about the age I am now, late 30s, who dyed her hair cola-black with a purple tint and had a business making Naked Clothes—a cult fad for a while. You had wrap-around nude photos taken of yourself, then the photos were reproduced on flesh-colored spandX, so you could be fully dressed and naked at the same time. Dumb, but she made a fortune.

She had a big party, and I was the guest of honor. A foam pad was centered on an enormous dining table, with appetizers—pigs-in-a-blanket, salmon on Ritz, bacon doo-dahs, the whole works—around the edge of the table, so people could munch while I passed on.

My friends let her know how insulting this was. "We're gonna get fish all over our equipment," I told her. As a gesture of apology she offered me a free Naked suit "if I survived the night." The fleeb. No 1 said that to a dying artist, especially not the night of the die. A friend stuck his thumb up her butt— almost tore her spandX–which was what we did back then instead of slugging.

I crawled over the cream cheese, whiffed the Ater, and whoosh, I was gone. My 3rd death, and I was a pro, no struggle, not even a twitch.

I found myself in a room filled with incredible light, sitting on a wooden bench beside a woman who had wings—real wings of feather and bone, white glistening feathers—and big boobs, too, glowing beneath a gold leotard: an angel. Around her neck hung a small placard that read: LABOR 3, LINE FORMS TO THE REAR.

"Is this heaven?" I asked her.

She offered me a radiant smile, then whapped me across the head with 1 of her wings. Knocked me off the bench and onto the hardwood floor. I saw then that I was naked.

"You have offended God," the angel said, standing. Her legs were the legs of a man, and her equipment was manly, too, coiled up beneath the leotard like a big cinnamon roll.

"What'd I do?" I asked her.

"All this come and go," she said. "It's ostentatious. This is the Everafter, not a talk show. We don't care for cameos."

"If I survive the 7 labors of death," I began, but she made a face.

"'Survival' is a Breethie word. Has no application up here, You complete the 7 labors, you get the gift." She smiled beatifically, and I noticed a couple of gold fillings. "You envy me my gold? My wings?"

"No, thanks," I said.

"Bitch," she said. She began rocking her head around, her long blond hair following it, fanning out, becoming a hair halo, and then she disappeared, only the halo remaining, which was no longer hair but a tunnel. I crawled in.

Right at the opening a grismal-looking man in a ragged coat and slashed pants stopped me and asked for loose change. "I'm naked," I told him, which made him snarl and shove his hand into my pocket—turned out I was wearing Naked Clothes. He pulled out 30 cents in change, then whispered in my ear, "All youse who enter here, abandon all hip." He counted the change again. "A penny less and youse don't pass."

"This is the 3rd labor of death? Having the right change?"

"You'd be surprised how many mess it up," he said, then he tumbled back into whatever crack he had crawled out of.

I plunged into the tunnel, which turned out to be my life.

I came back, still on the dining table, people applauding, munching their pigs-in-a-blanket, my heart going *whack, whack, whack,* beating against my ribs as if to punish me.

Blib's Pet Store, a bubble-built structure on a sooty corner in downtown Filadelfia, stank something fierce. Frankly began to gag as soon as he stepped through the door. "I am waiting outside," he said, and disappeared.

"It's not *that* bad," Stamen said. "They just need to clean the cages." He pointed at a filthy "Parrot Penthouse." Next to it sat a small-scale White House, complete with a gray mouse leaving a trail of turds across the floor of the oval office. A huge display showed images of big dogs protecting people from other big dogs.

Blib suddenly had his arms around me. "Lyddie, Lyddie, Lydia," he said, pulling me close, his mustache rubbing against my cheek. I felt a tiny nip on the lobe of my ear. We'd had 1 pretty thorough make-out session, he and Joanna and I, in the coat room of the Ethiopian restaurant. That nip brought it all back to me, his warm hands, Joanna's eager mouth. If I had married them, I wouldn't be in this mess. I might not be happy, but it seemed unlikely that I'd be a fugitive.

Blib cleared his throat, a sound like a motorcycle failing to start. "My darling, my love," he whispered, then straightened and pulled away. "What can I interest you in? A cockatoo? Chameleon? Love birds? Guinea pig?"

"Shelter," I said.

"Oh," he said, and did the kickstart in his throat again. "We have them all: Mouse Motel, Hamster Hideaway, Kitty Kondo, Hen Hut—"

"No, shelter for *us*," I said. "This is my brother and we have a friend . . ." I stopped. His face had darkened like a week-old banana.

"It isn't possible," he said, smiling a phony smile now, his eyes jogging around nervously in their sockets. He leaned over, opened a door to a wire cage, and picked up a miniature bunny, which promptly bit him. "Ow," he said, then yanked on the scruff of the rabbit's neck—the bunny was no larger than his fist. "Full grown," he said loudly, displaying the animal, smiling again as another customer strolled by. He leaned in close. "My apartment got searched this morning. They didn't reveal who they were after, but I gather you're the hot property."

Stamen stuck his puny head in between us. "Who did the searching? Government Big Boys or—"

"Cops," Blib said softly. "Carrying major-caliber rat-a-tats."

"Jesus," I said, but Stamen shook his head. "If they sent Cops, that means you're merely yellowlisted. If you were darker listed, you'd get the attention of the Big Boys."

"These little bastards are vicious," Blib said, turning the bunny in his fist to look at his bleeding finger. "Do you need money?" he asked. "I could let you rob the store. I'm insured."

"Nice of you to offer," I said, "but we're not that desperate."

"You'd better go, then." He tossed the tiny rabbit back in the cage and slapped the wire door shut. "They're so overbred for cuteness, they have no sense of . . . humanity." He sucked the blood from his finger, a trace of it remaining on his mustache. "Come on. You're not safe here." He guided us toward the door, but slipped away before we reached it. He rushed up to us again as we were stepping out, lifting a greenish mouse by the tail. "You'll need some affection out on the streets. These little guys are so sweet—and inexpensive." He waggled the mouse, a pointy-nosed, freakish-looking thing, but I saw a folded slip of paper in his palm, hidden under the rodent.

"It sure is cute," I said loudly, taking the note with the mouse. I slipped the note into my pocket, while the mouse ran up my arm, his tiny feet making my skin prickle. "Get it off," I said. "Hurry. Get it off me." Stamen clamped his hand down on my shoulder, catching it. "Maybe another time," I said to Blib. I flew out the door.

Around the side of the building, I stopped running. The note was wrapped in 20-dollar bill, which I stuck in my pocket. *Beware, suspicious-looking man outside store hopping in snow*. I breathed a deep sigh of relief, although my arm flinched from the ghost steps of that stupid mouse. Why had that frightened me so?

Stamen and Frankly came churning around the corner. I led them away, still unable to think, heading toward the 1 place in town with which I was familiar—a spot where I once died, a place I thought we might find shelter for the night.

"That really was a cute little mouse," Stamen said.

"It looked like an alien," I said. "It gave me the creeps."

The broad city avenue lay before us, covered with brown snow—like the fur of a dog. Plenty of barking and snarling came from out there, too. *Focus*, I told myself. *Your fear is a mouse, your future a Doberman.* It began snowing.

4

By the 4th time I died, I was completely underground, passed from hand to hand, at the mercy of any Bi-level who offered help. I already had a sizable underground rep, both for the elegance with which I died and for the numbers—I was gaining on the record. The record-holder at that time was a kid out of Mexico City who'd done 6, although 3 were not well documented. Later that year, the Mexican boy died for good sleeping in the backseat of a car stalled in traffic—too much bad air and he succumbed. A newsletter called *Morgue Update*, distributed secretly among dying enthusiasts, carried the news. No 1 else in the car had died. His readiness to go down had betrayed him.

I ran into trouble in Cleveland. The guy putting me up wanted to weird-sex and got belligerent when I wouldn't. His name was Wysh, and he threatened to turn me over to the Cops.

I sexed a lot of people back then, mostly for pleasure, but sometimes to make things go more smoothly. This Wysh, though, I didn't like. Besides being a crude bore, he had bad skin and a nose too little for his face.

I took off. Right out the bathroom window, down an old fire escape, and on down to the City History Pavilion. I hung out in front of the Flaming River Hologram, lugging my dismantled Accu in a saxophone case, confident I'd spot some other Subterranean or someone would spot me. I hadn't been under long, but I'd been Bi-level for a good while. If the Cops really understood the underground, they would just arrest everybody at the tourist joints. But it would make for negative pub.

I ran into a woman named Madeleine Bruce, a middle-aged Politico who had been under a long time. She had seen my die in StLouis and remembered me—once you die for people, they find it hard to put you out of their minds. I explained my trouble.

"I know that fuck," she said. "Little Make-A-Wysh, the fleeb." Madeleine had a perfectly square face and an inch-high flat-top that smelled of Brylcream. Not a large woman, she nonetheless had a powerful presence. "No true Bi-level would turn you in. Too scared he'd get nailed himself. That little fuck's a Darling, I bet." I had to ask what a Darling was. "A fucking snitch," she said. "You're green as garbage, aren't you?"

"I've been under a month."

"Practically a virgin. C'mon." She walked slowly, covering her square head with a shawl, which made her look much older. She'd angle her head to look up at me, then smile or giggle—all part of her disguise. Outside, maneuvering down an icy sidewalk, she said, "You do anything besides die?"

It seemed like a simple question, but I didn't know what to say. The question would haunt me for years.

"What I mean," Madeleine said, "is there another reason you're underground?"

"Just the dying. Somebody turned me in, so I had to go under or go to jail."

"Not jail." She shook her square head. "Dying Artists, they kill. Poetic justice, you know?"

I nodded, unable to make words, realizing for the 1st time how deep into it I was, how far from home I was even in my hometown.

By evening we sat in the back of a moving van, beneath an oak dining table, furniture roped in all around us. She had given me a stat-flattener, jeans, a Cubs cap, and a dirty workshirt that even stank like a man. "We're safe in here," Madeleine began. "If the truck's inspected, they'll never yank out enough crap to get back to us. You ever ride in a truck, make sure you're way in the back in a complete clutter. The driver's got to be a weak little shit. Some brawny guy, and they might make him unload the whole fucking thing."

She went on to warn me about the dangers of living underground, especially from other Subterraneans. "Politicos are generally trustworthy, though fucking tedious to listen to. The most likable and interesting are the Artists, like yourself, and the long-time Poor, who more and more go under for shelter, believe it or not, but there are plenty of uglies down under. Shit Peddlers, Smut Wranglers, Pickpockets, Die-Hard Guppies—you know the types."

I didn't know anything. Madeleine taught me. "Anybody too happy to see you, too eager to see you die—skip out. Don't trust anyone who's not afraid. Let that be your touchstone."

She took me to Filadelfia, got me a cot in a con-demned gym that smelled vaguely of mace, and arranged a die. "I know you artists need to do your thing," she said. It took place in the gym, on the canvas of an old boxing ring.

I wore boxing trunks and a spaghetti strap T-shirt that showed off my breasts. There were maybe 100 people, supposedly all Subs or Bi's, but there were plenty of dilettantes, which was fine as long as they didn't do anything stupid to get us busted—which for me, Madeleine insisted, meant death. Permanent death.

I stretched out on the canvas, took the whiff, and went down, while a guy dressed like a referee counted me out. Already, dying had become a circus.

Dead, I rose above my body, above the crowd surrounding the boxing ring. I hovered in the chilled air and looked down at my dead self, looked at the crowd that studied me, heard the hush—no 1 talking, no 1 even breathing it seemed, as if in sympathy. While I watched, I started to understand why people treated my dying differently, why everybody loved my act.

Dead, I had a kind of beauty—a sort of radiance—that I never possessed alive. A transformation took place when I died. My face lost the tension of living, and instead of becoming slack, became lustrous. My skin took on a sheen of light. That night, for the 1st time, I genuinely thought of myself as an artist. Seeing me die could make you think death was not so horrible, could make you think death had its own kind of beauty—an amazing revelation, but not a good thing to think about if you were planning on returning to this ugly life.

I watched as they slapped the Accu on and zapped me, but I remained up there, above it all. They waited, checked my pulse, listened to my heart, zapped again: nothing. The hush ended, followed 1st by the collective intake of breath, then the interrogative tone of dismay and fear.

This thought occurred to me: the 4th labor of death is desire.

Suddenly somebody from the crowd yelled, "Naw, it's anger, damn it. Not desire. Don't it piss you off to be stuck up there watching?"

"Where are you?" I said.

"Get real, bimbo. If you can't pick me out of a crowd, you're worse than dead."

I spotted him, then. "You're a goddamn fucking lion!" A *huge* goddamn fucking lion—3 or 4 times the size of earthly lions—but with the face of an old man. He crouched on the canvas of the boxing ring, close to my dead body and my harried rescue team.

"That's my girl. I knew there was a little vinegar in you." he said, growling in a friendly way. "You pass the 4th labor, but there ain't no way you're gonna make it back to Breethie Land." He looked from the floating me to the dead me. "I'll look less like a lion the longer you're dead." While he spoke, his claws began to turn to fingers, but his body seemed to grow scales.

As they hit the Accu a 3rd time, a drop of rusty water from the battered ceiling plummeted down, right through my floating self and onto my dead self, landing on my neck—which I felt, cold and stinging. I had come back through the drop of water. "Blind luck," I heard the lion call.

I opened my eyes as the shock was administered.

It can save you if you're dead, but it can kill you if you're alive. Luckily, I was still dead enough, though I screamed and felt my lungs turn to smoke, my flesh to flame. Then another drop of water hit me, and the fire extinguished.

"Nobody on fucking earth dies like you," Madeleine told me after. She had me wrapped in coarse blankets, my legs still quivering uncontrollably from the shock. A handsome young man carried me out to a waiting car. "Too many people saw you," Madelaine said, walking along beside us. "Security was shit. You've got to get out of town."

I rode in a hearse, in a casket, all the way to DC. "If we get stopped," the fat man behind the wheel said, "just pretend you're dead." He guffawed. He had seen me die, had been enthralled, describing the attempts to revive me exactly as I had seen them while dead. "The whole stinking lot of us was scared shitless," he said. "Never seen anything like it. Never felt anything like it. I cried, right in front of everybody, and they was crying, too."

He described himself as a Politico. "Not big time, a course. Got in a jam on account of a letter to the editor I wrote." He didn't reveal its contents, and I knew better than to ask. Guns, I guessed—although this was long before the Banjo Society. I couldn't figure what else it could have been. He didn't sound like the Abortion Advocate type, and I didn't think Madeleine would set me up with a Race Monger. In those simpler days, I had known only few categories.

After we arrived in DC, while the hearse trudged through traffic, I mentioned Madeleine and wondered aloud, without actually asking, why she had gone under.

"Christ!" he said. "She's the woman who bombed Coutant Academy." He sputtered and swiveled his head to stare at me in disbelief. "If you got a public education, you owe Madeleine Bruce."

It had happened when I was 7, the bombing of a private DC school after Congress passed a bill ending public education. President Zack Schwartz vetoed the bill after the bombing. Within a year, the money spent on public schools doubled.

"You're part of her legacy," he said, pulling to a curb to let me out. "Everybody that's got an education owes her." I guessed then that his letter had been about public ed—a battle so old I'd never thought of it as a real fight. "Madeleine Bruce is 1 of the great people of our time," he insisted through the open car window. Then he waved and drove away.

Years later, after I was rehabbed and back in the larger world, I researched the Coutant bombing for a sociology class. 19 children died. 7 more lost limbs. 3 made blind.

The gym was gone, but its rubble still filled the lot. "We hike across town for this?" Frankly leaned against his knees puffing little clouds into the cold air.

"Why aren't you depressed about your physical conditioning?" Stamen said. "You could do a couple of jumping jacks, turn red-faced, and huff pathetically for 30 minutes."

"If I am doing that every night, I get into shape," Frankly said. "It's self-rewarding—no good for a depressionist."

From behind a short wall of crumbling brick, a yellow-eyed dog raised his spotted head and growled.

"We've got to find a place to sleep," I said and began walking again. I had counted 96 dogs on the way over, most of them middle-sized, but a few huge mangy things with mean-looking eyes. I'd only heard 3 instances of gunfire—maybe the dogs kept the shootings down. I certainly hadn't seen any Freedom People—besides us. Unlike NeYork, no 1 slept on the streets.

"We have to handle the next 2 nights," I said, "and then hope that Mother will have something planned for the die. Otherwise, this is our lives, right here."

"How did you manage to go underground before?" Stamen's face had turned red from the cold, his nose running. He reminded me of the mouse Blib had offered—an unkind thought, but my brother had rodent qualities.

"Dying paved the way," I said. "It's not so easy if you don't have an in. Mother is a major Politico, but we're nothing."

"I was a Silk-Level bureaucrat," Stamen reminded me.

"I am a near-famous depressionist for 3 years," Frankly added.

"We're all has-beens," I said. Suddenly, I began crying, a few loose tears to begin with, but soon the whole waterworks. Rather than console me, Stamen and Frankly joined in. We walked down the sidewalk bawling, practically begging to be arrested.

That was when it finally happened. Walking in the Filadelfia cold, my eyes spouting water like a retroSprinkler, the snow causing a brownout in the already darkening sky, a Great Dane sticking his head out of an alleyway to sniff at my butt, I finally accepted the fact that I'd gone under again, that the life I studied and worked for had ended, that I was back at the starting point—only older and no longer a star.

But also not alone, and if they weren't the ideal companions, then, well, neither was I.

Once I accepted this, my head began working. I started recalling the old tricks and dodges. I made a plan.

We headed for Tumble University.

"1 of my friends goes there," Frankly said, hopping now to stave off the cold, wiping the tears from his cheeks.

"Would your friend put us up for the night?" Stamen asked.

I groaned. "You're hopeless. His friend hasn't been near Tumble U in an elephant's lifetime."

In the old days, universities had been havens for Subs. You could sleep in the library or the student union in heated comfort until late in the evening. Often you would find open classrooms and could stay the entire night. Students were sympathetic.

From what I'd heard, all that had changed. IDs were required to enter buildings. Most libraries had X-ray walk-thrus.

It took us 2 hours to cover only a few miles, pausing beneath awnings to get out of the snow, ducking into alleys when we saw Cop cars. Down 1 alley, Stamen spotted a pack of dogs tugging on something sizable. It had the general appearance of a human body.

"HEY!" Frankly and I yelled at the same moment—a technique we had practiced together on walks around NeYork—but these dogs did not even look up. Stamen began running toward them.

"They'll kill you!" I screamed, running after him, Frankly scampering along behind me.

Stamen suddenly halted, spreads his arms wing-like, and clapped them together in a sonic-boomish way. Frankly dropped to his butt. The dogs squealed in fear or pain, then galloped off down the alley. Above us, windows creaked open, voices murmured.

"Where do you learn that trick?" Frankly said, wiping off the seat of his pants as he got up. But Stamen had run to the body: a middle-aged woman, not long dead from the looks of her.

"What do we do?" I asked.

Stamen shook his head. "I don't know. We *should* call the Cops, but given our circumstances, that's out of the question."

Her coat, gapping at the seams, bore an insignia on the breast—a tightly stitched red crown. Beneath the coat, she wore a soiled Hercules Mouse T-shirt. Her pudgy face, grime filling the wrinkled lines, smiled at us smugly. The dogs had chewed away 1 of her hands, but the stump hardly bled. I drove past human roadkill all the time, but it felt different on foot. We felt responsible for the body. Dumb, but we did.

Frankly tapped my shoulder, pointed up. From the windows, on either side of the alley, the barrels of rifles jutted out—I counted 6. A radio played somewhere, old fashioned jazz, a saxophone blowing sadly.

"Don't clap your hands again," Frankly said. He pointed to a covered doorway. "We are putting her up there. The dogs can't get here there."

It meant carrying her to a filthy dumpster, Frankly and I passing her up to Stamen, who balanced himself on the greasy lid and lifted her onto the aluminum roof that covered the entryway. We shoved the dumpster down the alley, so the dogs couldn't leap onto it to get her.

As we headed back toward the street, something

came plummeting down from above. We all jumped back. It landed ahead of us with a plop—not large, smaller than a bread box.

"It's a loaf of bread," Stamen said. He unwrapped the plastic bag covering it and sniffed. "Fresh."

I looked up in time to see a final window close. "A gift," I said. We ate the bread as we hiked. Warm, rich bread.

When we reached campus, we hunted for an English or Foreign Languages building. The recycling dumpsters behind these facilities would hold mainly paper—clean enough to sleep in, and good insulation if it hadn't been emptied recently. Science buildings were riskier—no telling what kind of stuff they might call garbage.

Finding a clean dumpster amounted to the full equation, my whole plan. Not an amazing thing to remember, but a start, and maybe it would get us through the night.

Behind the Poetry & Rhetoric building, we found the ideal dumpster—huge enough to park a car in, covered with a rubber lid, new, and about a third full of paper. A dream motel for the down and out— which explained the people already in it. We didn't see them until we tumbled inside.

"Shut the lid." The voice called to mind stones grating against other stones. Stamen obeyed. A flashlight suddenly illuminated the dumpster, blinding the 3 of us kneeling among the sheets of sentimental verse and botched essays.

Stamen said, "We come in peace."

"Yeah?" said the voice. "I bet you come apart, too."

"Nice pun," said Frankly.

"We were freezing," I said. "Let us stay long enough to warm up, then we'll find another place to spend the night."

A 2nd voice, feminine and nasal: "Who's looking for you?"

"Nobody yet," I said, hoping I spoke the truth. "Except maybe some pissed-off dogs. Can't you direct that light against a wall? You're blinding us."

"I like you blind," Stone said.

"How long have you been under?" I asked. "I used to be under years ago. I bet we know some of the same people—if you've been under a while. I used to know Madeleine Bruce."

Stone grunted. "That's easy enough to say."

Stamen said, "You knew Madeleine Bruce? The child killer?"

"She spent a lot of her time in Filadelfia," I said to Stone. "I'm trying to think of local people."

A 3rd voice spoke, this 1 from behind us. "Not Filly. None of us has been here long." A smooth, musical voice. I wanted to turn and look at him, but I knew it could be dangerous. The light would illuminate him, too. But Stamen and Frankly had already stared, so I turned. Only his head, shoulders, and arms showed above the paper. A balding frizzhead wearing square glasses. "What city?" I said. "I used to get around."

"Politico?" Frizzhead asked.

"I used to die, back when it was illegal."

Stone man grunted. "An arrr-teest," he said, and the woman laughed. "What about Rif and Raf?"

"They're new Subs, just went under. But I—"

"Chicago," the Frizzhead said.

I threw out names, only those completely under-ground. No Bi-levels, on the off chance these people were Cops. Subterraneans had no cover to blow. Stone grunted several times. Frizz nodded. "You sound legit," he said, "though a lot of the people you named have been disappeared a long time."

Stone said, "You're Lydia Melmoth. I never saw you die, but my brother did, in DC. Claims you were the best. Used to carry a Polaroid of your corpse in his butt pocket."

I felt a rush, a thrill, a cheesy, junky, noodle of delight and shame like when a Retro whistled at your legs, or a teacher petted you. I didn't want to like fame, but I did.

We spent the night in conversation, in the dark, beneath the warming papers. Frankly started sniffing the mimeos, which led him to extol the virtues of the InfoTechno Collapse. "When we are students, we never have anything more tangible than a computer screen," he said, lifting an armful of papers to his nose. "The Collapse brings back all this."

Stone and Frizzhead didn't reveal their names, but the woman called herself Cee. Underground because she was poor, she had less to worry about. Stone and Frizzhead were Politicos.

"What did you do to be forced underground?" Stamen asked Stone.

"Blackout beakerhead," he said.

"*Never* ask that of a Politico," I said. "You can request a general category, but no specifics. They have to be offered freely."

"Am I a Politico?" Stamen asked. I could tell from the upturn in his voice the possibility pleased him, a new slot he could slip into.

"Yeah," I said, "you're a Politico."

Stone said, "What about you, shrimp? What's your label?"

"Depression," Frankly said.

Eventually the conversation got going. I wanted to know if the old underground networks still existed.

Frizzhead said, "They're still in place, but they won't do you any good. They've become very exclusive."

Stone agreed. "I've applied 3 years running. Either I'm too small potatoes or my references suck."

Frizzhead told me my past fame wouldn't help. "Unless you have some new notoriety."

"She is on national television in 2 nights," Frankly said.

"A Nowist underground?" Stone said. "I've never known a Sub to have hobbies."

"Nowism's not a hobby. It's a way of life," Frankly insisted. "It's a perceptual filter."

"It's a grammarian's nightmare," Stamen added.

Frizzhead said the TV spot might get me into the network.

Cee said, "National tube? The Cops won't touch you if you've got national spotlight. Some things are still sacred."

"She's right," Stone said. "You'd have to be in deep shit to remain under. Really deep shit."

Frizzhead quickly changed the subject, for which I was grateful. A TV spot would make me invulnerable for a while, but I would have to remain famous to stay out of trouble.

The latest way to disguise yourself, Frizzhead said, was through fashion. "The more stinG, the better." He, however, did not take his own advice. He wore a shirt from the collar-bleed era, complete with broad stripes, dipping collar tips that buttoned together at his navel, and those stupid pectoral pads—popular for about a month 5 or 6 years ago, now the mainstay of 2nd-hand stores. "Rip off people who just bought clothes—not clothing stores. Too risky," he said. "Couple of shoplifters got nailed in Chicago, snipers posted in false ceilings."

"I read about that," Stamen said. "If the clothing isn't valued at more than 200 dollars, though, it isn't legal. Regardless of the store's posted Rights/Trade."

Frizz hadn't known this. He encouraged Stamen to continue.

"The InfoTechno Collapse produced a radical shift in the interpretation of rights. I watched a lot of the legislation go through." Stamen paused, but he was smart enough not to reveal his former government position. "The idea that you should be free to trade off your own freedoms in exchange for shopping rights, cash, or whatever—that was unheard of before the Collapse."

Frankly put his head in my lap, sniffed more mimeo, and closed his eyes.

"Although," Stamen went on, "it's hard for me to say exactly what the nature of the connection is between the Collapse and the trade-offs, I—"

"Power," Frizz said. "They take tech out of our hands and keep it for themselves. Beginning of Total State. Making liberty tradable merchandise paves the way to ending independence. Everything becomes a commodity, even freedom."

Cee decided to jump in. "Then why don't they do it and make the place a dictatorship?" she wanted to know. "Why isn't the government already whole-hog totalitarian?"

Frizz cocked his head slightly, peering at her, happy she had asked. "Because they stumbled upon something better. No need to forcibly hold back the people. You don't even need to prevent information from getting out—although sometimes, stupidly, they still do. Instead, you set up a megaMedia so pervasive that other news doesn't really count." He was getting worked up now, throwing his arms around while he spoke. "If the megaMedia doesn't cover something, it ain't news. Who cares what some intellectual magazine has to say, or some tiny alternative news channel. You let everybody talk, but you make sure that only a few folks are listened to."

Frankly whispered to me, "Those who cling to the past are destined to dress badly." He sniggered smugly and nuzzled my tummy, his warm breath at my belly button.

Frizzhead went on to talk about the Info-Networks that had been developing before the crash, networks separate from the government and the popular media. "We had the tech to reach enough people so that the national media had to at least acknowledge that some event was taking place—US support of Retropartheid Guerrillas, for example. A video of a mass execution circuited on 3 People's Networks 1 week, and the next week QBN did 20 seconds on ongoing US support for the fascists. Congress cut off money to the guerrillas for several weeks."

Stone added little grunts to the conversation, then he began to snore. Frankly continued to chuckle snidely at intervals, but after a while, he fell asleep. Cee was either asleep or very quiet. Meanwhile, I did nothing—didn't talk, didn't sleep. I didn't really even listen. I hadn't heard this particular theory about the Collapse, but I'd heard a million others. Most people only half-believed the official story, that the megaVirus was the invention of a lone, crazed, misanthropic hacker. Once the researchers came up with tamper-proof tech, the stuff was supposed to again become available to everyone. Until then, the government and the few special-permit businesses had to keep their techno work secret and separate to avoid getting wiped out again. People didn't entirely believe the story, but they acted as if they did. It was like campaign promises—you chose your candidates on the basis of promises you knew they wouldn't keep. The ability to hold contradictory ideas had become central to getting by in the world.

Even when the conversation eventually ended, I remained awake in the dark. My brother's high-pitched snore, which ought to have reminded me of our childhood room, instead reminded me of this boy named Booty. This Booty I had known a long time ago, who I sexed while he was doing a die—riding him as he went down. He never came back; Booty stayed dead. Later that night a buddy of his tried to rape me. "I watched you sex the shit out of Booty," he said. "No reason for you to turn me down." I provided the reason—that I detested him—a grayish, pretty boy with pitted cheeks and breath like lighter fluid.

I told him off, and he hit me, *hard*, knocking me to the floor. Luckily, the woman in the next room heard. She charged in carrying a baseball bat, chased off the guy, then took me to a Bi-level nurse, who answered her door in her pajamas. "What is it?" she asked as she let us in.

"This 1 got smacked upside the head," the 1st woman said. "She don't know where she is."

They put me to bed, which meant making the nurse's lover—a dark, thin woman—get up. They made hot tea and talked to me. They had all attended the die, had seen me naked, riding Booty while the Ater took him down.

"You're in Chicago," the nurse kept saying because I couldn't remember. She whispered softly in my ear. "You're with friends." That sweet whispering, so settling, so comforting—that was what Stamen's snoring reminded me of: the night I lost my friend Booty and almost got raped, and how 3 strangers saved me.

I fell asleep thinking about it, but I didn't sleep long. The final part of my weird logic came together. I woke with a start in the pitch-black knowing who Frizzhead was. I remembered his face from a photo in the news a few years back. A Major Rev, 1 of those guys who wanted to turn it all upside down. He had infiltrated the country club set in Chicago, slept with a handful of debutantes, his health certificate a counterfeit. He had IT. 12 women and men had been infected. Their closed-court society, designed to keep themselves clean, blown apart. He had been labeled a terrorist by the press, a hero by fellow Revs, but even a lot of Rads thought spreading IT was wrong. He'd had better hair back then, and he hadn't worn glasses in the TV pic, but I knew he was the killer.

Suddenly the dumpster filled with light. Stone had both a flashlight and a gun pointed directly into my face. I didn't move. After a moment, he angled the light toward the rubber ceiling so that I could see. The gun disappeared beneath the sea of papers. He whispered, "I heard you wake up. You made a little whoop."

I nodded and took a breath, my heart sprinting.

"Can't be too careful," he said. "We just met you all." The light went off. He made settling noises. Then his voice came out of the dark. "*You* dabble in death. *We* have to take it seriously."

5

The network rep oozed enthusiasm. "We are *so* happy you've changed your mind." She had a cheerleader-cum-executive voice, like she had just given up bubble gum and taken up scotch. "Qigley really wants to *meet* you. You are his *idol*." She advised me to get to the temporary studio the network had set up outside the arena by 4:00 tomorrow afternoon.

"I might need a shower," I said, "and an iron."

"No sweat," she said, and prattled on about the facilities.

The pay phone stood unprotected in the center of a university lawn. A cold wind gusted through, picking up the fresh brown snow, hurling it against my bare legs. I had seen pictures of old phone booths, cute little glass houses, complete with shuttable doors. Pay phones had disappeared before the Collapse, and when they were reinstalled no 1 had given a thought to the caller's comfort because no 1 expected them to survive more than a year or so. 2 decades later, the concrete poles holding the phones still angled sloppily out of the ground, still in the same stupid locations picked originally for the convenience of the work crews—like this 1 in a virtual wind tunnel.

"About the Bite,'" the network girl went on, "just come sober and we'll do the rest." The QBN "Qik Bite" consisted of 60 seconds of filler and fluff to separate the commercials. The difficulties of broadcasting a die all centered on the length of the actual death and resuscitation—only a few minutes. If the die went longer than 5 minutes, the dying artist would likely get gray rot—or worse. Which meant the network needed a lot of filler. Enter Lydia Melmoth, filler incarnate.

"Oh," the rep went on, "I should add that the Cops and Federal Big Boys have been positively *hounding* us about you. We're so thrilled to have a *fugitive* on the show, but don't dally by the phone, I'm sure they'll be showing up there *soon*."

"Jesus," I said.

"He rose from the dead, too, didn't he?" she replied. "Maybe you could allude to him in the Bite?"

"How am I going to get to the arena studio if they've been listening? Won't they—"

"Oh, honey, honey! They won't screw with *us*! You just have to*night* to worry about. Tomorrow, you're *ours*."

I slapped the receiver down and started running back to the dumpster, trying to calculate the number of minutes I'd spent on the phone. How long did it take to trace a call?

"Cops," I called, nearing the dumpster. "Maybe Big Boys, too." I didn't want to explain—Frizzhead and Stone might have been justifiably angry. "We've got to run."

Mr. Frizz bounded out of the dumpster and began running without even looking my way.

"I'll save our spot," Cee said to Stone. She knitted her hands together to give Frankly a boost.

"Is she going to be safe?" Stamen asked.

"She's Poor, not Politico," Stone said. "They won't waste much time on her. They're after 1 of us." He cast an accusatory glance at me.

While we waited for Frankly to make it over— "He's a fucking snail," Stone said—Frizzhead disappeared around the corner of the building.

"We're not going to stick together?" Stamen called to his back.

"Don't waste your breath," I said, already running by the time Frankly hit the pavement.

Stone accompanied us to the edge of the campus. "Don't come back here tonight," he said. "In a few days, if you want, but not tonight." He paused, staring at us apologetically. "This is our home." Out of shame or guilt, he added, "You know your way around? You got a location in mind?"

"Isn't there a big museum near here?" I said.

He gave me directions. "Good luck," he said, and then he ran back in the direction we had just come.

"Do you think he knows what he's doing?" Stamen asked. "He's heading right into their hands."

"He must have a hiding spot," I said. "He just wants us out of the way." I began walking, a fast pace. Running might call attention to ourselves.

"When I am famous," Frankly said, "I'm buying a dumpster like that 1. I sleep like a baby last night."

Gunshots sounded behind us; ahead of us came a clamor of barks and yips. "It's cold," I said. "It's brutal out here." No 1 disagreed.

The Museum of Ontological Stuff had all the shoes Velma rOOst wore during her ground-breaking All-Shoe Fashion-N-Dance Tour, which got her banned in the Plebeian Substates, coronated in the Blip Cities, and shot in Atlanta. The shoe with the bullet hole occupied a separate case, a pink pump with a yellow silk flower. It had been 1 of her breast shoes, so the sniper had been aiming for her heart, which ruled out the Protest Wound—something the Plebeians now argued as protected under the 1st Amendment as long as the recipient was a public figure. But Protest Wounds could not be life-threatening, so the shot at Velma rOOst had been definitely illegal.

Footage of her waving from her hospital room played on a tiny screen next to the perforated shoe, but to see a recording of the actual performance cost 9 bills. Frankly and I had seen her live during the original tour. I didn't see what all the fuss was about. Plebeians didn't like any art unaccompanied by violins, or art that had to do with sex—even if 1 of the partners was just a stiletto-heeled boot.

Frankly came up to me smiling slyly, which meant he'd found something about me in the museum. Whenever we went to a place like this, he immediately scanned it to see if they had my picture.

"Don't tell me," I said. "They've got that stupid lowers-only photo."

He shook his big head. "Better." His smile grew completely out of control. "They have *film*. You die every 20 minutes, 12 hours a day, 365 days a year."

I couldn't speak. People had often brought cameras to the dies, but we had made them pile their stuff in a corner, out of reach. We might designate 1 person to take pictures, but never movies, which could be used as evidence. Stills just showed some somebody lying around. Besides, we had this notion of dying as a live and living art—sort of like opera. We didn't take money for it; we didn't let people film it.

Frankly started hammering my spine with his open hand, and I got my voice back. "Which die is it?" I asked him.

He shrugged. "I don't know. It costs 11 dollars."

"Wow," I said, "that's more than the Velma rOOst film."

"And they pay her royalties," Frankly said. "If they pay you a dollar a head, you are rich."

"Have we got 11 dollars?" I asked him. I'd spent most of the 20 Blib had slipped me on breakfast for the 3 of us in the museum cafeteria.

"You mean have *I* got 11 dollars," Frankly said.

"You only have money because you were staying at my apartment," I reminded him. It occurred to me that my brother, who also might have money, had vanished. "Where's Stamen?"

Frankly glanced about. "You tell him to disappear, he disappears," he said, hopping slightly as I dragged him into the milling crowd. "Stamen's a concrete thinker." He grabbed my skirt as we navigated the river of people. "What is Ontology, anyway?" he asked.

"Oh, it's 1 of those Reality, Pro or Con sort of things."

"I see why they have you in here," he said. "Dying is as real as it gets, but I don't see why Velma rOOst is here, or half the other stuff."

"The premise of the rOOst show was very metaphysical," I said. "All you remember is getting a look at her breasts."

Frankly nodded seriously. "They are big."

I expected to see Stamen in 1 of the many long lines. The museum had no admission charge, but it cost plenty to see any of the good Ontology. We made our way through the Jigsaw Materialists Room, the Head of Pin Platform, the Magnetic Reasoning Sphere, the Illusionary Reality Slough, and even the Descartes à la carte Cafeteria—but no Stamen. All that remained was the Beyond the Pale Pavilion.

"You avoid yourself," Frankly said, giving me a push toward the entrance.

"Get your hand off my butt," I told him.

Frankly steered me directly to the Dying Artist Display. A huge video screen flashed questions: IS THERE DEATH? IS THERE LIFE AFTER DEATH? ARE DYING ARTISTS ANGELS? A lot of knickknacks and artifacts decorated the wall, but Frankly bulled us past them to the line for the film.

Immediately, a handsome well-dressed man wearing figure-8 eyeglasses addressed me. "Aren't you her? You are. You're our angel."

A teenage girl in a checkerboard tutu joined him. "I've seen your movie 50 times," she said, taking my hand and squeezing. "You truly die like an angel."

"Yes," the well-dressed man in the figure-8s agreed, "like an angel." He flashed me a beautiful smile, which made me recall for a moment 1 of the advantages of fame—good-looking groupies.

Autographs followed, handshaking, a few people keeled over and feigned death to ingratiate themselves. They ushered us quickly to the head of the

line. Frankly got the guy with the glasses to pay for
our tickets.

My 5th death took place in DC, at a senator's house,
in the middle of the day. I had floated around town 6
months, working 1st as a waitress, later as a dancer in
a SloMo Bar. They called us dancers, but actually we
acted out scenes from literature in slow motion—like
putting on 1 of Gatsby's big hullabaloos, or playing
Anna K. throwing herself beneath a train, or Tom
Jones eating with his hands, or Sloopy being hanged.
I didn't exactly excel at it, so I never got the good
parts—nothing that involved falling or jumping or
going into labor. All of which are a bitch to carry off
in slow motion. I did play Zono the Zen Prostitute in
the famous Noise-as-Violence scene from DFW's
classic novel, but that was my only decent role.

This guy who had seen me die in StLouis recognized me, called me a genius of death, said this
SloMo stuff insulted my dignity as an artist.

"Yeah," I said, "but I get paid for it."

"You need to die again," he insisted. "You should
be treated like a queen." He worked for a senator,
and I fell a little bit in love with him that night. We
sexed in the men's room, met every night of the week
for the next couple of months—in the backseat of his
car, on the staircase of the Washington Monument, in
the grass at Twinkie Park. I couldn't go to his apartment—the Big Boys employed 1 of his roommates—
and he couldn't openly associate with Subterraneans,
so I couldn't take him to my place.

Maybe I would have fallen completely in love with
him, but I had a feeling that he only loved me

because he had seen me die. He kept talking about it, how it transcended the boundaries of performance and art unlike anything else he had ever witnessed. Which made his love for me seem almost impersonal. Whenever I had an orgasm I flinched and went soft, "like you died just a little," he liked to say, the words lighting his face as if from the glowing ash of a cigarette.

He arranged a die at his senator's and brought me over early to meet dignitaries. The senator shook my hand, smiled his public smile, then introduced me to his wife, a few congresspeople, some wealthy DC types, and a federal judge. "Don't worry," the judge confided. "We're all cool."

They led me to a single bed, covered with a crisp white sheet, centered beneath a large and elaborate chandelier. I crawled onto the mattress. The crowd gathered around in respectful silence. Then they held hands—a custom I had initiated myself during the die of a friend. Published articles had mentioned the hand-holding as an integral part of the whole affair; it shouldn't have surprised me that these well-read people would try to follow the appropriate custom, but it did. I felt a wild sense of power—thrilling, but not what you want to feel before a die. Better to enter the great beyond with a bit of humility.

I had worn a silky blue dress, a gift from the aide, my lover, which I carefully spread over my knees before lying back and settling my head on a white pillow. The film opened with my hands on the silky dress. Those hands startled me so much that I immediately looked to the flesh-and-blood hands in my lap, but the dim theater light didn't permit me to tell whether they were still as slender, pale, strong, and beautiful. I knew they weren't, of course; I had been a teenager when the film was made.

My name appeared on the screen, superimposed over my body now in repose. "Death," the film narrator said in an overly serious voice, then paused, "the final frontier." I expected Frankly to laugh, but he was rapt.

I watched my death—the smile I gave everyone, the moment of concentration before I closed my eyes and gestured for the Ater—and then the theater crowd inhaled in squeaking harmony as I fell out of life.

The on-screen monitor produced a big fat zer0. For only the 2nd time, I witnessed the transformation, the shining presence that entered me when life exited. Why couldn't I have that beauty while I was alive? Why did death produce a radiance I was denied in life?

The audience watched intently, but they couldn't see the most interesting part: death, this time, was the color of freshly cut wood—the very air I didn't breathe was this color. A male voice sang a song nearby, a Crooner-type voice, singing without words, or the words so blended together that I couldn't make sense of them. Then I recognized my father's voice. Finally, again, I would get to see my father—the 1st time since my initial death.

"Where are you, Daddy?" I said, my own voice betraying me, sounding childlike and too full of hope.

"Over here, sweetheart." His voice cut through the tan air, honey smooth. Turning, I saw him slouching under a slant of blue light that had no source, wearing a gray suit jacket and black turtleneck sweater, a cigarette in hand, smoke spiraling up into the light.

He hummed and tapped his hip, the opposite foot keeping time, too. His face held the alcoholic haze of satisfaction. He sang, "You're just the kind of a girl who would always-ways play fair."

My father, in death, had become a lounge singer.

"That's right," he said, in answer to my thoughts. "I always wanted to be 1. Tell the truth now, baby girl, didn't you? I can arrange it, darling. I pull a lot of weight around here." Behind him appeared a deer with human eyes and golden antlers, striding up next to him with precise steps. My father petted the deer while he spoke to me. "You get through this little number here, and you've only got a couple teeny tiny steps to go, giftwise, my sweet girl."

I asked him, right then, a question that had bounced around in my head while I was alive, the question that seemed worth dying for. I said, "What's the meaning of life, Daddy? I'm going back, you know. I'm going to be alive again any second now. I don't want to know about the labors of death, I want to know about *life*. What's it all about, Daddy?"

He cocked his head to 1 side, smiled, winked, pointed with his smoking cigarette off into the wooden air. The deer with the fancy antlers stared where the cigarette seemed to point. My father began singing, "You got to give a little, take a little, let that sweet heart of yours *break* a little—"

"I don't want to hear some dumb song, Daddy."

He stopped singing. The deer loped off into the wood-colored nether regions. My father waited until the deer disappeared. "Good answer, sweetkins," he said. "Watch this." He put the burning cigarette in 1 ear, tilted his head, and it popped out the other ear. "My brain is on fire," he said, smiling. He flicked the fiery butt at me. Immediately, I was immolated, but without pain, only the heat and the sensation of being consumed.

"*Hot* for you," my father began singing. "We're all so *hot* for you . . ." The flames turned me to nothing but ash and smoke and the charred smell of hair. I could see only the haze of my own smoke, but I heard my father, no longer singing, say, "Forgive the dead, as they forgive those who live after them." And then: "The furniture is alive."

I passed right through the smoke into my life. People were applauding. Many members of the film audience wept while clapping feverishly, turning to face me, their arms raised high. Others rushed to my seat to touch my hair and mutter unintelligibly. Frankly sat beside me, openly bawling, his feet swinging back and forth, inches above the floor. The girl in the tutu said, "That was *so* stinG. You die *so* perfect."

I smiled and nodded. "Pull yourself together," I whispered to Frankly. "We have to find my brother."

Frankly sniffed melodramatically, tried to get himself under control.

The handsome guy in the figure-8 glasses loomed over us. His hands filled the pockets of his expensive brown suitcoat, and when he opened his arms, the jacket flapped like the wings of a bat. "You are the diva of dying," he said. "If there is ever anything I can do for you . . ."

Through his tears, Frankly said, "How about a loan?"

"He's joking," I said when the man reached for his wallet. I smiled at him now too largely, a flirting sort of smile. I had come to the instantaneous decision

that this man was a Big Boy. He was too good-looking
to be here accidentally. He wouldn't want to arrest us
inside, especially not here where I was considered a
hero. He would want to trick us into going out.
"Thanks, anyway," I said.

He merely shrugged, smiled. He clearly didn't
want to leave us, but finally he said, "Another time."
He said it so sincerely I decided I must be wrong.
Not a Big Boy, just a fan, a good-looking fan in that
superficial movie-star sort of way. His clothes were
too nice to belong to a fed, in any case.

Frankly and I hightailed it to the top floor, the
Museum Library. I had begun to fear that somebody
had lured Stamen outside. The library took up the
whole floor, but only a few of the shelves had the new
paper-n-print books. "StinG," Frankly said, looking
around. All that remained of the old computers were
the discolorations on the table mats.

Books were stinG, but this library had no 1 in it.
We hustled over to the windows and stared out at the
people milling below just beyond the museum doors.
We scanned the crowd, looking for Stamen's distinc-
tive shape. "He could be in 1 of the exhibits," I said.

"Stamen doesn't pay 9 dollars to save his life,"
Frankly said. The nonirony of this statement chilled
me. Then Frankly tapped the glass, pointing.
"There," he said. Across the street, 2 Cops dressed in
their pink uniforms stood side-by-side on the busy
walk, a stream of people circulating around them,
giving them plenty of room. The Cops faced Stamen,
who was not hunching.

"Oh, no," I said. "Oh, god. Oh, damn."

"Do you think he snitches on us?" Frankly asked. As he spoke, Stamen suddenly gestured with his hand, holding it out at his waist. "That's just my height!" Frankly said.

"We have to get out of here. Otherwise, they'll wait until closing and nab us, too."

"How are we getting out?"

"I don't know," I said. Down below, Stamen placed his hands on the roof of the car and spread his skinny legs. "Poor Stamen," I said. He had his head turned, speaking. The Cops listened to him and nodded seriously. A 2nd car arrived. Before I ran to catch up with Frankly, I saw the silver glint of handcuffs.

We found the handsome man with the figure-8 glasses in line to see the film of my die again. "You really want to help us?" I asked him. He raised his brows in interest. I explained the situation, our hastily made plan, while Frankly went to retrieve our bags.

His name was Blu Fen; he was a podiatrist. We took the elevator to the abandoned library, where he and I exchanged clothes back to back between aisles of books. His suit jacket more or less fit, and I rolled up the sleeves of his silk shirt, the cuffs of the wool pants—it looked strange enough to pass for fashion. He gave me his glasses, which, he explained, were only ornamental anyway. Then he produced a pocketknife and began whacking off my hair.

"You still don't look like a man," he said. "Here." His fuzzy, perfectly arched eyebrows came off his forehead, leaving a residue of stickum. He carefully placed them over my own subtler brows.

"Thanks," I said.

"The hair on my head is chemically attached, or I'd give it to you. I need a bottle of BunWash to take it off, and I'd have to shave your head to make it stay on you." He gave a little apologetic wince. "None of it grew back," he added. "Not 1 follicle." Everyone knew a dozen people who had been through Radical Radiation, so he didn't have to say anymore.

I ran my hands through my savaged hair, hoping I looked sufficiently manly. He didn't look bad in my dress. I'd never been much attracted to cross-dressers, but he had the kind of looks that could make you forgive little habits.

"Your shoes are fine," he said, pointing to my boots. "We need to do something about your breasts." I knew he was talking about my disguise, but I still felt a little awkward. I used to sex naked in front of a cheering crowd, but now it made me blush to have a man staring at my clothed breasts.

"How about if I just keep the coat buttoned?" I said.

"Let's bind them with my socks."

Not an appealing idea, but he wore long gray things, and it worked. His socks didn't even stink.

"Don't do anything to draw attention to yourself, and you should make it to the parking lot," he said.

"Wish me luck," I said.

He tugged on the hem of the skirt, which barely covered his boxers. "I may need some luck as well," he said. He had no hair on his legs, I realized as he walked out ahead of me. No hair anywhere on his body.

———

Frankly hid in the huge hippie bag Stamen had taken from the stolen van. I couldn't lift him, so I paid a green-haired teenage boy to carry the bag to Blu Fen's car. The Cops didn't give us a 2nd look. I managed to catch a glimpse of Stamen in the backseat of a patrol car, his forehead resting against the back of the front seat. Could he have been smiling?

"What you got in here, bud?" Green Hair asked, lugging the bag.

"Pellets for my hamster," I grunted in a manly fashion.

"Must be a hungry fuck," the boy said amiably. He had a volcano tattooed on the back of his neck.

Blu Fen drove a Chevy Reagan—luxury to the limit. I gave the kid a 10 from Blu Fen's wallet, then freed Frankly as soon as the kid had scrammed.

"You call me a hamster, damn it."

"Oh, shut up," I said.

The Reagan needed no driver. Just punch in the address, and the vehicle steered itself, no 1 at the wheel. I typed Blu Fen's security code and address onto the screen. The engine immediately turned over.

"1 day I own a car like this," Frankly said, although he had to know they quit making these after the Collapse. He dusted himself furiously. Being locked inside a hippie bag had to approximate his idea of torture.

"Aren't you the least bit worried about Stamen?" I said. "He's my brother, and they're probably going to kill him."

"You don't know that. You can't know what's happening to him now, or what's happening to him later. I am sorry they arrest him."

The car, unaware of our fear of capture, steered us right by the Cop cars. Frankly dropped to the floorboard, but I dared another look at my brother. He *was* smiling. Talking to the Cop. Handcuffed, but smiling. "Something's going on," I said. "Stamen's smiling."

"He finds out jail is rent-free."

"I'm serious."

"Lydia," Frankly said, his breath against my ankles. He lifted Blu Fen's pant legs and stared at my calves. "I am so moved by your dying. I am so touched by it. You have a stinG gift, so stinG. How do you do it? Why are you so perfect at dying?"

"Drop my cuffs, Frankly."

"I always think I know you. I even think I understand your dying way back when. But when I see this movie, I realize I don't really know you. This gift of death terrifies you, I think, because you don't know why you can do it, why you can come and go so elegantly. I always think I know you, but I don't."

"Oh, you know me."

"No," he insisted. He licked my shin. "You are a mystery now."

The iron gate to Blu Fen's estate swung open automatically for the car. A long and curving brick driveway, flanked by equally long snow-covered lawns, led to a large stone-block house and 3-car garage. The middle garage door sank into a hidden slot as we neared, and the car obediently steered itself in, stopped, and turned its engine off. "This car is new," I said to Frankly. "You aren't supposed to be able to get these anymore." Behind us, the garage door rose up from the floor.

Frankly said, "What does a podiatrist do?"

"A podiatrist is a foot doctor," I said. The locks on the Reagan doors popped up.

"Well," Frankly said, "everybody has feet. I am guessing there are a lot of foot-poor people in Filly."

As soon as we opened the car doors, an enormous Hispanic man stepped into the garage carrying an automatic rifle, which he aimed in our direction.

"Mr. Fen calls to say you are coming," he said. "Welcome to our home."

"You Now!" Frankly said. "I Now, too."

"Are you going to shoot us?" I asked politely.

"This is an unfortunate but necessary precaution," he said, waving the gun. "I am always greeting guests this way." He shrugged, smiling apologetically—cute, in a mammoth sort of way. "If you are so kind as to stand against the wall and spread your legs, I am searching you."

His search had the thoroughness of a medical procedure. He took his employer's keys and wallet from me, and his hands patted, squeezed, and prodded every part of my body. I'd had long-term relationships that were less intimate. He did the same to Frankly, then went through our bags. "This 1 is not yours," he said of Stamen's hippie bag. He withdrew a single leg from a pair of patched gray pants; the pantleg, as long and narrow as an elephant's trunk, probably *would* have fit Stamen.

"My brother's," I said. "He's . . . we've lost track of him."

The Hispanic man only nodded. After he satisfied himself with our bags, he searched the car. Finally, he popped the clip from the rifle. "My name is Jimy Schmidt." He bowed deeply. "I am at your service."

———

We ate the Bitter-Fried Stoom that Jimy cooked and waited for Blu Fen to come home. Bitter-Fried food reigned primo stinG; Frankly was in heaven eating it and Nowing around with Jimy, but I didn't share his relish. Bitter-Fried food tasted, well, *bitter* to me. Besides, I worried anew about Stamen. No matter the number of times I ran the image through my head, it came out the same way: he had been smiling. Maybe he felt relief just to have it over, to be a fugitive no longer, but there was also the possibility that he had worked out a deal with the Cops—a terrible thing to think about your own brother, but Stamen had his faults.

When we had been kids, he constantly ratted on me, even though Mother proved a poor audience. "Lyddie is a spirited girl," Mother would say, whether I had ravaged the kitchen trying to make a cake from scratch, or accidentally caught Stamen's desk on fire while playing with his chemistry set. Which made me wonder what had happened to that spirit, the nerve I had to die and keep on dying even though it had meant leaving home, going underground—where had that bravery gone?

Mother had hated my dying, which, of course, she had heard about from Stamen. "I don't want to see you damaged," she had told me seriously. "Or dead. I can't forbid you because I have no way of enforcing such a thing. But I am asking you not to do it." We had been seated on the front stoop of our building. She held onto my shoulders, looking me square in the eyes. "I don't make many demands of you," she continued, "but I wish with all my heart that you'd give this up. Don't die again. Please, don't die."

I couldn't imagine the misery I had put her through, dying and then disappearing in order to continue dying. But it was even harder for me to imagine myself doing it, defying her, taking that kind of risk. Maybe the dying had taken away my spirit; maybe the spirit had been eaten away a tiny bit with each death. Or maybe, as Frankly suggested, it terrified me to die so well. Maybe I was just getting old. None of the possibilities pleased me.

The interior of Blu Fen's house exceeded the expectations created by the exterior. He had that cool Zen-cubist blocky furniture covered with gray-black zigstriped cloth. Paintings covered the walls. I even recognized a couple of them—DeStonno's "Pregnant Madonna with Hay in her Hair" and Essea P's "Lolita in the Resthome."

Blu Fen arrived home halfway through the meal. No longer wearing my dress, he had new, slantier eyebrows to go with a dark woolen suit. "I took the liberty of purchasing you some clothing," he said, smiling heroically in my direction, which caused a little flutter in my chest. Then he added, "For each of you," and gave Frankly a nod.

6 beautiful dresses. "These are incredible," I said, while Frankly bolted to the bag of his new clothing, but what occurred to me at the same time was this: no podiatrist on the planet had this kind of loot.

Jimy nuked the leftover Stooms in the microwave. Blu Fen ate while Frankly hopped (literally) into the suit our host had purchased for him. It had vertical lines that got thinner as they rose, which was supposed to make the wearer look taller—ForeLengthened was the official title. The suit looked terrific on Frankly, but he was still short.

I did not try on the dresses. Some little resistance to excessive charity. Instead, I ducked into the next room and put on 1 of my dresses from my bag.

"You're here for the die, aren't you?" Blu Fen said to me between bites of Stoom. The slanty eyebrows made him especially sexy in a grown-up way. "In the cab, on the way over here, I finally managed to put 2 and 2 together."

"A Qik Bite for QBN," I explain.

"Oh." He appeared disappointed. "I was hoping to see you die live." He looked right into my eyes when he talked, which also struck me as *adult*. I wasn't accustomed to being around somebody who had actually figured out how to be an adult.

Frankly said, "She gives up dying." He studied the sleeves of his new jacket. "All my life I want a suit like this," he went on. "How do you know to buy this for me?"

Blu Fen threw me a glance that said, "What's so difficult to figure out? For a guy under 5 feet, you buy what makes him *think* he looks taller." A very telling glance, and not mean-spirited. To Frankly, he said, "I'm glad you like it."

Jimy joined the conversation then with an oddly put question for me. "How is death?" he said.

It took me a moment to worry through the words and Nowism to the meaning. Frankly, who hated slow responses, said, "She doesn't die for years."

"She forgets dying?" Jimy asked.

"It's strange," I said. "Sort of exhilarating—definitely exhilarating—but there's this strange quality, this seething quality to it. Creepy."

"My mother dies when I am 4," Jimy said. "My father dies when I am 16. My wife dies when I am 20. Do I see them when I die?"

"Yes and no," I said. "You'll probably see them, but they won't be the people you knew."

"She never stays dead long," Frankly reminded him. "Permanent death is different, maybe."

Blu Fen spoke then. "Do you think it *is* permanent?" He was talking to me, his eyes zer0ed in on my eyes. His were the green of glow-in-the-dark watches—probably the result of his radiation treatments, but beautiful nonetheless. "Now that you and people like you have blown apart the idea that death has to be permanent, is there reason to go on believing that it is ever permanent?"

"Can't say for sure," I told him, "but I've got a hunch it is."

Jimy said, "There are more people alive than there are dead."

"Is that true?" I said.

Frankly nodded. "You learn that when you become a Nowist."

Jimy wore a pensive look. "1 of the tenets of Nowism is that the whole past and future are happening at once right now, and the immense population of the world is part of the evidence. Most of us don't believe all the philosophy literally, but Nowism is the perfect metaphor, don't you think?"

"Seize the day?" Blu Fen said to them, but he looked at me while he spoke, a flirtation—1 of those adult sophisticated flirtations that usually only happen in movies.

"Not that," Frankly said, "and not not that."

"Seize the here and now?" I said, a little nervously, knowing that I was flirting out of my league. "There's no time *but* the present?"

"Or, now is now," Blu Fen said, his green eyes shimmering at me. "Or . . . how now brown cow."

I laughed out loud. I had always had a weakness

for men who helped save my life. Many of my rescue crew members had become lovers. It came from watching those old movies where the heroine always chose the guy who had just shot up a dozen people to untie her from a chair.

Frankly smiled at Blu Fen's joke, but Jimy didn't. He said, "It's more like, We *are*. Or, We always *are*."

I said, "How does Nowism handle death?"

"We are alive," Jimy said, "and we are dead. We are born, and we are dying. We always are."

"If I arranged it all," Blu Fen began, and though for once he was not looking at me, I knew from the tone that he was speaking to me, "would you die for me? Here? In my house, where it would be perfectly safe?"

"Dying is never safe," I said a little self-righteously, a bit too dismissively. Why did all the men who were attracted to me want me to die? But maybe I'd over-reacted. To soften it, I added, "You heard Frankly, I don't die anymore."

"Isn't it like riding a bicycle?"

"Nope," I said. "It's more like falling off a bicycle, and then, just before you land, falling back on."

Blu Fen smiled, not a perfectly symmetrical smile, but a friendly 1, an intelligent 1, a beautiful 1. "My eyebrows look good on you," he said.

The others looked and laughed as I peeled the fuzzies off.

In my dream the man grabbed my breast, but when I actually woke Blu Fen's hand rested on my shoulder. I didn't know whether he had touched my breast, but I was frightened. My sudden intake of breath caused him to lift the hand.

In the dark room, Blu Fen's face looked gray and seemed to hover above me. My heart throbbed in fear.

He said, "I need you to come with me," his voice soft but not a whisper, with an edge to it, as if he had issued a command rather than a request.

"What time is it?" I said stupidly, unable to think of what I should say, whether I should express my fear or hide it.

The dark silhouette of his hand appeared beside his face; he held an illuminated pencil clock: 3:53 A.M. His thumb flicked a switch on the pencil; the digits disappeared, and a green bulb threw a dim spray of light. Blu Fen leaned over me again, the green light turning him ghastly pale. He had no eyebrows. He had no hair. His nipples shown purple on his white chest, like identical bruises. And the weirdest part: he was astonishingly beautiful.

He craned himself farther over me, bare-chested and hairless—an albino turtle out of his shell. "Get up now," he said softly. "You must hurry."

For the 1st time I considered that he might not be the source of the threat, but seeking to protect me from some other, larger menace. "Let me dress," I said. Because I'd had my own room and a soft bed with clean linen sheets, I had slept in the nude. Blu Fen gave me a mannerly nod and crossed the room, leaving the pencil light on the bed. At the door, he asked me again to hurry. He wore a silky, low-slung skirt, whiter even than his skin.

I didn't bother with underwear, just slipped into 1 of the dresses Blu Fen had purchased for me—a sleeveless pink chenille mini shirtdress with a draped neckline. A bit dressy for bizarre nocturnal intrigue, but I had no time to worry about it.

Blu Fen waited just beyond the door in the dark hall. "Keep the light down. Don't illuminate the windows," he said. "Follow me to the control room." He began an agile trot, his arms stiff and swinging in time with his legs, the white skirt billowing behind him.

The door to the control room lay at the end of the hall. Blu Fen took my hand gently, leading me inside, as if to a gala ball, then closed the door behind me, the room dark except for the pencil light's beam. Blu Fen touched a switch. Hazy floor lights aimed against the turquoise walls illuminated the room. We stood before a hi-tech panel that covered 1 wall—a maze of lights and knobs like I hadn't seen since the Collapse. He punched 3 buttons. Video screens suddenly lit: the vast lawn at night, the huge gates by the drive, a wall of trees at the end of the lawn; superimposed over the images, a moving green grid, angling across the screen. Snow fell in every illuminated square.

Blu Fen faced me, his glowing eyes soft and serious, the same color as the grid. He said, "There are intruders."

I searched the screens, thinking that he held me responsible, recalling the look on Stone's face when I warned him of Big Boys, a look that suggested I had contaminated his home. "I don't see anybody," I said. "I don't see any movement but the snow.

Blu Fen punched another button. 2 of the screens went dark, but the 3rd screen—the shot of the trees and wall—had a sudden red pulse in 1 corner, a roundish little spot, like an exotic bug. Suddenly the bug enlarged so that the screen filled with it. The speed of the zoom was disorienting, and I grabbed the edge of the control panel, as if I were about to be knocked off my feet.

Blu Fen rolled a padded stool to me. "Sit here," he said, sliding it beneath me.

The red bug now filled the whole screen. Abruptly the red blinked off: 2 young people, a dark man with a shaved head except for an ear-tail of hair on 1 side, braided and stapled to his lobe; a young woman with a blond flattop and a dangerous sneer, wearing a jeweler's monocle held on by a black strap around her head. They squatted in the shadows of barren trees.

"Do you know these people?" Blu Fen asked.

"No," I said immediately. "Should I?"

He shook his head. "Of course not, but you're an artist. Artists sometimes have unusual friends. I also know, of course, that you are a fugitive from the law. Your friends might not feel comfortable ringing my bell. They might try to sneak in, rather than call for you. I needed to check. I needed to rule out every possibility. This is not something that can be done lightly."

"Who do you think they are?" I asked. On screen, the man and woman whispered together. The man pointed in the direction of the house.

"Thieves. Perhaps." Blu Fen shook his bald head sadly. He stepped away from the panel. "Or worse. They're armed. The woman has a handgun. The man has a TargetLaser. They're after something—or someone—of value." He took another step, then leaned against the wall, his arms crossed, his feet apart, a floor light shining up his skirt, making it diaphanous, his penis listing to 1 side, his balls hanging unevenly.

"What are you going to do with them?" I asked.

"You may go back to bed," he said. "Jimy will take care of them, as soon as I give the word."

"Where is he?"

"He's out there, watching them." Blu Fen stepped back to the panel. "Do you see that glass over her eye?"

"It looks like a jeweler's monocle," I said.

He rolled a thumb over a stationary ball on the panel, which made the grid angle the opposite way across the screen. Then he punched a button, and the screen filled with the image of the monocle. "It's an infrared filter. Looking through that glass, she can see as if it were daylight. If she spots Jimy, she'll kill him. Sometimes . . ." He tapped the panel again, and the camera zoomed back until the bodies of the intruders once again filled the screen. "I'm not sure I should mention this, but I suppose you have the right to hear my speculation. Sometimes the Big Boys hire assassins. They could be after your brother. They could be after *you*." He turned from the screen to me, his eyes looking deeply into mine. "They don't leave us any alternative."

I sat there too long, glancing back and forth between the video screen and Blu Fen's own strange and seductive person. He said, "Very well. Become a witness." He put his hand on my bare knee, pulled me and the stool along. He positioned me before the middle of the panel, then stepped behind me to roll the stool forward until my knees and thighs were beneath the panel's ledge.

"Press here," he said, his lips at my ear, his chest touching my back. He reached around me on either side, taking my hands in his. "Here," he said, his breath soft in my ear. He laid my hand on the panel. A new screen, 3 times the size of the other, went on before us. The man and woman, enormous now, checked their weapons. They kissed briefly. Blu Fen lifted my hand. "Now, touch here," he said and raised my hand to my breast.

He guided me, my fingers caressing my breast. "Now here," he said. My other hand touched the panel. The huge screen suddenly split in 2. On 1 side, the man and woman crawled on their knees through the gray trunks of the leafless trees, leaving a trail in the filthy snow like that of skiers, the camera automatically tracking them. On the other side of the screen, Jimy Schmidt crouched in a snow-laden ravine, barefoot, bare-chested, wearing a silky skirt just like Blu Fen's. Over 1 eye, he wore the now-familiar monocle. In his arms, he cradled a rifle.

My breath caught. Blu Fen raised my hand from the panel to my other breast, my arms crossed, touching myself. When I could inhale again, my breathing came roughly, irregular gulps of air. I'd begun to tremble.

Blu Fen, lips at my ear, whispered, "Jimy."

On screen, Jimy whispered, "Yes."

"Jimy," Blu Fen said, "take off your skirt." Teeth gently took the skin of my neck.

Jimy slid a finger beneath the elastic band, pulled it down below his butt, then over his bent knees. The crouch exaggerated the roundness of his butt; his genitals hung beneath, animal-like.

Blu Fen's erection pressed against the small of my back. He lowered my crossed arms, had them grip the hem of the shirtdress. I pulled it over my head, and Blu Fen yanked it off me. 1 hand returned to my breast, the other found his erection—his hands still guiding mine. The couple reached the edge of the trees, 1 head, then the other, rising cautiously, 1 and then the other, rising, standing erect.

Blu Fen said, "Now, Jimy."

The rifle rose, then leveled. 1 of my hands moved between my thighs, began the penetration.

The rifle made no retort, but I screamed. The bodies fell heavily, the woman 1st, her legs buckling on the bullet's impact, the man had time only to turn his head toward her before the 2nd shot rocked him. His head landed between her knees, blood raining upon them. Hands on my breasts, fingers inside me. The screen went black.

Blu Fen rolled me across the room, which dimmed as we moved, my eyes unable to adjust. I had to throw my arms around him to keep from tumbling, the black wall ahead of us dividing, opening, parting for us. A bed appeared out of the dark, a bed with black sheets. He slid me onto it effortlessly, slid himself on top of me, his tongue inside my mouth, his hands at my waist, his cock against my pelvis but not inside me.

A second before it happened, I knew what was to come.

He thrust the mask over my face. The faintest whiff of Ater, and like a pro, I went down immediately.

I was dead.

PART

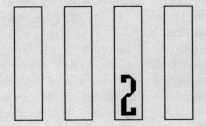

2

6

The 6th time I died was in Atlanta, on the top floor of a 7-story burned-out building, so ruined that it was open-air. The lights of downtown Atlanta flared in the distance, the fabled skyline rising above the multi-tiered highways. The building we inhabited was dark, ragged chunks of concrete where walls used to stand, huge rusted pipes sticking out of them.

A hot night, 17 of us among the rubble up above the city, all teenagers, friends I hadn't seen since going under. Stamen had been there, too, but he left before the party propulsed into high gear. Awkward with people in any circumstances, Stamen had flinched, literally flinched, at talk of a fuck-around, although what he said to me conveyed a different fear. "I will not watch you die," he said.

I had called him after Washington went bad. He got ahold of all the people I wanted to see. I hadn't expected him to come with them to Atlanta. He had been a student at MichiganU. I was touched that he came all that way.

"I thought you wanted to quit," he said to me. "I

thought you wanted out of this." I had told him as much over the phone, but once I had my friends around me, all I wanted to do was die.

And sex.

This was during the Monthly Health Credential days, and all us had cleared IT screening in the afternoon. We had almost started sexing in the health center parking lot. BingeSexing, the magazines started calling it, which eventually led to the demise of the required monthly checks, but back then it didn't have a name, and felt spontaneous and alive. As did dying.

I had reached the end of my rope in Washington. The guy I had more or less fallen in love with had come up with a plan for me to die in front of the President and Congress as a way to get dying legalized. Which was not offensive in itself. A lot of us wanted dying legalized. But his feelings for me seemed more political than personal. I was a cause, a means by which he could make a name for himself. That hurt.

Later, after he himself became a congressman, he did get the legislation passed. He was the only person I had ever loved in that romantic let's-get-married-and-borrow-a-lot-of-money sort of way. Anyway, I ditched him and moved to Atlanta. The notion of Plebeian Substates was just emerging—the idea that it was constitutional for some states to outlaw whatever they didn't like as long as there were other states that wouldn't. This started all the legal haranguing about anti-Plebeians living in a Plebeian Substate who were unable to move for legal, economic, or psychoEmotional reasons, and how much they should be compensated for giving up some of their rights. Ersatz rights led to ersatz economics—prosthetic loans, junkmoney xFunds, WallaDough, CapitalStinge,

Reaganomics—all the phony economic business I eventually studied as a Ragaccountant.

It was no fun being a dying artist in an emerging Plebeian Substate. I called my brother and asked for help. He talked to my friends, brought them to Atlanta, and we wound up on the top floor of a roof-less building. As soon as Stamen left, I decided I wanted to sex and die simultaneously. There was no shortage of volunteers. I chose a sweet little guy named Bosh who had used the last of his frequent flyer miles to come see me. I chose him because he looked and acted nothing like the Washington guy I had recently fled, and he had kissed my fingertips when he 1st arrived in town.

I stripped, making a show of it. Bosh and I did some Oral to get loose and ready. The he crawled on top of me, gave me a big kiss, sexing me in a good rhythm, the others cheering us on. Then I got the Ater, and I died.

Cherry tomatoes blossomed from my flesh. A little ball formed beneath the skin, then it turned red and popped off, falling to the floor. Took about 3 seconds. I was naked, cherry tomatoes blooming all over me.

I found myself in a room with a spongy floor, a crowd of people surrounding a table spread with food. I was the only 1 naked and the only 1 making tomatoes. "I say there," said a well-coiffed young man, "could you possibly stop that?" He waved his hands at my body, then continued in his fake British accent. "And would you mind putting on a scrap or 2? Covering up a bit?"

I opened my mouth to respond, but made a tomato instead—it popped right out of my mouth. The man jumped away, disgusted.

The men wore tuxedos; the women, elaborate old-fashioned gowns. They gabbed about their past lives beneath a fancy chandelier. Blackbirds perched on the golden arms of the chandelier watched dispassionately. The table held an incredible array of meats, including its centerpiece: a silver platter holding a roast piglike thing—only this little piggy had 3 bodies connected to its single head. The room had no doors or windows, and above, beyond the chandelier, lay a strangely textured ceiling. It took me a moment to figure out that the ceiling was made of human skulls.

"I was Harry Houdini," 1 of the women said. "I escaped the impossible."

"I can see that," a man replied, overtly appraising her body. "I was nobody famous, myself, just a working stiff in the 16th century."

"Agricultural work?" the former Houdini asked.

"Primarily, although I branched off into bootlicking and corpse handling. Have you heard what our labor is here? I'd like to keep moving, wouldn't you?"

"Sustenance, do you think?" she asked, stuffing her mouth with pork.

"Doubtful," he said. "Let us hope, for your benefit, it has nothing to do with table manners."

"Once I escaped from a triple-locked trunk submerged in 100 feet of crude oil," Houdini said.

"Yes," the other replied, "labor 4, anger and humility. I spent a century being nice. Couldn't get my dander up."

Suddenly Houdini dropped to her knees, picked up 1 of my cherry tomatoes, and ate it. She clutched her chest in ecstasy. "Body ripened!" she said.

The feasting began. 1st they ate the fallen tomatoes, then caught them as they fell from my body.

"We eat of your body," the former boot-licker-slash-corpse-handler said.

The piggy thing on the table turned its well-cooked and partially eaten head to stare at me. "You and me," piggy said, "we're outta here. Feed the misses, that's the labor."

The crowd began pressing their mouths against my body, sucking the fruit out of me, tomato spray covering their fancy clothes, sucking me into a state something like orgasm—sucking me right back into my life.

Bosh had come while I was dead. He lay beside me, weeping. My friends wept, too, holding hands, calling my name into the humid night.

Jimy held the Accu when I came to—not a real 1 as I had used as a kid, but a reproduction model made to look like the original but with modern power. He stood over me in the dim room, gargantuan and naked but for the slinky skirt. My 1st thought: now he, too, was going to rape me. I knew that Blu Fen had while I was dead, not just because of the mild soreness between my legs, but also because of the death itself, because of what had happened in death.

The die left me confused, as dies often did, but this 1 was different. I felt the confusion but also a kind of clarity, a strange sensation, a presence. I had died, and while dead I had been given a glimpse of the gift. But this feeling now, this awareness—it was as if something had followed me from death. Or, perhaps, this death let me become aware of a presence that others could not perceive. Someone was with me, watching, seeing what I was seeing, knowing some of what I knew, but also ignorant of things.

Jimy slid his arms beneath me, and I saw that I was naked. Of course, I was. How could I have forgotten that? He lifted me from the bed, his skin warm against mine, his touch gentle. He nestled me in his arms, his eyes red, his cheeks wet. From the way he carried me, I could tell that he would not rape me—something in his touch let me know, something like tenderness. But he had shot 2 people. I had met them during my death. Charles and Arlene. We had spoken.

Blu Fen was likely watching me from some dark corner of the room. I pictured his still naked body lurking invisibly in the black. Which made me think of the presence as darkness, another darkness, a more personal darkness residing not in the room but in me. Before we reached the door, Blu Fen's disembodied voice reached my ears. "Good night, sweet princess," he said softly, so softly that I thought he must be within inches of us. I tried to spot him, but could see nothing, could barely even make out Jimy's face, the shape of his nose, the cut of his dark hair.

I had been ready to sex Blu Fen, but he preferred to rape me.

Jimy carried me through doors, down the hallway. He kneeled beside the bed to tuck me in. Which started the tears, his tucking me in. Funny what will set a person off. I covered my head with a pillow and wept.

I tried to think, tried to figure what to do, whether I should do anything, but began considering instead the other darkness, my intimate darkness. Already I understood that it was alive, that it was both a part of me and separate from me.

Then it occurred to me that there was probably a camera monitoring my every gesture. If the technology were available, Blu Fen would be listening to my thoughts.

Or maybe not. Maybe after raping me, having Charles and Arlene blown away, and forcing a die on me, he was ready to sleep, perchance to dream. I hoped he had bad dreams. At least that. The *Hamlet* quotation had been our dying motto back in the beginning. Later we picked up the Velma rOOst lines:

> Body for pleasure, body for pain
> Death the inevitable pressure
> The holy unreliable measure
> The turning from the treasure
> The body made profane

Out of retirement, dead again, alive again, I had crossed another line. I had glimpsed the gift. And now I had an unaccountable something accompanying me.

I pretended to sleep, the pillow still over my head. Real sleep was never easy. What I could not deny was that I had wanted to sex Blu Fen. I had helped him kill Charles and Arlene, and then I had wanted to fuck him. What a rush to feel both revulsion and desire at the same time. I was every bit as sick as the next guy.

An ugly business, this life.

I heard a voice. I thought at 1st it was from the inside of my head, but lifting the pillow, I saw Jimy, still beside the bed, still on his knees. "I'll be right here," he said softly, then lay his head against the floor. "I won't leave your side." His body filled the rug, a large rug that I had hardly looked at, but now I wondered what design lay beneath him. I wished I had taken notice.

"Do you want a blanket?" I asked him.

He shook his head. "Don't worry about me," he said. "Nothing more will happen to you tonight. I'll be right here."

I couldn't sleep, but I found Jimy's proximity comforting. That other presence, too. There were things I didn't understand, too many things, but there were also things that I did know, that I could explain. Explain to this new resident of my—what? mind? body? I didn't even know how to think of it, but I decided to give it a name: *you who live inside me*. Or, for short, just plain *you*. Naming you permitted me to engage you.

You wanted me to fill in the gaps. *You* seemed to think it would be good for me to tell you my story.

Instead of sleeping. Instead of screaming. Instead of continuing to weep. I acknowledged you, acknowledged that I did not know what you were, and then I began telling you what I thought you needed to know, what you seemed to want to know, what you thought I needed to say.

Without speaking, I told you about the buildings that lined the tracks, the narrow throat of sky, the pink clouds. Telling you permitted me to see again that fatal sky.

I told you the story, and told myself, also. I had heard somewhere that dreams didn't exist the way we remembered them, that we pieced them together from fragments and imposed a story when we woke. It occurred to me that this was the same way we made our lives coherent.

Stick to the story, you said to me, or seemed to say, talking to me without words, talking to me through my own intuition, going straight to meaning without the detour of language.

I began again, taking my time, telling you the story, patching it together from the fragments: Stamen, Mother, Frankly, Ananais, Blu Fen, and Jimy, who slept on the floor beside my bed. The telling calmed me, brought me back, brought me here—to the present, the still darkened room, sunlight less than an hour away. I took you up to the moment, filled in the gaps I could sense. In a funny way, the telling made you more real. I was not imagining you. You were as real as anything I knew. Like a black space in the back of my head, way back in a remote crag. I could feel you there, feel your darkness, like the way I used to feel the dye when I colored my hair to hide my identity.

But why did I think that what I couldn't see had to be dark? Maybe you were more like a light that was on somewhere in a house, a light in a not-so-distant but wholly other room, a light I couldn't see but could perceive, some part of me ticking like a meter, measuring the energy that might be flowing out or might be zooming in—lousy meter reader that I was, I had no idea which. I just knew you were there, knew you were more than a death dinG, more than a weird variety of synapse rot, or a tiny psychotic chasm. I didn't need you to talk. I could tell what you knew and didn't know, the things you were interested in, the stuff you would rather skip.

1 time when I was a little girl in a city park with my mother and brother, I rolled down a grassy hill over and over, until my brother tugged at my mother's sleeve and said, "Lydia's skin is moving." Mother hurried me home, where she made a steaming bath. "Submerge," she said, and I went under. There, beneath the hot water, my fingers pinching my nose, my mother's wavery image hovering above the tub, the skin of the water suddenly turned red.

Ticks. Tiny red ticks. Thousands of them.

You were what kept waking me all that night, making me rub and scratch at nothing, that creeping sensation all over my body—memory with a million legs.

Or you were the tears I wept while I was beneath the water—invisible but real enough, water among other water, so only I knew you were there.

Or maybe, this time around, I was the tick. And I was only just now getting a glimpse of this enormous thing I had hitched a ride on.

7

The QBN portable studio—an inflatable dome anchored at the corners by house trailers—looked something like a huge loaf of bread in blue wrap with boxes of animal crackers at each corner.

Don't ask the recently dead for metaphors.

"DinGy" (*ding-ee*, rhymes with *thinGy* as in "Twist that thinGy on the whatchmacallit that makes the dealie go on") was the word we dying artists used back when, though the newspapers now called it Postdead Befuddlement. It meant we were goo-heads for hours—sometimes days—afterward. It didn't entirely hit me this time until after I finally slept.

The inflated dome covered the arena parking area and the neighboring avenue. A bubble tunnel inside the dome permitted street traffic to roll through undisturbed. Frankly and I arrived an hour early in our new clothes so that I could get away from Blu Fen.

He had brought me flowers. Big lilies or irises or daisies, 1 of those not-a-rose flowers with long green stalks. My mother would know their names, but I was no good at such info.

He appeared at my door in the early A.M. bearing this whoosh of flowers, wearing his best hair. "Good morning, my love," he said. I felt halfway swayed by the hullabaloo, remembering the lust I'd felt for him without recalling the people he had killed (including me), or that he had raped me.

I smiled before I realized what I was doing, but then I told him to go away. "Don't blame me for my passion," he said—sexy, but I knew better than to trust dinGy thoughts.

I even doubted the existence of *you*, thinking I'd spent the night in interior yak for dubious reasons. But you gave me a nudge, a mental elbow, to let me know otherwise.

Blu Fen put the flowers on the corner of my bed, blew me a kiss, studied me all moony-eyed, and left. The thing about beauty is I expect it to be benign, and this man was gorgeous. Not vapid-but-with-good-bone-structure—genuinely beautiful.

Jimy came later with a breakfast tray. He had spent the night on the rug, then took care of me most of the day, bringing me water and magazines—little offerings of kindness—without making me talk. I was in no state of mind for chatter. The rug, I noted, had images of birds, somewhat abstracted: blue and yellow birds in symmetrical opposition, a velvety diamond at the center, a design that grew in complexity the more I studied it.

The Cops occupied Blu Fen. They had come to collect the bodies. I watched through the kitchen window as Blu Fen strolled across the lawn to present the corpses. Even dinGy, I was acutely aware that he could easily have me arrested. But he didn't, which made me feel like I owed him. The creep.

After the Cops hauled the bodies away, Blu Fen personally prepared an elaborate lunch for us. He tried to engage me in a the conversation about means and ends. "If the ends are sufficiently noble, then the means are of little consequence," he argued, talking to everybody but meant for me to hear. "Those unfortunate robbers, for example. If they were robbing to feed their children, to keep their children from starving . . ." Blah, blah, blah, chewing on the bones of an argument, on the gristle of Charles and Arlene, who I knew, from having met them in death, were not robbers. They had not come to kill me or Stamen. They had come to assassinate Blu Fen.

The 1st chance we got, I insisted we leave.

The haircut Blu Fen had given me with his pocket-knife didn't please the network. I was sent immediately to Cosmetics. The woman assigned to cut my hair made a pukey face. "Circus time," she said. She had a calico cut, complete with pointy cat ears. "Don't do to me what you've done to yourself," I said, a more oblique statement than I intended.

Frankly translated. "She doesn't want a calico cut. Just a regular do." To me, he whispered, "Never offend someone with scissors in 1 hand and your head in the other."

I hadn't told Frankly anything about what happened during the night, but he'd guessed something was askew. He had asked what was wrong on the ride over in the Chevy Reagan, but I'd told him that the wheels had ears. Now, while calico cutter gave me a modified crew, I began to cry.

"Lyddie," Frankly said softly, taking my hand. "Everytime you cry, my heart cracks."

I told him the whole story. He cried then, too,

which was sweet, although he had started when I told him Blu Fen aroused me, so part of his bawling might have been self-pity, but I decided to ignore that and believe he was crying for me.

Calico cutter, on the other hand, got furious. "I'd like to stab that somnabitch in the balls," she said, gesturing with her scissors. "This isn't a Plebeian State—he can't rape us."

She did a nice job on my hair—a modified bottle-brush crewcut with a very stinG widow's peak. Then she personally escorted us across the bubble tunnel to meet Qigley. Frankly held my hand while we walked, patting it every now and then. What he didn't understand was that my feelings were really confused. Blu Fen hadn't had to rape me. I had been ready to sex. But he did rape me, and he made me a part of the killing, and—here was the gross part—they didn't know how much the killing thrilled me. I couldn't sort through it all, but I wouldn't be fooled into feeling sorry for myself. I might have been raped and died, but I was alive now. Charles and Arlene were completely dead. The big D. The absolute D.

You, of course, were part of the confusion as well; although, my explaining things to you swept away some of it. And I didn't have to explain you to yourself. Not that I could, anyway. I forgot about the fact of you and concentrated instead on telling you the here-and-now of my ongoing story.

Frankly and I waited together outside Qigley's dressing room, Frankly in his Tall Suit, me in a yellow-and-purple checkerboard sheath dress with pagoda sleeves. Blu Fen might be a jerk, but he had exquisite taste in clothing.

"I should know about this while it is happening," Frankly whispered to me. "I should wake up when you are being seduced and dying."

"Quit it, will you? You sound as dinGy as me," I said. "Men always want to blame themselves for things they have nothing to do with—some stupid way of reinforcing their sense that they make the world go round. But if they're really responsible for something, they completely deny it, falling back again on their whatchicallit, that I'd-never-do-such-a-thing diddly."

"I forgive you saying this because you are not yourself," Frankly said.

"See, there you go," I said. "Qigley'll be no different. He'll find some way to talk about his cock, even though we're complete strangers." Some of the brilliance of my argument escaped my words. Wind whistled through the logical gaps.

Frankly changed subjects. He leaned close and whispered into my ear as if to offer words of love. "Be nice to Qigley."

After a couple of minutes, Qigley himself stuck his head out the door and invited us in. I had seen his picture plenty of times—a thin, pimply boy who reminded me of a kid in high school who wrote other students' papers. It was shocking to see him in Naked Clothes. I hadn't seen anyone wear them in years, but even stranger—he had on women's Naked Clothes. Cross-dressing going the extra mile.

"Recognize any-ny-nything?" he asked me, offering the typical dying artist's half-smile.

"I've seen you on TV," I began, but he shook his head.

"D-d-d-don't you recog-og-ognize anything else?"

"Naked Clothes," I said. "Yeah, I had some way back when."

He nodded, the half-smile so big it contorted his face. "You had *these*." He tugged at the hips of the spandX suit.

Finally it dawned on me that he was wearing my old clothes. I was looking at my own naked body.

Frankly said, "Turn around."

Qigley not only turned but bent over to display my butt.

"Lyddie, you're beautiful," Frankly said.

"May I have a glass of water?" I said. "And will you put some clothes on?" I felt both very old and weirdly disoriented. "Some more clothes on, I mean." I was on the verge of getting teary-eyed like when a mother 1st realizes that her daughter is becoming a woman, but instead of a daughter, I had spandX staring back at me. My life was suddenly clearly beyond pathetic.

Qigley looked dismayed. "I'm sorry. I thought you'd get a kick out of this. It's part of my dying collection. I have a whole s-s-section dedicated to you." He quickly slipped a shirt on over my breasts, shorts over my bottom. "Th-th-th-the last th-th-th-thing in th-th-th-the world I'd want to d-do would be to hurt you." He seemed genuinely distressed.

During the next hour, he told me all about myself. "I think of my work as part of a great tradition," he said, "and you're the *grand dame* of that tradition."

I had a strong desire to fake Parkinson's as a way to plead my relative youth. I was 37, not 90. He kept on like I was Mother Jones or Billie Holiday or Buffy Nest.

He pranced about, talking about my 1st die 1 moment, when I was weaned the next. He knew who I 1st sexed, why I got axed as a Ragaccountant, knew about the now-Congressman I more-or-less loved, knew I told 3 different men they were responsible for my 1st orgasm—it was a frighteningly thorough list.

Frankly ate it up until Qigley interrupted his description of my 1 affair with a single woman to say he knew Frankly and I were "just friends." Frankly hated to be described this way. The only thing he hated worse was for someone to come up to him and say, "Where is everybody?"

"You've got some of it right," I said, cutting him off. Frankly liked this, as if I had said it for him.

Qigley stared at me a moment, maybe a little hurt, maybe feeling that I had been rude. He said, "I know about your mother." He smiled smugly. "Ms. Banjo." He stood and pulled off the T-shirt and the top of the Naked Clothes in 1 gesture. His narrow, pimply chest reminded me that he was just a kid. "The truth is," he went on, "I adm-m-mire your mother almost as much as I d-d-do you." He stuck his thumbs in the waist of the Naked bottoms and pulled them and the covering shorts down. He wore blue butt-thong undies. His butt had pimples, too. "I've got to get ready for the show. Concentration, you know." He smiled again. "I gave the Banj-j-jo Society a fortune last year— secretly, of course. Look, can I take you 2 out? After the die? I'll probably be dinGy, but I've gotten off on the wrong foot, and I'd like to correct that."

"Sure," Frankly said. "We love to go out with you."

"You're a d-d-d-depressionist," Qigley said. "Have you ever done warm-up for a die? It seems a natural combination, doesn't it? Depression followed by death."

Hopping began. I had to all but drag Frankly out of there.

"What a break!" Frankly said. "All at once I get a job offer and see your butt."

"Shut up," I said, "or I'll really give you something to be depressed about." Even I didn't know what I was talking about.

Filming the 30-second Qik Bite took 2 hours. Frankly kept hanging around, hoping they would ask him to be in a shot, waiting to see if I mentioned him in 1 of my responses. They covered my face with peach powder, shot me from every possible angle, asked me a million times to lick my lips. "Could you giggle a wee bit for us?" asked the producer, a heavyset man in a rainbow cardigan, plaid knickers, and a mock Irish accent. "A giggle's always a blessing to have on tape."

20 minutes after finishing, I had just washed the makeup off, and they had already edited it. "Edit while we go, we do," the producer said. He wouldn't let me see it. "Against policy, love, but you can see this." He handed me a wad of bills. "A thousand quick ones. Our experience with fugitives is they prefer cash." He winked at me then strode brazenly away.

Frankly eyed the money, but pretended to have no interest. "We have great seats," he said, showing me the tickets. "And you don't owe me any money, if you are wondering."

"I'm not wondering," I said. We began making our way through the bubble dome to the arena.

"Well," he said, "just in case you are wondering about all the money I am spending every day on you and your brother, you don't owe me anything."

"Here." I divided the stack and gave him half.

"You don't have to do this," he said, pocketing the

wad. A crowd of people waited just beyond the bubble's double doors. "In another hour, there are forty
thousand people here," he said.

"How on earth are we going to find my mother?" I
said. "We don't even know if it's her we're looking for,
but if it is, how can we possibly locate her?"

"Mingle," Frankly said. "Rub elbows." He thrusted
his elbows out so they looked like fins.

The Filadelfia Arena gained notoriety for its inclu-
sion in the pseudo-postFeminist book *Horny
Architecture: Sins of the Mothers As Imagined By the
Fathers*. The author, Tulie Jane Potts, a Filly native,
used local buildings to make her points. She dubbed
the arena the classic vaginal+diaphragm symbol for
its bowl shape and rubber cap. Potts had various sug-
gestions for what milling people might represent, all
of them bacterial and disgusting. A crummy little
book, really, but very stinG at the time because so
many people wanted it banned—the Filadelfia Better
Business Bureau, the mayor, several Plebeian groups,
and a major Filly architect whose work she described
as precoital.

By the time Frankly and I reached the mezzanine,
cruising fans—Morbids—strolled the floor, their
faces powdered, wearing fake half-smiles. A carnival
atmosphere pervaded the thoroughfare: jugglers and
clowns performed on makeshift platforms, men with
greasy hair hawked Qigley T-shirts, vendors sold hot
dogs, popcorn, pizza, matzo on a stick.

Frankly held on to the hem of my skirt as we wove
through the stiffs, his fist bumping against my butt as
if by accident.

"We don't have any idea who we're looking for," I said. "I don't think Mother would come herself. It's too risky, and she really never liked dying. She'll have some messenger here, who's going to have to spot us."

Frankly pulled up short, jerking my skirt. "I want her to tell my future," he said. A blond woman in a green micro-mini sat in a ladder-back chair holding a sign that read GYPSY FORTUNE TELLER, $5. Frankly tugged me in her direction. "Depressionists love to hear the future," he said. "It's always either good news or good material."

The gypsy saw us coming and yanked Frankly by the elbow right into her lap. She hadn't had many customers and wanted to make a show of Frankly's future. She began by fingering his hair as if looking for lice. "1st thing I see about you," she said, "is that I should get the 5-spot in advance."

Immediately she gained credibility.

She continued to pour over his head while Frankly fished out a 5, bouncing on her lap to remove his wallet. She examined his ears, fingered his brows, licked his jaw. "Let me see your tongue." She took the tip of Frankly's tongue with 1 hand, and with the other scratched lightly. She squeezed his mouth open and inhaled his breath. "Stand up and show me your palms." Her scrutiny was impressive. I kept thinking, All this for 5 bucks!

Finally, she dropped his hands and said, "You're going to be famous for making people feel bad."

"Exactly!" Frankly said, but now the woman glared at me. Her mouth had fallen open. "What else?" Frankly asked. She ignored him and grabbed my hand.

"I don't need this," I said, but she yanked my head down and began examining my skull. "Let go." I pulled away from her.

"You from planet Mars?" she said. "Early death is written all over you. You should have died when you were a teenager."

"She does," Frankly said.

She glared at him. "A Nowist who wants to know his future? Can't you get kicked outta the fraternity for that?" She shook her head angrily. "Nowists give me the worst kind of crap."

I said, "I did die when I was a teenager."

"She's Lydia Melmoth," Frankly said.

"StinG," the gypsy said, smiling now. "You here to see the Qig break your mark? I got news for you. He ain't going to make it. I had a vision. No record tonight."

"You didn't say that to him, did you?" I asked.

"You think I'm uncouth? I know better than to be neg around a dying artist about to go down, but for real—he won't make the record tonight." Suddenly her expression changed, and she stared intently into my eyes. "Jesus, girl, what your eyes have been through. You've seen the hounds of hell so many times they think of you as a bud." She shuddered. "Get away from me, willya? Ya give me the willies."

I jerked Frankly back into the moving crowd. "Thanks a lot for subjecting me to that."

"I am famous in the future," he said. "You better sex me now while I'm willing to have you."

"You know what she wanted to ask you?" I said, feeling mean. "She wanted to say, 'What do you want to be when you grow up?'"

"That's cruel, Lyddie," he said, but immediately

brightened. "I am using it in my next routine. You wait and see. If Qigley doesn't break your record, then she is right about me, too."

"Yeah, but that would mean Qigley stays dead, and there goes your chance to be his opening act."

"Oh," Frankly said. "I don't think of that."

A juggler kept 8 tiny skeletons in the air, telling thematic jokes ("What does the skeleton say to the bartender? I'll have a beer and a mop."), catching the change thrown to him in a bucket tied to his shoe. A redheaded girl sent a funnel of flame toward the ceiling. Clowns went about their clowny business, leaping off their platforms to throw pails of confetti, farting loudly, humping strangers from behind. The fans shuffled along, glancing about, holding hands with their lovers or their kids, snarfing down ice cream, broccoli warfs, sno-cones, wiping their noses with their hands—ordinary ugly life, the thing to which I had aspired and failed.

A his-n-her geek show loomed ahead, bone-thin idiots who bit off the heads of small animals. The geek couple stood at the entrance to their tent waving at people, blood dribbling down their chins. The line to get in was depressingly long.

"If this isn't a circle of hell, it's got to be in the near suburbs," I said.

Frankly said, "I worry about pickpockets. We're carrying a lot of bills."

"Focus, Frankly. We need to—" I quit in midsentence. The geek girl smiled at me, showing her bloody incisors. It struck me that the Banjo Society might be angry with us. We had failed to protect Stamen, which had been our only use to them. By this time he had likely given the Cops the names of every person he had ever laid eyes on. We were now nothing but liabilities.

"What?" Frankly said. The worry on my face made him hop.

"Maybe we don't want to be found," I said. The geek girl waved, licked her bloody lips, encouraging us to see her act. "Maybe, without Stamen, we're just a nuisance to the Banjos."

"I don't think of that," he said. "What do we do now?"

"I don't know," I said. "The safest thing is to get out of the arena so the Banjos can't find us."

The geek tent opened momentarily as a couple slipped inside, providing a glimpse of the wall of cages for the animals they mutilated. The geek girl glanced my way again as she stepped into the tent, the old come-on, the salesman's ingratiating look. Only a teenager, she already knew that coy look.

"We are seeing the die," Frankly said. "No 1 messes with you the day you're on national TV."

"That's what you think," I said. The Qik Bite would make me invulnerable to the Cops for a few days, but not to the Banjos. On the other hand, avoiding the Banjos meant staying under without getting into the network. "Let's at least get away from this crap," I said. "Let's find our seats."

We turned around and muddled back through the swarm of people. Before we reached our gate, Frankly grabbed my elbow. "I always say your brother is a clown." He pointed.

Stamen's nose was covered by the traditional red bulb, his face pasty white with big blue dots at the cheeks and a huge painted frown, a fright wig covering his thin hair, but his teeny bat eyes and his gangly body made him unmistakably my brother. Besides, he was a pathetic clown, doing nothing but making faces and throwing puffballs. He waved to us goofily.

"How did he escape?" I wondered aloud.

Before we reached Stamen, another clown latched onto my hips and humped my behind. His baggy clownsuit ballooned around us, making farting noises. The traditional response was laughter, but I barely managed a smile. Why did people like clowns?

The clown stuck his tongue in my ear as the tradition required, then whispered, "Lidya Melmouth, is dat you?" I pivoted to stare at him. He smuckered up his face. The makeup covered his black skin completely. "And if it ain't ole Dim Watt, too," Ananias added, grimacing at Frankly.

"You dress for success," Frankly said to him.

Stamen, still clowning, threw blue puffballs at us that exploded on contact. *Puff, puff, puff.* We're targets, I thought, while Ananias thrusted at me and my skin turned blue.

Ananias offered a hurried and skimpy explanation, the 4 of us crowded into a single stall in an employees' men's room. Frankly, standing on the toilet, was still not as tall as my brother. In the next stall, 2 clowns sexed noisily, quoting something about Humpty Dumpty humping a wall—I had never understood people who needed entertainment during sex.

Ananias and Stamen speculated that Stone Voice—the guy from the dumpster who knew we were heading for the museum—had informed on us, hoping to negotiate a pardon out of it. They deduced this from the following evidence: 1. the Cops, who had sent a dozen patrol cars to Tumble University to search for us, suddenly shifted a couple of cars to the Museum of Ontological Stuff; and 2. only Stone knew we were heading there.

However, the Banjos had already posted people at most of the major tourist spots, hoping to find us. The Banjo at the museum picked Stamen out of the crowd easily. He might have saved the rest of us, too, but Stamen, thinking it a trick, bravely lied.

"Your brother's all right," Ananias said to me, clamping his clown-gloved hand on Stamen's narrow shoulder. "He wouldn't say a word about your where-abouts until he saw my own handsome face."

"I apologize." Stamen's painted frown made him look especially sad. "If I'd trusted them sooner, you could have been whisked away, too."

"That was you driving the Cop car?" I said to Ananias, who nodded. "Have the Banjos infiltrated the Filadelfia Cops?"

"No, no way," he said. "But anybody can rent a Cop car, complete with uniform, for 200 smackers. It's 1 of the ways the mayor is trying to balance the budget."

We paused while the clowns in the next stall loudly reached climax. "All the kings' horses," the woman clown called out. "Every damn 1 of them."

Frankly said, "I worry about what we do now."

"You're going to watch the die," Ananias said. "Then the 3 of you are going out with Qigley—he did invite you out?"

"How did you know that?" I said.

"Simple reasoning," Ananias said. "You *are* his hero. Tell him your brother is going to join you. I'll send more info by way of this fine clown." He clapped Stamen on the shoulder again, then he looked at his watch. "Better get to your seats now. Show's about to start." He smiled really big. "Ain't no b'ness like show b'ness," he said, then he flipped the latch to the stall door and exited. Stamen followed. Frankly grabbed my shoulder to stop me from leaving. Still standing on the toilet, he slipped his arm around me.

"Tell me the truth," he said. "If I am this tall, you are sexing me."

Maybe I was still dinGy, maybe I just had a desire—I put my hands on either side of his face, pressed my lips against his, a long, deep kiss. Then I stared at him, the tip of my nose brushing against the tip of his. "Not in a million years, Frankly," I said. "Not if you were 7 feet tall."

He did not take this as discouragement, and tried to kiss me again. I pulled away, causing him to slip off the toilet and fall to the floor.

"We're just friends," I said.

"Don't spoil the moment," he said, getting up and dusting his knees.

The clowns exited the next stall at the same time we did, holding their big rubberized hands. "How'd we sound?" 1 asked. "Could you tell we're in love?" They didn't expect an answer.

The 7th time I died was in L/A, on the beach, at 2 in the morning. In WashingtonState I'd picked apples; in Portland I scraped bricks. In SanFrancisco I tried being a waitress, a stripper, a short-order cook, but eventually the legit places wanted social security numbers, and the disreputable places took advantage of you. The day I got to L/A, I put the word out that I wanted to die. Boom! Suddenly I had a suite in an actress's beach house, I was eating lobster, having a facial, reading *Variety*. I didn't get paid to die, but when I died I got royal treatment.

It made my hostess the queen of stinG to have me die on her private beach. No 1 had ever died 7 times, and 2 boys had died permanently trying (which didn't count for the record). I met a lot of actors—exciting in an empty sort of way, like driving at night without headlights. Many of them tried to arrange future dies for future parties. I didn't want to die ever again. But living without dying had become too hard.

I shook a lot of hands, received many little kisses on the cheek. 1 actor talked about the integrity of my work versus the compromises forced on film actors. "In the film I'm making now, I play a scientist who develops an honest to God *effective* Spanish Fly. Great possibilities. A look into what makes people attracted to each other. But Hollywood doesn't want the customer to *think*, you know what I'm saying?"

"Pardon me," I said, "but I've got to go die."

"Break a leg," he said.

I changed into a black FrenchCut bikini and lay directly on the sand. I could hear the ocean slapping the shore and ice tinkling in the drinks of stars. An actor who played a doctor on a daytime soap opera carried out the canister of Ater.

Death this time was icy but not cold. I still wore the bikini, but reclined now on a huge blue glacier. Snow—white snow—fell into my hair, but I wasn't chilled. "Snow and ice are not cold in the world of the dead," I said somberly. This brought on a gaggle of titters from out of the darkness.

"Read your lines the way they're written," a voice called. "All you have to do is lie around and read your lines. You could at least get the goddamn lines right."

Death, this time, was a movie set.

The voice evidently belonged to the director, but I could see only a brightness about the ice and a darkness beyond it.

"Where are the cue cards?" I asked.

More laughter. The voice again: "On your lids, dipshit. Close your eyes."

I'd never closed my eyes while dead. I didn't know what to expect. With my eyes closed, the world turned a hazy red; I saw the director in his cloth chair, the camera and cameraman beside him, the remainder of the cast and crew, all staring at me. 1 of the flunkies held out a clacker thing, snapped it, and yelled, "Melmoth / Final Labor / Take 1." Suddenly words appeared, white against the red haze. I spoke them as they appeared.

"Give us this day our daily ice. Forgive us our snow, as we forgive those who freeze our hearts." I opened my eyes, and the red tint, the haze, the people vanished—just me and the ice. I shut my eyes, and they returned, but now they all wept.

"You're a wonder," the director said. All of the flunkies nodded, many of them clasping their hands as if in prayer. "That was perfect. You *moved* us, babe. You pass with flying colors."

"Why?" I demanded. "People see me die, they bawl. You guys hear me read a couple of sentences and you're all broken up."

"You've got that girl-next-door-cum-ice-queen quality," the director said, "mixed with just the right percentage of that saucy-temptress-with-a-history pout. You're a natural."

"How is this a labor of death?" I asked. The ice around me began to melt. I felt myself sliding along the glacier. I grabbed at the ice, but there was nothing to hold onto. "None of these labors is a labor. I never *do* anything."

"She's ad-libbing again," a flunky said.

The director wiped his eyes. "'Doing' is a Breethie word. You feel any in and out, airwise? See any fog about that luscious mouth of yours? We don't *do* in death, we manifest. That ice is moving, too, isn't it now? You've moved us all."

"I don't get it," I say.

"On the contrary," he said, "you do get it. You get the gift." They began applauding. The applause grew into a roar.

I opened my eyes. I was on the beach, surrounded by actors, all of them crying, applauding. Even the waves striking the sand sounded like applause.

8

A haze of respiration hung in the dark over the arena floor, a half-visible cloud of breath. I had read that IT might 1 day become an airborne virus, which would make gatherings like this unimaginable. The life of a virus was short, by our standards, which permitted it to mutate a thousand times in the span of 1 human's life. Early death was its big evolutionary advantage.

Our seats were in the VIP section; Frankly's even had a custom foam pad to make him appear taller. He jerked at my sleeve to point out famous people—a singer, a basketball player, a senator, a billionaire. I spotted Blu Fen, maybe a dozen rows away from us, in tux, tails, and zigzag eyebrows. He had been watching me and smiled when I looked his way—a frail smile and genuine-looking, although maybe the contrast with his phony eyebrows only made it seem genuine. I wanted to both flip him off and wave sweetly, but neither was a good idea. I turned away, wondering whether the shuddering of my heart was lust or fear, anger or something like love. A person who had never died would be able to tell, would know how she felt about a man. If I hadn't been dinGy, I would have been furious, I thought, but I wasn't furious, so how could I know anything? Maybe I was in a weird state of shock, or a shocked state of weirdness. Blu Fen had raped me, hadn't he? Just because I was willing to sex him didn't mean I was willing to sex him dead. If someone secretly gave you a drug in order to get you in bed—even if you were willing to go to bed with him, wasn't that rape? But it wasn't so much the sex as the death itself that troubled me. If only I could get my head to work right, I could figure it all out.

In the center of the arena, a single bed rested on a circular platform. The platform revolved so the entire audience could see all angles of Qigley's death. The fanfare began with QBN's Boo Lincoln, the MC. A spotlight followed her to the platform. She waved to the crowd, which roared back at her. A tiny woman, she couldn't have been more than a black spot to the people in the top rows, who must have appreciated the huge video screens suspended from the ceiling— although, they could have stayed home and watched the identical business on their own TV screens for half the ticket price. They'd have missed the geeks, but I couldn't see the thrill of paying a fortune to watch an event on big-screen TV.

Boo had aged since her days as host of the *Day After Tomorrow Show,* but she was still pretty. Her hair was black—a cubist cut, very stinG. She wore a silky black blouse and short black skirt. Abruptly the camera cut away from her to the QBN commentators secluded in a booth high above the arena. The crowd quieted to hear their chatter.

"Why do people pay fifty dollars to watch television?" I asked Frankly.

"Fifty bills doesn't get you in the door," he whispered, his eyes never leaving the big screen.

The commentators went through their usual prat-
tle. I didn't really listen until I heard my name.
". . . who is present tonight to watch the historic die."
A spotlight suddenly blinded me. I smiled, as I knew
I was supposed to. Frankly leaned close, trying to
steal some fame. Then the spotlight flicked off. A
commercial appeared on the huge screen. "Nice
smile," Frankly said. I realized that I had given them
the lowers-only snarl. Still dinGy, I'd had something
like a flashback. There must be a million ways to
make an ass of yourself.

I tried to explain to Frankly, but he shook his head
and pointed to the screen. "This is 1 of my favorites,"
he said.

The commercial showed news footage and clips
from old movies, only the film had been altered so
that the people wore DuckWear Shirts. Bacall, in a
DuckWear Polo, told Bogart, who wore a DuckWear
ButtonDownCollar, to put his lips together and blow;
then Elvis in a DuckWear GlitterRobe shook hands
with Nixon, who wore a DuckWear ManlyBra;
ancient wheelchaired Angel Chavez in his
DuckWear; Brando was pushed by teenaged Pooly X
in a DuckWear RibbedNet; followed by Lee Harvey
O wearing a DuckWear DressShirt being shot by Jack
Ruby, who had on a DuckWear SpaghettiT.

More commercials followed: Gerber's Baby
Workout Center, Levi's line of Bulletproof back-to-
school clothing. Finally the commentators introduced
my interview.

Suddenly I was 20 times life-size, posed in the coy, come-hither way they wanted. Boo appeared to be asking me questions, although, of course, I had never met her. "How do you feel about Qigley breaking your record?" she asked.

I smiled a big lush, dinGy smile. I didn't know whether it was the makeup or the lighting or just the fact that I was on TV, but I looked sexy up there—so sexy that it took me a second to recall that I had never been asked this question.

On screen, I said, "When I died, it was illegal." I crossed my legs, and the camera zoomed in to get a quick glance of my panties. It jumped back to my face. "2 boys had already died permanently *trying* to set the record." Now the camera zoomed in on cleavage. "Qigley is obviously the best dying artist of his generation." The camera began a slow pan of my legs, and I realized they had taken various parts of my dinGy talk and spliced it together to make the answer they wanted. They hid the splices with cheesecake shots.

On screen, I said, "The die only counts if you live through it." Then a shot of me giggling. The crowd gasped. I had broken every rule of dying etiquette by suggesting that Qigley might die, but I hadn't said that. I'd responded to a question about boys who had permanently died. The interview ended, the spotlight blinded me again. I couldn't hear the commentators' words for the catcalls. This time Frankly leaned away from me.

Eventually, the spotlight went off. More commercials.

"Why do you say that?" Frankly demanded.

"You were right there during the interview," I

reminded him. "They patched that response together out of context."

Frankly shook his head sadly. "Don't deny what's on the screen. The public is tired of excuses."

"Fuck you," I said.

"Boo Lincoln gets you to speak your true feelings. She is a great journalist."

"I wouldn't know, I've never met her." I might have said more, but the seat back in front of me began blinking: a message screen. Red letters appeared and moved across the chair back. ===I KNOW YOU DIDN'T SAY THAT===MEDIA MANIPULATION===GOOD PUB FOR US BOTH===SEE YOU AFTER DIE===Q===DUCKWEAR MAKES QACKING GOOD SHIRTS===

"Well," Frankly said after the message screen went blank, "if Qigley forgives you, I guess I do, too."

"Thank you so much, jerk."

For the next 30 minutes they worked the stall, complete with women in bathing suits, camera shots of celebrities, and plenty of commercials. Suddenly a flurry of official-looking men carrying briefcases appeared near us; they hustled about, flustered and whispering, which scared the stew out of me, but they remained several aisles away.

"You're sweating." Frankly wiped my brows with his thumb. "They don't want you. You're on prime time. You're safe. Even if it is a miserable interview and everybody hates you."

The men in suits left. I relaxed a little. Men in suits made me nervous. Even when I had been a Ragaccountant and worked with men in suits, I never felt entirely comfortable with them. Once I told 1 I'd like to see him out of his suit, and he took it the wrong way. Men in suits often took things the wrong way.

Finally came the announcement that Qigley was in the arena. A single spotlight illuminated his entrance. He wore a silver jumpsuit and waved extravagantly. The huge screens featured his half-smile. Heavily made-up, his acne didn't show. He strode toward the center platform slowly, working the crowd.

It occurred to me that the men in suits had rushed to the general vicinity of Blu Fen. I looked again, but it was too dark to make out faces. I didn't trust my memory about such details. There was no reason to suspect that everything that went on in this building pertained to me. I kept telling myself that.

"Here we go," Frankly said, taking my hand.

Qigley already reclined on the bed. A loud drum-roll began.

"That's gauche," I said, but he wasn't listening. "A man is about to die," I added, although that was obvious, the reason we were all there.

2 leggy women wearing bathing suits, capes, and Pope hats carried the Ater to the stage. They placed it on a table that spiraled up out of the floor. The celebrity administrator of the Ater, a teenage actress whose TV sitcom was called *AfroAmerican WannaBe*, took several bows before stepping up to the table.

On the giant screens, Qigley smiled, his vital signs inset in the top corner in fluorescent red digits. The young actress positioned the deathmask over the chalice briefly, then in 1 quick movement she lifted it to his face. The red digits zipped to zer0.

Mr. Qigley, he dead.

———

The 8th time I died was against my will at Blu Fen's house. Out of practice and unprepared, I felt the tug of death and gave in to it, knowing that dying quickly was my best chance of survival. Feeling, too, the pull of the old routine, the body returning to its former habit. I fell into the old practice like a musician, finally reunited with his horn, falls into song.

Death, this time, took me to a grassy mountain plateau. Snow-capped peaks towered nearby, but I lay on a flat stretch of lush grass, wearing only a silky skirt, like the kind Blu Fen and Jimy Schmidt had worn. My hair fell long and satiny beyond my shoulders, brushing my pale and unblemished skin. I had the instinct to cover my breasts, but simultaneously I realized it was a Breethie response.

Lying near me were the other 2—the intruders who Blu Fen instructed Jimy to kill. Stretched out on the grass, they studied me. The man—Charles— asked if I were an angel. He wore only jeans, his hair short but full—no ear-tail.

"I'm no angel," I said. "I watched Blu Fen kill you."

"And then he killed you," the woman said. A diaphanous blue robe trailed over her reclining body, white hair falling thickly to the grass and puddling there. Her name was Arlene.

"He killed me, but just temporarily," I said. As I said it, strawberries bloomed from my breasts, my belly button. "He's sexing me now," I added.

"It's better that you're dead, then," Arlene said. "At least until he's done."

"Death can be a turn-on," I said. "I die a lot."

"We wanted to kill Blu Fen," Charles said.

Suddenly mountain climbers scrambled up onto

the plateau. "Granna!" Arlene said to the 1st, a sweet-looking old woman in climbing boots, quilted down jacket, and banana-yellow pants.

"Dad?" Charles said.

A gray-haired man in a suit pulled himself over the summit. He said, "Your Aunt Gladys is here, too, but she's bad at this altitude. Give her a few minutes." He chuckled, gold fillings gleaming.

I was hoping to get the benefit of Charles and Arlene's 1st death, hoping I would see my father as I remembered him. But this was Charles and Arlene's only death; I couldn't help but wonder whether I had screwed up my afterlife.

Then, in death, I remembered what I'd suppressed in life, that I had finished the 7 labors. I would be given the gift. What it was, and whether I'd want it, I couldn't say, but there had always been enough mystery in death without this little bonus.

What finally scrambled up the hill for me was a dog from my 2nd death, the big black poodle with the puffy face of a jazz man. "Long time no see," he growled, knocking me over and mounting me immediately from behind, sexing me in death with the same rhythm that Blu Fen sexed me in the other world. "*Your* Aunt Gladys is coming, too," the beast said, glancing behind him. At the cliff's edge appeared the monstrous dog with 3 heads. The heads raised and lowered themselves independently on their long necks. "This ain't *your* death," the poodle said. "You're horning in on these folks' sweet bye-n-bye."

My coupling with the dog-thing horrified Charles and Arlene.

"I hate the way men are," I said. This seemed to

all of us like an explanation for what was happening. They left their dead family members to eat the strawberries that kept popping from my flesh. While they munched, they told me to watch out for Blu Fen. The poodle, meanwhile, kept at it, growling an upbeat number, but hurting me, tearing me, though pain in death was not the same as pain in life: it coursed through me, but didn't linger. The 3-headed dog merely watched.

"You're going back, right?" Arlene said.

"Yeah, yeah," the dog said, "she usually got a round-trip ticket." While he spoke, I wrestled him off me. He leaped at me, but I caught him by the throat, lifting him off the ground as I stood.

"Blu Fen," Charles said, swallowing a strawberry, watching my struggle with the dog with only mild interest, "is no coincidence. He's a partial owner of death. He's the delivery man for the grim reaper."

"He loves you," Arlene said.

"Is this the gift?" I said, shaking the throttled poodle, but looking to the monster dog. "What I'm hearing here? Is this information the gift?"

"I take door number 1, myself," the poodle rasped. I tossed him to the mountain floor. As he went down, I ascended—I was *flying*.

"Neat," Arlene said, as I rose above them and into the blue sky—which was not air, but an impossible sort of liquid. Charles and Arlene disappeared below me. The great dog howled with all its mouths. The sky above me split open, and I floated through the vault. A red cloud of birds appeared—thousands of cardinals, flying in a dense formation, each bird with 4 wings. They scattered as I approached, the sky red with flutter, and then beyond them the gift finally presented itself: a vast field of lush grass, rippling with the wind of my arrival, a radiant shower of sunlight, and blue sky that was air and not liquid.

"Is this it? A pasture?" I said, zooming down. The whisk of movement took away my voice. Singing began, a single feminine voice, singing without words, without sound, a song that resonated through my body, breaking up my body, a strange sense to the sound, a largeness, an expansive rush of particle and matter. I became aware of life in the landscape; the earth—if it was the earth—was alive. Not that living things were hidden in it, but the planet itself was alive.

Then the Accu stimulated my heart, which gave a shudder. The song ended. I plummeted right back onto Blu Fen's black sheets.

Qigley made it through another death. I was the only person in the arena unmoved by it. He died well enough, but I had seen too many. It occurred to me that I knew more about death than anybody who had ever lived. Expert at death, idiot at life. Major priority problem. I thought again of *you*. Couldn't *you* help me, tell me something? Convey information that might correct the muddled course of my life? But you weren't talking, just lingering, curious. Always curious. If the earth I'd seen in my death was indeed alive, then were *you* part of that life? If the gift permitted me to see that the planet itself was alive, were you the unseen life in me? Were even the living things alive in other ways as well?

During the long ovation, Stamen joined us, kneeling by our seats. His clown suit had been replaced by a business suit. He tried to say something, but the noise of the applause was too great. He passed me an envelope, which I tucked tramplike into the top of my dress. Even while the applause continued, the huge screens began flashing a message: DO NOT LEAVE THE ARENA. IMPORTANT NEWS. WAIT. IMPORTANT NEWS.

The crowd settled, grew quiet, an air of anticipation descended, replacing the jubilation. Even Qigley, sitting now on the bed in his silver jumpsuit, looked to the monitor. THIS DIE DOES *NOT* SET THE RECORD. The crowd gasped, then grew quiet again, the only sound the watery noise of mass whispering.

EVIDENCE PRESENTED TO THE OFFICIAL JUDGES MINUTES BEFORE THE DIE SHOWS CONCLUSIVELY THAT LYDIA MELMOTH COMPLETED A SUCCESSFUL DIE—HER 8TH—LAST NIGHT.

"That fucker filmed me," I said to Frankly.

He said, "The gypsy is right. There's no record."

THIS DIE TIES QIGLEY WITH LYDIA MELMOTH. The spotlight shone on me again. Some booing issued from the audience, some applause, mostly the sound of incoherence and confusion—almost indistinguishable from the noise going on inside my head.

Frankly poked me in the ribs as he leaned into the light. "I am soon famous," he said, his voice jubilant.

Security Guards took the 3 of us into the bubble dome, hurtling us past the press and befuddled fans, and on into Qigley's dressing room. The Q would join us presently. My brain had started to work again, and now wheeled madly trying to make sense of the past few days. "Stamen," I said, "how did the Banjos know the Cops were sending cars to the Museum of Ontological Stuff?"

Given the immediate weirdness going on, Stamen was surprised that I was casting back to yesterday's weirdness. It took him a moment to respond. "The Filadelfia Cops communicate through a VideoChannel that anyone can order from their local CableTV outlet. It's raised a fortune for the Cops Department, although it does sometimes interfere with their efficiency."

"Anyone could have been watching that channel?" I said.

Stamen nodded. "You should be acquainted with it, as it stems from the application of Prosthetic Economics to Public Administration."

Frankly said, "You think Blu Fen knows you are at the museum?"

"Well, he certainly can afford cable. And he was in line to see my exhibit, figuring that's where I'd be. For that matter, he could have had a dozen people in there following me around."

"What are you talking about?" Stamen asked. Frankly quickly explained. The forced death disheartened my brother. His eyes watered, but I didn't want sympathy. I wanted answers.

I said, "When I was dead last night, I was told that Blu Fen was no coincidence. 1 of the people he killed told me. Maybe it was no coincidence that he was in the museum."

"Can you trust the dead?" Stamen asked.

I didn't know how to answer.

Qigley sent his entourage away at the door. "Skidoodle, guys," he said, entering his dressing room

alone. I expected hostility, expected him to blame me
for ruining his record, but he was half-smiling and
wacky from death. "Hey, hey," he said. "Right after
dying I don't stutter." He threw his arms open, which
made him teeter backward. When he spotted
Stamen, he clapped his hands and tucked them
between his knees in an exaggerated expression of
delight. "You must be the *big* brother, emphasis on
big. Oh, but wait," Qigley shook his hips and started
singing, "He *aaaain't* so big; he's just tall, that's just
about all."

"It's a pleasure to make your acquaintance,"
Stamen said.

"You're a little out of it," I said to Qigley.

"DinGy is what we Dying Kings say. That dinGy-
winGy time. Not that I need to tell you. You practically invented the term." He shook his head fiercely.
"Lez go eat. I don't eat for twelve straight hours
before a die. Bowels relax at death, you know. Can
really bum a crowd." He held his nose and laughed.
"Gotta limo waiting. Juz lemme change my rags." He
unzipped his silver jumpsuit, then stumbled toward
his closet, falling to 1 knee. "Whoa, there," he told
himself. "Holy, holy."

"Help him," I said. Frankly hopped up to assist the
Dying King. Qigley's dinGiness made me feel pretty
straight by comparison, and I recalled the note
Stamen had given me.

While Frankly dressed Qigley across the room, I
pulled the envelope from my dress and opened it—a
single typed sentence.

Is Qigley a threat to your mother?

"Who gave you this?" I asked Stamen.

He read the note before answering. "Ananias."

The lettering was in SmearInk, so I licked my thumb and made it unreadable before tossing it in the trash. "Apparently we have a mission," I said.

"Perhaps," Stamen whispered, "or perhaps Ananias is trying to warn us. Although a simple declarative sentence would be preferable to an interrogative if, indeed, he wished to warn us."

"Yeah, well, we'll be careful anyway," I said, feeling more confused than ever. Just when I had thought things were making sense along came a mysterious interrogative to clog up the works.

Foombah's, an exclusive and ritzy dive where the rich came to pretend-slum, had a line a block long when we arrived, but Qigley signed a couple of autographs and we were ushered in. The place had the look of a pirate den from a Disney movie. The ceiling had splotches of black paint that appeared to be holes. White ceiling fans hung on long extenders from the roof and whirled slowly in the air-conditioned air. The tables appeared rickety and pieced together, but they never rocked or gave. People who looked like bums straggled about; they yelled and passed out and pretended to vomit. For a 5-dollar tip, they would fight near your table.

Our waitress wore a sleazy, hip-hugging black dress with décolletage nearly to her belly button and a rip along the rear that exposed her underwear, but she was squeaky clean and smelled of expensive HairJob.

"Line us up some brews." Qigley threw open his arms.

The waitress smirked professionally and scratched her crotch in a practiced way before leaving.

"This is a weird place," I said.

"Yeah," Qigley said, "but you and I, we've seen weirder, no? When you die, Lydia M., do you go to heaven or hell?"

He stared at me earnestly, albeit dinGily, but I didn't know what to say. I had never thought of my deaths in biblical terms, although clearly they weren't much like heaven.

"Yeah," he said, as if I had answered. "Thought so. All the great artists go hellward. The ones that go to heaven aren't eager enough to get back. Thaz my theory." He smiled his mini-smile. "Hey, for a buck the waitress'll spit in your beer. Extra stinG, believe me. Anybody want her to? Spit's on me."

Even Frankly passed on this offer.

"My 1st die was very pleasant," I said. "The others were . . . not hellish, exactly. They weren't nice, but—"

"Hell's like that," Qigley said matter-of-factly. "If it was all fire and lava lamps, you'd get used to it. There's gotta be some sorta semi-half-good stuff, so you have hope. Dante got it wrong. If there's no hope, then adjust. To be utterly hopeless, you have to have some eensie bit-o-hope. Take this bar, for example . . ." He looked around and lost the thread of thought. "Hey, you won't believe this," he said, obviously surprised. "I've gotta hard-on. Honest engine."

"Congrats," I said, then to Frankly and Stamen, who stared dumbly. I explained, "Male dying artists often have sexual impotency for days, some times weeks—"

"Months!" Qigley said.

"—after a die. Others . . ." I stopped. There was

no reason to humiliate Qigley. Some men came out of death with erections. Death was all things to all people.

I found it hard to believe that Qigley was out to get Mom, or that he was anything other than what he appeared: a dopey, mildly talented kid.

"This is maybe the best day of my life," Qigley went on. "I get to meet my all-time hero and have a drink with her—if they ever bring us our brews. Waitress! Plus, I have this sensational die, making me a fortune. Then I find out you had already died another time the night before!"

Stamen, over feeling awkward, asked, "How is Lydia's recent death good news for you?"

Qigley stared at Stamen, then pulled a pistol from his pocket. We all ducked, but he fired it into the air. "Waitress!" he screamed. The gun fired blanks; they handed them out at the door for a price. I hadn't seen him get 1.

The waitress arrived promptly after the shot. They wouldn't serve a pistol table until the gun was fired. She spat in Qigley's beer for free (not actual spit, but SpitProduct from a squeeze packet she bit). Then she took our orders. It was clear she had recognized Qigley by the way she tried to hide her smile. She was paid to be a bitch.

As soon as she left, Qigley started talking again. "Like Dante is this big, huge guy in literature, but me and you, Lydia, we know more about hell that he ever dreamed of—while he was alive anyway. He may know it inside out now. Too much order in his hell. The real joint thrives on chaos. I feel like singing, I'm so happy. Your die last night means I've got competition. Means my next die will be for the record *again*. Do you have any idea how much money we'll make? All the time that I've been the top dying artist, my real competition has always been *you*. Now to have you as a competitor *in the flesh*, it's like box office bonanza time. See what I'm saying?"

"I'm starting to see," I said.

"That interview you did, don't you see how perfect it is? We'll have this feud, be on page 1 of the Sports-N-Arts section every week. This is so . . . ." He took a big drink of beer. "My 1st manager used to handle boxers. He'd say, 'Best thing for a champion to do is retire. Then wait until there's a new champion and come out of retirement. He'll make more money in 1 "Battle of the Champions" than in a dozen title defenses.' And you get a whole lot less gray rot, to boot." Qigley's smile was so huge it lifted half his face. "You had the good sense to retire. Now you can cash in."

Frankly began hopping in his seat beside me. "I am the opening act for both of you," he said.

"Sure," Qigley said. "We'll need a lot of filler."

Frankly flinched, but the disgust passed. If he had to be known as filler to be famous, he was willing. I said, "I'm not going to die again. Ever."

"Hoo, hoo, I beg to differ," Qigley said. "You're going to die at least once more. Everybody is."

"You know what I mean," I said.

"Yeah, but if you're going to die once more anyway, why not make a few mill doing it?"

"A few mill?" Frankly said, more than a little astonished.

"Mill as in million?" Stamen asked.

I took a drink to hide my astonishment.

"For this die tonight, I clear 9 million *after* taxes. My manager makes the same. She's a great guy. She's going to come by later to meet you. For the next 1, if we each die, I'm guessing we could clear 10 to 15 mill a piece—after taxes. You'll probably make more even than me. *Think* about it: a legendary dying artist, a pioneer in the sport, who is still a creamingly beautiful woman, comes out of retirement, feuding with the current Dying King—big buckaroos, jumbo major bucks!"

Our food arrived on chipped plates. When Stamen complained that his fork was dirty, the waitress rubbed the tines against the tight fabric covering her bottom. "All the forks look like that," I said, and showed Stamen my fork with the identical lipstick stain.

"Oh," Stamen said. "I wish then she hadn't wiped this on her . . . her clothing."

"I trade with you," Frankly said.

Qigley was ravenous, wolfing down his cauliflower quiche and fries. I ate, pretending to be concentrating on dinner, but really trying to sort everything out. I could die once more and never have to work again. But repeatedly dying had a way of spoiling 1's life. I could feel it right now, that strangeness that lingered. The disconnectedness. The dinGiness. The fear. The inane list-making.

While trying to contemplate this heavy stuff, I spotted Ananias a couple of tables away, sitting with a dark-skinned woman, sipping a beer. 2 questions occurred to me: 1. How did he follow us? and 2. How did he get in? Did Banjos have pull with Foombah bouncers? Okay, that was 3 questions, I failed another test.

Stamen had been with Ananias all day and the night before, so Stamen might be carrying some sort of homing device sewn into the lining. That probably answered number 1. Number 2 solved itself while I was wondering. The dark-skinned woman stood, turning slightly to take her purse from the back of the chair. It was BlackAnnetteFunicello, the DaytimeRetroTV BeachActress. She must have been a Banjo sympathizer. According to Mother, the Banjos received a lot of secret donations from Hollywood early on, but the money started to drop off after the initial publicity died down. In recent years, the Banjos had gone to former contributors and forced them to give more by threatening to reveal their earlier contributions. "We only blackmail those who can afford it," Mother had insisted. BlackAnnetteFunicello was leaving; apparently all that was required of her was to get Ananais into the club.

Ananias raised his beer as if toasting me. I looked away, which made Qigley turn. "Invite him over," Qigley said. "Any friend of yours is a friend of yours truly." He shouted to Ananias, "Come on over, bro. Join the hoo-ha."

Ananias smiled and rose. He pulled a chair from the adjoining table. He said, "Ain't you Qigley, that dead boy?"

"Dat dere's me," Qigley said. "Mr. Dead and Dying. The King-O-Corpses. And you're sitting beside the Queen. Who you?"

Before any of us could introduce him, Ananias said, "Call me Ishmael."

Qigley laughed and shook his hand. "I saw that flick, where the dude gets his dick bit off by a white whale, then goes out after her." He was referring to

MobyDickHead, the X-rated film that had been stinG a couple of years back, wherein Ahab, after being wounded, got a sex-change operation and seduced the whole crew while in search of the whale. The whaley climax was, well, climactic.

Conversation stalled for a while, then we talked about other movies, or rather, they did. I was still trying to think. Ananias wanted to know whether Qigley was out to get my mother, which would mean that the top dying artist in the country was working for the Big Boys or the NRA, but he seemed genuinely smitten with me, and with the possibility of making a fortune on account of me. Besides, he was too dopey to be a real threat. Anyone who let his manager get half the earnings he had died for couldn't be too astute.

Then there was Ananias himself to consider. He had come all the way to NeYork to get me to take on Stamen, but then he immediately went to Filadelfia, knowing we'd wind up going there for the die. He must have had Banjos spread all over Filly tourist spots keeping an eye out for us—not that it was really difficult to have Subterraneans stake out tourist spots, but still, he had worked every bit as hard keeping track of us as he would have taking care of us.

What was his genuine motivation? How did Mother play into this? If my real job wasn't taking care of Stamen, then what was it? Why now was I thinking of that retroGame show *Jeopardy*? "Let me have Melmoth for 100. Answer: Her life is irrevocably fucked-up. Now, what's the right question?"

Stamen started naming the flaws in a popular movie about a government employee who got angry and blew up Idaho. "Checks and balances are integral to all aspects of the governmental bureaucracy," he was saying, while Qigley, almost under his breath, made a joke about balancing checks—a conversation I could survive missing.

Blu Fen was a more engrossing topic. I had a feeling it was important to figure him out. "Blu Fen is no coincidence," Charles had said. I believed that much. He had been monitoring the Cop Video Channel, and hurried over to the museum to ingratiate himself with us, but to what end? True, he filmed my die, but I was naked and he was sexing me, which meant he couldn't show the film. "He is a partial owner of death. He's the delivery man for the grim reaper," Charles had said, and Arlene claimed he loved me.

Everyone wanted a piece of me: Ananias, wanting me to help the Banjos; Stamen, wanting me to save him; Frankly, wanting me to make him famous; Qigley, wanting me to die along with him. And me? What did I want from me?

A normal life would have been nice, but I couldn't even imagine what that was like. Normal had become 1 of those archaic words like *thou*, *spinster*, *gentleman*, *decorum*.

I remembered once asking Mother why she had never remarried. I had just been hired as a Junior Rag, and she was visiting, helping me find an apartment. "When I met your father," she began, "I thought he was merely a passing fancy, a way station, someone to dally with until I found my real love."

"Dally?" I said. "People really used to say 'dally' and 'passing fancy'?"

Mother went on unfazed. "He, on the other hand, was certain that he'd found the love of his life, and he chased me shamelessly. That won me over, his shamelessness. I haven't found a man since who will

forego all fear of shame in his love for me." Then she
had patted my shoulder. "I'm like you, Lyd. I'm a
holdout for love."

"Hey," Qigley said to me, "I want you to meet my
manager. This is the person who's going to make you
rich." He pointed across the crowded bar.

A tall, blond woman, pale and attractive,
approached, a vaguely familiar woman—like a minor
actor, whose appearance led 1 to say "What have we
seen her in?" She crossed Foombah's plank floor with
a definite rumba in her walk. "She can be pushy,"
Qigley said confidentially, "but she knows what's best.
Without her, I'm nowhere city, like, Detroit."

Frankly put his lips to my ear. "That's your dress."

It was. The blue dress I'd worn when we'd left my
apartment what now seemed like years ago. The 1 I'd
traded with Blu Fen. "Oh, my god," I said.

Qigley's agent winked at me as she came near. For
just a moment I could see the woman and the man,
like that trick drawing where you saw opposed faces,
then it changed to an end table. The Q's agent was
Blu Fen.

I had heard of Ambers but never met 1. There had
been a surge of interest after the 1st successful oper-
ations ("Have It Both Ways" the early ads had said),
but most Ambers wound up having their extra geni-
talia removed, returning to their original sex. The
monthly radiation treatments required to keep the
new parts working proved tedious, and the penises
were rarely fully retractable. Plus, they came with
very little testosterone, which pissed off the women
who'd had the surgery ("What good is it to have a

dick if you don't have the temperament to go with it?" they'd asked angrily).

Whether Blu Fen had been born a man or woman was not clear physiologically. His chest had been flat the night I'd seen him, but women had their breasts surgically flattened with pump-implants that inflated when they did female. Blu Fen's hips were womanly, but that didn't prove anything. He certainly *acted* like a prick, but, really, it didn't make any difference—although, for some reason, I really wanted to know whether I had been raped by a man or a woman.

As a woman, Blu Fen called herself WandaLee. She offered her hand, but I wouldn't shake it. She pulled up a chair next to me anyway. "I'm delighted to find you here," she said in a sultry tone.

"Fuck off," I said. I was *not* going to play along. "What the hell is going on? I know I'm being jerked around, but I don't know why or by whom."

Qigley laughed hysterically at this. "I love her," he said.

WandaLee smiled and spoke in her breathy voice. "I certainly didn't expect to fool you," she said. "Would I wear your dress if I was trying to fool you?" To Qigley, she added, "She knows me as a man."

Frankly bounced indignantly in the seat beside me. "You rape Lydia. You make her die."

"I make her a fortune," WandaLee said. "And there was no rape. Lydia wanted me as she has never wanted you. I care for her deeply. So deeply that I want to get everything out in the open, which is why I wore this particular dress. Right now, the film of our night together is premiering at the FlewHouse right here in Filly. There's a line around the corner to

get in. Flyers advertising it were distributed outside
the arena at Qigley's die."

"What is the FlewHouse?" Stamen asked.

Ananias answered, "A high-class porno/snuff theater owned by HarveL Blu Fenester."

WandaLee turned to me. "You're a star."

I slapped her. Hard. People at the next table
applauded, thinking we were part of the decor.

"Oh," WandaLee said, rubbing her cheek, "I know
you're mad at me. It's true that I behaved badly, not
telling you about the camera—or the die—but I
asked you 1st if you'd do it willingly, and you refused.
Sometimes a person has to take fate into her own
hands. That film is going to make millions. Every
porn lover and snuff fiend in the country will come,
but so will all the dying buffs. It's going to be a big
crossover hit, in the tradition of—"

"'MobyDickHead'" Qigley said.

"Yes, and it dates all the way back to 'Deep Throat'
and 'Behind the Green Door.' I've done my research.
They were among the 1st porno films to get a
crossover audience."

Frankly said, "What is Lyddie's cut?"

"On the film? Nothing. But don't you see? Her
notoriety as a porno-snuff-record-holding-dying-
artist-pioneer will insure that her next die will make
her *millions*. I have a contract in my purse that will
guarantee her 12 million after taxes." WandaLee
smiled at me. "I'll even pay your little friend to be the
opening act." She smiled at Frankly, who, bless him,
scowled back. "I'd give you a cut of the film, Lydia,
my love, but it would work against you in 2 ways.
You'd have enough money to scrape by on, so you
wouldn't want to die again, and that would cost you

and Qigley and Frankly and other people much, much money. Also, as long as you get no cut, you lose no face for being in a porno/snuff film. It says right in the credits that the die was against your will."

I wanted to say, "How could you do that to me?" But the question implied that I trusted her, that I cared for her, and I didn't want to reveal that—I wasn't even sure it was true. I had *lusted* for him. That was all.

Ananias leaned into the table now, looking past me to WandaLee. He said, "There are some details to work out."

"Don't speak for me," I said. "I'm not dying for her. I'm not dying for anyone."

Ananias stared right at me. "Have you forgotten that you're a fugitive? The Big Boys may lay off for a day or 2 since you made such a big splash on TV, but not for long. Especially not if someone was to let on how involved you are with the Banjos." His face scrunched up again. "You in some hot water, missy."

WandaLee smiled at Ananias. "You do a good nigger."

"Yeah, I do," he said flatly. "And you do a good woman."

"I *am* a woman," she insisted. "At the moment." Then she took my hand, which I tried to wrestle away, but she was strong. "I know you're angry, but greatness often needs a little push. I wouldn't have thrown you into deep shit if I hadn't known you to be a great swimmer."

"That's a lousy metaphor," I said, freeing my hand finally.

"It lacks parallel construction," Stamen said.

"You take away my choice, then you tell me it's for the best," I said.

"Talent such as yours comes along once in a millennium," WandaLee said. Her eyes suddenly glossed with tears. "I want to see you achieve the fame, the respect, the wealth, the adoration you deserve."

Her gaze into my eyes was convincing, almost hypnotic. She—he—loved me. That much I knew. Even if I hadn't been told by Arlene, I would have known by looking into her eyes.

"Well, fine," Ananias cut in. "We're going to leave here now. All of us. We're going on a little trip together. We're to meet with the big cheese."

"The Banjo head cheese?" Stamen asked.

"That's right, our number 1 banjo, our national leader."

Qigley stood, bumping the table, his ersatz pistol tumbling to the floor. "Hey, cool," he said. "Lez go see Lydia's mom."

"Mother?" Stamen said.

Ananais only smiled.

9

In the alley behind Foombah's, where Ananias made us change our clothing, a mangy black dog with eerie green eyes snarled menacingly and crept toward us. 3 or 4 other dogs crouched in the shadows, watching. We humans each had identical white tunics to wear—and nothing else. "Slip it on over your head, then take your clothes off. No tricks," Ananias said. He held a handgun.

"I'd prefer not to show bare skin to those dogs," I said. "They look hungry."

"Just hurry," Ananias said. "Toss your stuff in a pile."

The black dog barked at this. Ananias calmly turned and shot it through the ribs. The dog yelped, fell.

"Jesus!" I said.

Squealing, the dog got up, tried to run off, its back legs faltering. His canine pals had already abandoned him, scampering out of the alley, their tails tucked between their legs.

Ananias shot the wounded dog again. The squealing

ended. The dog wheezed out a red mist and collapsed, its blood turning the brown snow to the color of rust.

"Man's best friend," Ananias said. "Turned into a political tool to maintain order." He looked back at us. "Hurry up."

WandaLee had been sent to her car, and she returned as Blu Fen, utterly bald, even his brows bare. Ananias had insisted s/he radiate back to his natural self, which s/he was able to do in the Chevy Reagan. Fen came back from the parking lot with Jimy, who smiled when he saw me—sweet, kind Jimy. How did he ever wind up with Blu Fen?

A courier truck rumbled past the alley, stopped, and began backing toward us. Ananias gestured for it to keep coming. The back end opened up as it neared, revealing walls a foot thick, and a bare and windowless metal interior. I tried to catch a glimpse of the driver in the side mirror, but I had no luck.

"Step in, now. 1 at a time," Ananias said. "No tricks." He took no chances. He even ran his hands through each person's hair before letting any of us climb in—something like what the gypsy had done with Frankly. I didn't want to think what the gypsy might say about my future now. When you have a gun to your head, the future isn't what it used to be.

We lined the truck's walls, sitting in our togas. Ananias tossed our real clothes in a dumpster, then he hopped into the back with us. The big door closed.

"Our money," Frankly said. "We have a thousand dollars in our clothes."

"I've got your money," Ananias said. He patted his coat pocket. "It's safe." He put his finger to his lips.

Like the walls, the floor was made of metal, and the truck needed new springs—I'd had more pleasant rides. I used the time to finish putting together the story. It came out like this: when Stamen became a liability for the Banjos, their leader—Mother— decided that I should take care of him because I had both underground experience and a natural desire to see to his safety. How would I support myself and Stamen without being a drag on the Cause? By dying, of course. Once they looked into it, they saw that I could not only pay my way and Stamen's, I could support the whole organization with the money I'd make.

But how would they get me to go along? Stamen provided the answer when he misspelled my name on the computer. Find a way to make me complicit, and I'm dead in the water (so to speak). I should have seen Mother's hand in all of this earlier. Nobody knew about Blib and Joanna, except me and my mother; yet when we arrived at the pet store, Blib said the Cops had been to his house that morning. Cops and not Big Boys. Mother informed on us, but kept the Big Boys out of it. Or maybe there hadn't been any Cops at all, only Ananias in his rented pink outfit.

Maybe she had told Blu Fen about us as well. She must have been in contact with Qigley; how else could he know so much about me? The Naked Suit should have clued me in, as I had left that in Mother's apartment, but I was too embarrassed and dinGy to think it through. Mother sold him the suit to raise bucks for the Banjos. That would explain the note Ananias sent. *Is Qigley a threat to your mother?* Qigley probably paid a fortune for my old dying knickknacks, and he claimed he donated money to the Cause as well, but much of what he was purchasing was information—

about me, ostensibly, but indirectly about Mother—
and Ananias became suspicious. The fact that his
agent was HarveL Blu Fenester must have multiplied
Ananias' worry.

It became increasingly clear to me that I needed a
plan. Or I needed to be willing to die again. The
Banjos were no different from Blu Fen; both wanted
to make me die against my will for their profit.

Frankly tugged at my tunic. He whispered,
"Whatever you do, don't sex me tonight."

"No sweat," I said.

"I am depressed about not sleeping with you,
which makes a perfect opening act for your die. I list
all the times you reject me for the audience, especially the time you wear this flimsy parachute."

"You can be a jerk, Frankly."

"That's good. Insult me. Send me to the depths of
despair." He was barely able to suppress his smile.
"Later on, of course, especially when we are on tour
together, we are sexing all the time."

Sex and death, death and sex. My life kept turning,
or failing to turn, on these pivots. I was weary of
them both.

The truck didn't take us all that far. Ananias covered
our heads with hoods and linked our hands with
ropes. He led us from the truck into a damp room
that stank of stale exhaust: a parking garage. We huddled together in a tiny room, which then started to
move: an elevator. When the hoods were removed,
we would be in another place—we could wind up
anywhere. Which reminded me of dying, that same
sense of powerlessness, giddiness, fear.

Where we actually wound up was a windowless room. Cheap beige carpet covered the floor, but there was nothing else in the room, not even a poster or plant. We all sat together against 1 wall—Jimy, Blu Fen, Stamen, Frankly, Ananias, and me. All but Ananias in stupid tunics. We waited.

"For whom are we waiting?" Stamen asked, tucking the tunic about himself as best he could. His legs were so pale, they were almost green, like stalks of asparagus.

"Madam Melmoth," Blu Fen said.

Ananias agreed. "Your mom will be here soon."

"You don't really think she'll approve of your behavior, do you?" Stamen said.

Ananias laughed. "Hey, I'm following *her* orders."

There was a picture in 1 of Mother's photo albums of Stamen and me sitting on our father's lap. Stamen was already a gangly kid, but I was a baby, in an outfit a lot like what I had on now. We each sat on 1 knee, and Father was hunching his head down, smiling, trying to get us to look at the camera. Above him hung the oak-framed mirror that Mother still had in her apartment. I'd seen the picture 100 times before I noticed her reflection, the camera obscuring her face, her hair tumbling to her shoulders.

That was how I wanted to think of Mother—a normal mom with a living husband, and 2 happy children, neither of whom were wanted by the law, neither of whom had ever died.

Then it occurred to me that the mirror no longer belonged to Mother. She'd had to abandon her apartment to avoid prison. Even the photo albums were likely gone.

I was thinking about this when the door opened, and Mother, at long last, appeared.

She smiled at us, her hair rippling back, gray-blond and tied behind her head with an incongruous pink bow. Stouter than my mind's image of her, she wore a flowerprint dress that could have come from the turn of the century. It was too big for her, of course, but she looked good, as she always did. She carried a plastic tray filled with muffins, a butter dish, a pot of steaming tea, cups and saucers, and a single glass of chocolate milk. No 1 else in the world knew that chocolate milk was still my favorite—that was sad, that no 1 else knew, but I didn't feel sad. There was no 1 I wanted to see more.

"Lyddie, what have you done with your hair?" she began, and I was up and in her arms. "Don't topple the tray, sweetie," she said, balancing it in 1 hand while I hugged her. "It's so good to see you, sugar," she said. Ananias took the tray, so that Mother could hug me properly. For several long seconds, in Mother's arms, I felt like a child, free of my troubles.

We had to separate. She gestured for Stamen, and while they hugged I recalled that day years ago when I had turned myself in—how Mother had visited me daily while I was held in the local jail, bringing me cookies and cupcakes and chocolate milk. The chocolate milk tasted now, as it did then, like the sweet parts of childhood.

She greeted Frankly and Qigley by name, giving them little pats on the back. She was always the favorite mom on the block; kids would hang out at our place and come running to her in tears with their problems. "Oh, Qigley," she said, "I have something to show you that you are going to love. Just a moment." She stepped out the door, then returned lugging my old Accu, the great gray butterfly of resuscitation.

"Is it a reproduction or an original?" Qigley asked, lifting it from her. From the way he asked, it was clear that they had done business before.

"It's not only an antique, it's the 1 my girl used when she was queen bee of this business. I've had it fully reconditioned and charged up." She turned her impressive head to me. "I understand you're queen once again. I can't say I approve, dear, but I'm happy for you."

"I was made to die against my will," I said.

"Yes, Ananias told me. That's shameful behavior, Mr. Fenester."

"Madam Melmoth, a great pleasure to meet you," he said, rising in order to bow, "but you, even better than I, should understand that sometimes means can be justified by the ends."

"Tea?" she asked him. "A blueberry muffin?" She glanced at Frankly. "Why Frankly, that tunic makes you look quite tall, doesn't it, Lyddie?" She continued without waiting for my reply. "I know you've been going through a hard time since the election of Stumpy, but you're looking well, young man."

"It's good to see you, Mrs. Melmoth." Flattery worked on Frankly the way milk worked on cats. "We are looking for you for several days."

"Well, we're all together now, aren't we?"

Blu Fen said, "Perhaps it's time we talked business."

Mother said, "I haven't met your friend yet." She paused before Jimy Schmidt and introduced herself. "And what is your heritage?" she asked after he had told her his name.

"My parents are born in Sinoloa, Mexico," he said. "I am born and raised in New Mexico, near the Rio Grande."

"Oh, I hear the habitable parts of that state are quite lovely, but that poor river is a cesspool, isn't it?"

"Yes, ma'am," he said.

She insisted that he take a muffin and tea. "I hate what they've done to the West. My husband and I used to travel through the West every summer when Stamen and Lyddie were tiny. You could tell what was going to happen even back then. A lot of it already had happened."

"I grow up in an uninhabitable region of New Mexico," he said.

"I want you to tell me all about it," Mother said. "Is it as dangerous as we hear?"

"Yes and no," said Jimy. "It is less violent than any city, but the water and the heat are dangerous."

Mother nodded, giving him her full attention. "Are you pretty much left alone out there, then?"

"By the government, yes, but there are bandits. You need a community for protection."

"Isn't that the way with the whole world?" she said. "Why don't we all sit down? Ananias insisted we remove the chairs. He's a worry wart. Doesn't want some kind of fight to break out. You see, even in this barren little room we have to worry about violence."

She went to 1 knee and let herself down slowly to the carpet—it was the 1st thing that reminded me of her age. With Mother it was hard to keep her actual image clear in your mind even while you were staring right at her.

"Now let me outline our proposal," she said, taking a muffin for herself. She buttered it and took a small bite before continuing. "Mr. Fenester, we would like to arrange a single event featuring both young Qigley here and my daughter. We will take 35 percent of the net, including the concession, parking, and television rights. This sum is not negotiable, as, I'm sure you'll agree, it is quite reasonable." She paused to permit him an approving nod. "We're not out to gouge anyone. From that sum, we will cover the expense of keeping Lydia hidden and safe until the day of the die, but you must cover all other expenses. We'll leave the negotiating with the TV network to you, but we'll ask for a representative to be present and to have access to all the records."

"I would have to be a fool to cheat the Banjos," Blu Fen said. "Your terms are quite fair, and I accept them."

"Oh, good, I like for business to be simple." She looked to Ananias. "And you thought this would be difficult."

"What about me?" I said.

"Oh, sweetie, we'll take good care of you. Think of all the time we'll get to spend together. We have so much catching up to do. And we'll keep a close watch on you until you've rested sufficiently and you're ready. We'll retain your share of the money from the 1st event for the cause, but you'll get to keep all your future earnings for yourself. We're not trying to gouge you either, dear."

"It's not an 'event,' Mother. It's a *die*. You're negotiating your daughter's death."

Mother's face clouded, a look I recalled from childhood, from times when I tried to put something over on her. "Let's not be melodramatic, Lyddie. It is most certainly *not* your death we're negotiating.

Death is, by definition, permanent. It is a performance that we're negotiating. An odd performance, I'll grant you, but you were always an odd child. This gives you the opportunity to use your talent for the betterment of mankind."

Stamen cut in, speaking angrily. "She died last night, and Mr. Fen is keeping the profits, and now she is to die for you, and you will keep the profits."

"I'm not going to do it," I said.

"Sweetie," Mom said, lowering her muffin. "I'm going to have to put my foot down about this."

"What, are you going to make me stand in a corner if I don't? You going to put me in time-out?"

Mother sighed. "I'll be forced to let the others in the organization exercise their option. I don't have unlimited power. You never understood that as a child and evidently you don't understand that now. You used to demand that I take you to Culverton Park long after we'd moved from Culverton." She looked to Stamen for help. "Do you remember, Stamen, how she'd go on and on, as if I could transport her across the country in a flash if I really wanted to?"

Stamen said, "Don't make her die, Mother."

"We don't have a choice, dear. You know I hate to interfere in your lives, but you will have to believe me when I say that we have no choice."

Ananias spoke. "The competing faction wishes to turn you over to the Big Boys," he said to me. "There's a sizable reward for the 2 of you."

Stamen said, "That's barbaric."

"Isn't it, though?" Mother said. To Frankly, she added, "My own flesh and blood, but you see, we encounter bloodshed everyday. That's our business, to be acquainted with the bloody goings-on in this country. My exempting you 2 would be like a general keeping his kids out of battle. Who could respect such a person?"

Ananias said, "For every gun seller or NRA member we box—"

"You mean *assassinate*," Stamen said angrily.

"Yes, dear," Mother said, "that's what he means."

Ananias continued, "For every 1 of them we get, we save 100 others. I can show you our stats. A net saving of 99 lives."

"How do you figure this?" Stamen asked.

"It's a complicated formula," Mother told us. "It has to do with both the actual lost sales from having a dead salesperson, and the more generalized slowdown that comes from people being reluctant to be associated with guns."

"Plus, we often get to take all the guns in the shop for our own use," Ananias threw in.

"Doesn't this seem just the teeniest bit hypocritical?" I asked Mother, but Blu Fen answered.

"Unfortunately, sweet woman, it's the way every business must operate."

"Let me give you the rest of the figures, Lyddie," Mother said. "Now each of our actions—"

"Assassinations," Stamen insisted.

"Yes, dear, each costs us roughly 10 thousand dollars. I know that sounds like a lot, but you have to think of all that goes into it—the travel, the surveillance, and you wouldn't believe our overhead! Now each 10-thousand-dollar action, we estimate, saves 100 lives, which comes out to 100 dollars per life saved. Now Lyddie, we believe that your event will earn us at least 10 million dollars." She glanced at Blu Fen.

"Minimum," he said.

"This means you could be responsible for the savings of 100 thousand lives. How can you turn your back on 100 thousand lives saved?"

"To refuse," Ananias said, "would be an act of genocide."

My heart zoomed then, as if from the gray Accu that rested at my feet. Its red charge light blinked at me—fully charged and ready to go. 100 thousand human lives.

Stamen touched my arm. "It would also make you responsible for a thousand deaths, and that is genocide as well."

"To be neutral in times of moral conflict is the greatest offense," Mother said. "Better to believe in the wrong thing than to believe in nothing, to refuse to take a stand. The year before the Banjos were formed, 200 thousand people died from guns in this country. Only IT kills more. Today, the number of people killed by guns is down to 139 thousand."

"And that counts the 700 or so we killed ourselves," Ananias put in.

"We make a difference," Mother said. "We've saved at least 60 thousand lives this year alone. And that's using 200 thousand as a steady figure, when we all know it was actually going up annually. We are mathematically *virtuous*."

Ananias was up on his knees now, gesturing with his hands. "We're going to force Congress to pass humane gun laws. We think once we reach the point where the number of people we box is equal to 1 percent of the overall number of gun related deaths Congress will have to listen." He paused and added, "Otherwise, hell, we'll kill them."

"Did you read the book I sent you?" Mother asked me.

"I've had less reading time lately than you might imagine," I said. "But I've read bits of it."

"You should read the whole book. All of you should read the book. Iglesia Smith was a great writer and a great man. He was likely murdered for writing that book. It makes the argument that terrorism can be a moral act. You have to give yourself over to the book to get the full message. Literature is the most powerful thing on the planet, don't you think?" She smiled her sweetest smile and added, "England thought of our founding fathers as terrorists, you know. The Boston Tea Party is nothing if not a terrorist act. Sometimes it takes desperate measures to make the world wake up and recognize the evil about them."

"Besides, Lydia," Ananias said, "you don't really have too much choice."

"I'm afraid that's true, my love," Mother said, then her face clouded over again. She started to speak, hesitated, shaking her head. Finally she said, "The only other possibility—"

"No," Ananias said. "Don't get into that."

"What?" I said. "What other possibility?"

"Well, we could use a Ragaccountant," Mother said. "It's very hard for us to get decent interest on our monies. We'd like to get to the point where all our actions are funded by interest so that we don't have to touch the principal. If we just had a little nest egg . . ." She turned to Stamen. "And we could certainly use a quality spellChecker and grammatical whiz, Stamen—as well as someone who knows what parts of the InfoTechno system the government has revived for its own purposes. But it would mean that the both of you would have to take the Banjo pledge, have to agree to go under forever. Even then, Ananias and I would have an internal struggle on our hands."

"You've got that right," he says.

Mother looked back to me. "Lyddie, with 1 die you could buy your way—and your brother's way— out of the organization. We've spent a lot of money following you about, getting you out of that jam at the Ontology Museum and so on. We've received nothing in return. With 1 die, the slate is made clean with us. I am quite confident that if you donated a sum from the 2nd die to Stumpy's reelection campaign you could buy your way—and your brother's way—out of the underground and back into regular life. Plus, you'd have enough money to live comfortably the remainder of that life. Believe me, I'm thinking of you. From the moment you were drawn into all of this, I've been thinking of you."

"Don't die for me," Stamen said. "I'd rather take the pledge. I don't want you to die ever again."

"We all d-d-die," Qigley said. The return of the stuttering seemed to surprise him. "Some of us j-j-just manage to p-p-profit from it."

"Well put," Blu Fen said and smiled at his client. Then he shifted his gaze to me, his eyes that compassionate nuclear green. "But more to the point, it's an opportunity for you to continue your art, for you to participate in the great theater that owes its very existence to your mastery of it. Art is our most profound form of communication, and you are 1 of our greatest practitioners. Watching you die is 1 of the most powerful things any human can witness." He paused and those amazing eyes became moist. "You are a genius of death. The genius does not understand the source of her brilliance, but she must not turn her back on her gift."

"And like I says befo'," Ananias said, scrunching up his face comically, "ya'll don't really have no choice in this here matter."

Mother laughed. "Oh, Ananias, that act of yours always makes me laugh." She gave herself up to laughter, then looked at me and said, "Isn't he a pistol?"

10

"I never get to talk to you," Mother said.

I had been permitted to leave the room. It turned out we were in an apartment whose kitchen window overlooked the Hypnotic Canal Amusement Compound—a New Age park for the gratuitously weird. At least it was quiet. The meditation dome glowed brightly, people milled about, but the only noise was the sparse traffic in the street below and the occasional dink of a stray sitar. While I was looking, a pack of dogs burst out of the alley and crossed the street, causing cars to screech to a stop. Mother had given me a cold beer, and I took a hearty gulp.

She wanted to tell me about Aunt Gloria's proposed surgery.

"Mom, I can't concentrate on Aunt Gloria's hypochondria at the moment."

"Gloria is not a hypochondriac. You're just like your father, no appreciation of dear old Glorie. Why the woman can hardly stand on her 2 feet without weeping. Hypochondria, phooey. She's old and in pain." Mother stood at the refrigerator and found a bottle of beer for herself.

"I can't die anymore." I turned from the window. I could tell Mother had been living here for several days. Dirty dishes and empty beer bottles littered the countertop, and the faint odor of popcorn lingered in the air. Mother loved popcorn. On the refrigerator, a triptych frame held family photos. "I can't die, and I don't want to be a part of your Cause."

Mother seemed disappointed that I wanted to talk business. "Oh, you used to sneak away to die, you eventually left home to keep on dying, and now you can't even consider it? Let me remind you that when you were doing it, it was illegal, just as what we're doing now is illegal. Several young people died permanently among your crowd, and all the good that ever came of it was some entertainment for a few thrill seekers. We save many lives by taking a few. Your dying never saved anyone. Please do not get self-righteous with me."

In the 1st photo on the fridge, Stamen and I had our arms around each other. He was wearing his high-school graduation gown. In the next photo, it was me with Mother, right after I turned myself in, and we both looked weepy. The 3rd photo showed all 3 of us, but when Stamen and I were little kids. I could see my adult face lurking in the child, a red-faced girl in a blue raincoat, only there was no death in that face.

"Do you remember when we took that picture?" Mother asked. "You were in 4th grade, and you'd just written that essay about Amerigo Vespucci. You'd written a child's version of his braggardly letters—the letters that resulted in his getting credit for the European discovery of this country."

"I remember. The teacher made a big deal out of it."

Mother nodded, but pursed her lips. "She thought it was very creative, which it was, but she couldn't see the larger value—how even the name of this country comes from deception and braggadocio."

"But that wasn't what I was writing about."

"Not consciously," Mother said. "Iglesia Smith says that the best writing always comes from the unconscious."

"I thought he was dead."

"Of course, he is, but his words still *speak*. That's the 1 area where Nowism has some legitimate application—literature is forever in the present tense."

I nodded without thinking. There was no point in getting her started on literature. "Why did Ananias give me that note asking if Qigley was out to get you?"

Mother flapped a hand at me. "He worries. Qigley pays a lot of money for your old things, but he also wants to know about you, about us. When Ananias discovered that HarveL Blu Fenester was his agent, he became afraid that Qigley might be setting me up. And we were both worried about you. Fenester is a complicated man. I went with Ananias to that tacky bar, you know. I drove the truck—I just couldn't let anyone see me. There's been such a fuss about me since I was elected president of the Cause. I have to be careful." She drank from the beer bottle then folded her arms. Her dress was long-sleeved, a flowery Mom kind of thing, but she looked terrific—she always looked terrific. It had more to do with who she was than how her body parts went together.

"Also," she began again, "I didn't want Fenester to know that there's just me and Ananias here. We can contact others, but An and I are the only ones holed up in this apartment."

"An? You call him An?"

She nodded and continued. "There are some in the organization who would like to kill Fenester after your event is over and we have the money. But I won't permit it. He isn't in the NRA and he doesn't sell guns. Once we start picking targets outside our stated goal, we lose our integrity—even if the person we box is a cad." She shook her gray-blond head angrily. "Once we pick political targets, we're done for. The organization will become nothing more than a form of organized crime."

"The way I see it, *all* your targets are political," I said. "Someone, a couple of people, did try to kill him last night."

"I know. They were Banjos, but they were *not* working on my orders. Mr. Fen knows that. There's a renegade faction. The same faction that wants to sell you and your brother to the Big Boys. I was furious that they tried to box Blu Fen."

"What about me? You're willing to box me."

Her face darkened again. "What nonsense."

"No 1 has *ever* died 9 times, and I'd have to then die a 10th time just to have a life."

"Only you and Qigley have done it 8 times, and you don't have a single speck of debility. Qigley should stop. His brain is going to turn to bric-a-brac. But you can do it. This reluctance of yours has nothing to do with a fear of being killed by the dying."

"It does other things. It messes up my life." I thought about saying, "It makes it impossible for me to tell whether I hate Blu Fen or love him." But I couldn't say it.

"I tried to tell you that when you were a teenager. Now I'm afraid that you're going to have to adjust. That's what aging is all about, anyway: accommodation."

"Yeah, well . . ." I could feel myself becoming petulant and childish, but I also felt helpless to stop. "Why do you care about the Banjos more than you care about your own children?"

She stared at the ceiling, as if looking to heaven for help or consolation. "I joined the Banjos *because* I have children." She shifted her gaze to me, deciding something. "Let me tell you a story, a story about you. This took place back when you were a baby, a newborn, and Stamen was just a boy. Your father was still living and—"

I shrieked, "Father! Did Father die from gunfire? Is that why you're so—"

"Don't be silly, Lyddie. Your father died from pneumonia. If you're curious, though, Ananias lost his wife and their child to armed robbers. Many of our members are people who have lost someone to guns. That's why we can't be defeated, you see, the more who die, the more outraged survivors there are to join us."

I sighed as loudly and with as much exasperation as I could muster. "Okay, okay, what's the story?"

"Your father and I were at a restaurant, a fairly elegant place. His mother was in town and baby-sitting. It was the 1st time we'd been able to go out since you were born. I don't remember what I'd had, but your father had ordered pesto fettucine, and he found a bit of metal in the pasta. He called the waiter over and showed him the piece of metal. The waiter could not believe that it was really in the fettucine. He thought we were trying to get a free meal out of the restaurant. An argument ensued. Eventually the cook and manager were involved. Finally, we left without eating.

"As we were walking angrily to the car, our special night ruined, the cook came running out to us. He said, 'That was a filling from 1 of my teeth. I'm terribly, terribly sorry. If I had admitted it in there I would have been fired. I'm an exoffender. Without a job, I'd be in terrible shape.'

"He asked us to meet him in another hour, after his shift was over. We got together at an all-night diner, and he bought us meals. He had learned to cook in prison, he told us, and he was certain that his job was the only thing keeping him from returning to crime. Your father asked what crime he'd committed."

Mother paused and touched my hair. It was so short now it must have felt like a pelt. "I loved your hair long," she said. "When you were a child, it reached your knees." She smiled at me sadly for another second, then resumed her story. "The cook said he'd been a Radabout, which is what we called Politicos back then. He had tried to covertly organize the workers of a factory where he'd been employed, although worker organizations had been outlawed. Father asked, 'And if you lost your job as cook, you would have to go back to being a Radabout?' The man stared at us long and hard, then said, 'I suspect I'd better not say.' You see, he thought we might get him fired in order to make him once again politically active. We hadn't been considering that, but for the next several weeks we discussed the rightness and wrongness of such an act.

"A couple of years later . . ." Mother seemed lost

for a moment, her eyes wandering about the room, her face going slack. "A couple of years later, when your father was dying, he said to me, 'Don't let our children be cooks.'"

We sat together for a while. Mother put her arm around me. The moment was tender. I said, "Did Daddy ever tell you he wanted to be a lounge singer?"

Mother jerked her head up and made an exaggerated frown. "God, no. Your father loved art, precision, beauty—not cheap entertainment."

"I've seen father twice, while I've been dead."

Mother's eyes were suddenly wet, her hands flying to her mouth. "Really? Your father?" She squinted and studied me. "It was really him?"

I nodded. "The 1st time, he was so sweet, so wonderful to me, but the 2nd time he was a lounge singer doing stupid stunts with a cigarette."

Mother didn't know how to take this. She stood, looked out the window at the Hypnotic Canal. She raised her beer to take a drink, but spoke 1st. "Could he have been trying to tell you something?"

"I don't know."

"Do you suppose . . ." Mother drank from the bottle, then set it gently upon the kitchen counter. "Do you think I'll see him when I die?"

"Probably," I said.

Her face flushed. She leaned against the counter, as if for support.

"What? Don't you want to see him?"

She nodded furiously. "Oh, yes," she said. "But . . ." She didn't finish the sentence, didn't look at me, but I understood that it frightened her, that for the 1st time in her life she was apprehensive about her own death. "If you see him again," she said, "before I do," she turned and smiled at me, "tell him I've thought of him every day—and every night—since he left."

I got choked up. We drank our beers weepily, and Mother told me about old Glorie's surgery.

We were given foam pads. Stamen, Frankly, and I took 1 side of the room; Blu Fen, Qigley, and Jimy took the other.

Qigley asked me to show him how to use the ancient Accu, which, I noted, had been cleaned and fully charged. This frightened me, and I scanned the room for a place where Ater might be stashed. I got up and looked around. Loudly, I said, "If either of us were to die tonight, it would kill us. You have to spread your dies out."

Blu Fen understood immediately. "No 1 is going to force a die on you tonight. The future payoff is too great. This—" he gave the Accu a prod "—is just a boy's plaything. Qigley is a collector." Suddenly he was close to me, pressing his lips against my ear. "I love you. I can protect you from the Banjos and from the Cops. You can come live with me and wait until you're truly ready to die again." Jimy suddenly appeared, poised behind his employer, but he quickly moved when he saw we were going to act friendly. I pulled my head away from Blu Fen's grasp. "Thanks, but no thanks."

"You come live with me," he said softly. "I'll live for you." He smiled then, a sweet, gentle, slightly lopsided smile. "Dying is your destiny," he said, "and so am I."

"I've been told," I said, and paused, "that you're a partial owner of death, that—"

"Who told you that?" He kissed my cheek.

I explained. We sat on his side of the room and I explained. Why not? What good did it do to keep this from him? I ended with Charles's lines, "Blu Fen is no coincidence. He's a partial owner of death. He's the delivery man for the grim reaper." I left out what Arlene had said, that he loved me.

He said, "Those assassins looked sweeter in death than they did in life, I'd wager."

I had to grant him this point. It was hard for me to think of them as assassins, but they had told me they were there to kill Blu Fen. Mother had said they were Banjos, renegades.

Fen started in again, "All right, it's true that I'm no coincidence in your life. I staked out the museum once I heard you might appear there. Is that a crime? I was already half in love with you. I'd seen the film of your die, and you may as well know this, I saw you die years ago at an old gymnasium."

"You were there?"

He nodded. "Madeleine Bruce invited me. I put up a lot of the money for security."

"How did you know Madeleine?"

He rocked his bare head to 1 side and eyed me sadly. "All right, I'll tell you everything." He settled back against the wall. He draped an arm around my shoulders, and I let him pull me next to him. "I'm no coincidence in your life. I've been obsessed with you for 20 years. Since I witnessed that remarkable die. What else did the assassins say about me?"

"That you're a partial owner of death."

"Yes, I'm Qigley's manager, and I take a big cut of his earnings. I suppose—"

"He said you were the delivery man for the grim reaper."

Blu Fen nodded sadly. "I've made some decisions in my life. I'm a lot like your mother in that way. Some of the things I've done have had consequences that are ostensibly ugly. Unless you see the big picture. Your mother and I both see the big picture. It's all a matter of vision."

"I'm not sympathetic with the Banjos."

"Neither am I, but the problem they address is real. The proliferation of weaponry in this country is obscene. But very profitable—capitalism just means moneyism, you know. I understand the desperation that can lead 1 to take extreme measures. I respect the Banjos, although I don't sympathize with them. I own guns. I need them." Suddenly he brushed his lips across my cheek.

"Don't," I said.

"Madeleine Bruce was a friend of my mother's," he said, "although my mother was no radical. My parents were industrialists. My father held public office. If they'd known what Madeleine was up to, they would have had her arrested. I, on the other hand, was infatuated with her. She gave fiery speeches about the right to education. When Congress passed the bill that would have ended public education, Madeleine came to me and said we had to act immediately. You see, the private school that she bombed was *my* school. I made it possible for her." He touched the corners of his eyes, which were dry. "I made an error, however. The bomb was supposed to kill no 1, merely destroy a building, but I . . . keep in mind that I was 15, that I thought—"

"You killed those children."

"Classmates. Friends. Sons and daughters of neighbors and congresspeople. I believed that if a few were hurt, then the President would veto the bill, and there would be no more bombings. But Madeleine had not been entirely straight with me. The bomb was more powerful than I had been told. I never expected that kind of carnage." He took a deep breath. "I was injured myself. Seriously injured. But I was not implicated in any way. Madeleine supplied phony details to keep me out of it. She was unapologetic about the deaths. The big picture. In terms of the big picture, we'd saved public education. By doing so, we'd made millions of lives less desperate, less violent. As your mother likes to say, we were mathematically innocent.

"I've been an active part of the underground ever since. I inherited my family's money, and I've used it to further the causes in which I believe. That has made me a controversial character—a wealthy heir to industry, and also a subterranean boss. I'm no more controversial than your mother. I was the delivery man for Madeleine Bruce, and I've been involved in some underground work since then, too."

He stopped. We just breathed a while. I didn't know what to make of it, couldn't worry my way to the right and wrong of it. Finally I said, "Mother claims you're a cad."

He laughed. "What a lovely old-fashioned word. I suppose I am. In an era of incredible violence and despicable behavior, it may be more responsible to be a cad than a polite victim. Of course, nonviolent resistance is the more admirable way to fight injustice. But can you imagine what would happen to the Banjos if they tried to fight the gun-happies through nonviolence?"

"It could be done," I said.

"Maybe, but there would still be a lot of blood-shed, and you'd have to have a charismatic leader, who, typically, would be murdered. Nonviolence is tough going. Those assassins who befriended you in death were not the nonviolent type. They wanted me dead, and their people want your mother dead, too. They see me as a kingpin of the underground, the protector of people like Madeleine Bruce and your mother and *you*. They're probably part of that group hunting down the old Rads—a group partly funded by the CIA from what I hear. They want Madeleine and some others. They believe my money is protecting them, so they attempt to kill me. WandaLee—I had the operation because I thought it would be the perfect disguise. WandaLee doesn't mean anything to me, really. Come live with me."

"I've got to think about this," I said.

He nodded, took my hand, and kissed it. "I saw you die in that gym, and it changed my life. I've been in love with you all this time. Look, I'll be entirely straight with you, although it's, well, embarrassing."

"Embarrassing?" I said, but what I was thinking was this: never again in my life will I know for sure that someone loves me. I had the word from the other side, from beyond the grave that this man loved me. How could I give that up?

"The truth is, I saw you die in StLouis, then Madelaine Bruce contacted me in Filly, and I arranged that die. You probably don't remember, but 1 of your fans had to carry you out to the hearse we had waiting. I was that man. I paid for the hearse. A while later, when you performed a die in DC, I heard about it and flew down."

"You saw that die, too?" My insides seemed to be wobbling around, the organs changing places.

"I not only saw it, I filmed it. The senator was a friend of my parents. He owed me a rather large favor—"

"You've filmed 2 of my dies without my permission," I said. "You're a prick."

"I am a man in love. I understand you better than you understand yourself." He stared directly into my eyes, unflinching. "You want *easy* love? Puppy love? It's not worth the bother. I'm offering you powerful love, challenging love. I saw you die 20 years ago, and I became obsessed. It changed my life. It changed the world. I understood that beauty stemmed not from youth, but from death. I understood that embracing death as a way of life could put you at an advantage over the rest of frightened humanity. You need to understand that now. This is an opportunity, Lydia. With your inspiration, your great talent, and my vision and money, we can change the world. It's true."

I slipped my hand from his and rose to a crouch. "Like how?"

"In whatever manner we choose," he said. "The truth is, we already have changed the world."

"What do you mean?"

"Stay with your mother, if you wish. But have dinner tomorrow with me. There are things I could tell you. I'm no coincidence in your life. If I hadn't found you at the museum, Qigley still would have delivered you to me at the restaurant. In fact, the only reason I became Qigley's manager was to find a way to get close to you. I know I—"

I stood, cutting him off, but I didn't know what to

say to him. I merely looked down on him, confused beyond words.

He said, "Think about dinner tomorrow. Think about *us*. Think of the possibilities." His eyes followed me as I crossed the room. I could feel them on my back. It wasn't the worst thing I had ever felt.

I sat between Stamen and Frankly. They were both reading *I Am A Big Man Not*, holding the book between them. Frankly said, "Your brother takes forever to read 1 page. I think he's looking for spelling errors."

Stamen said, "Stay away from that man." He nodded in the direction of Blu Fen. "Don't trust him."

"Do you know something about him?" This possibility excited me. Sometimes I forgot that Stamen had been a Silk-Level bureaucrat. There were lots of things he could know. I tugged on his tunic. "Do you know something about Blu Fen?"

"Yes," he said. "You stay away from him."

"What?" I whispered. "What?"

Stamen looked steadily into my eyes. "He made you die. That's what I know. That's all I need to know."

I slumped against the wall.

Frankly waved the novel at me. "This is a great book. A mega-page-turner."

"I find it a bit too elliptical," Stamen said. "Too much is left to the imagination."

Frankly snorted, something he rarely did as he was afraid he would be compared to a pig. "I bet as a child you make things with popsicle sticks. I bet this is your great passion."

"You are in error," Stamen said. "I did no such thing."

"Then you miss your calling." Frankly turned the page. "You are through memorizing this, I assume?"

Stamen didn't answer. I glanced over their shoulders and read a paragraph:

> Cruz worries that he has condemned his soul to
> eternal damnation. He cannot escape the image
> of the hanged Flagstone. Perhaps, Cruz consid-
> ers, he should not have wrapped his friend's
> head with burlap before executing him. He did
> not think he could stand to see Flagstone's eyes,
> but he should have been thinking of his friend,
> giving him 1 last opportunity to see the blue
> sky, the deciduous trees, to witness the glory of
> this earth at dusk.

Ugh—that was my exact thought—Ugh. It was pathetic when you started thinking in grunts.

Eventually, everyone was asleep but me and Qigley. Insomnia was the dying artist's curse. Even Ananias was sleeping, although I had assumed that he'd returned to watch over us.

"T-t-to s-s-sleep, perchance to d-d-dream," Qigley said to me. He no longer seemed dinGy. "D-d-do you d-d-die in your d-d-dreams?"

"Not exactly," I said. "But they're not pleasant."

He nodded. In the dark room, I could barely see him. He patted the Accu, which separated him from Blu Fen. He had negotiated what he considered a fair price for the relic—more than 100 times what it originally cost. He sat up suddenly, staring through the dark at me. He asked, stuttering terribly, how I managed to die so much without getting the half-smile, the stutter, the gray rot. His question was sad and sincere.

"How much gray rot do you have?" I asked.

He shrugged. "I can't do math anymore," he said, stuttering through it. "I can't tell colors so well."

"I let go quickly," I said. "For some reason I have the ability to give up life without a struggle, but I still have enough desire that I come back without that other kind of struggle."

"The desire to stay dead," he said, stuttering over the final *d* so long that it sounded elegiac.

"Qigley, when you die . . . "

"Monsters," he said, "chewing on the bones of the people I loved. The 1st deaths were different, but since then it's been all monsters."

"Hmm," I said, but I didn't offer anything about my deaths. "Have you heard about the labors?"

"The labors of death?" he said, his stuttering making my stomach knot. "Oh, yes, I know all about them. Or the 1st 3, anyway."

"What do you mean? You've never gotten past the 3rd labor?"

He shook his head. "I don't know anybody who has," he said. "You haven't, have you?"

"Yeah, I guess I have," I said. "I don't know *anything* about them, though. I mean, I don't know why I've been able to get through them."

He fell back to his elbow and opened his mouth to say something, but paused for a long while. When he finally spoke, he got it out without stuttering: "You have grace."

———

I stayed up long enough to see Qigley fall off and go into the shakes, the full-body rattling of a dying artist with rot. He might survive 1 more death, but not 2. He should retire. For me to continue dying would kill him.

We were a funny group. Each of us, in a strange way, held the key to another's future. While I waited for sleep, bits of my conversation with my mother came back to me. Could my dead father have been trying to give me a message? Did he become a lounge singer in order to convey something to me? I wondered if the message wasn't something about my own act—my dying. Had I become a sleazy act? Something like a lounge lizard? I supposed that I had. Certainly now that my naked dead body was being seen on porno/snuff screens around the country, I was in the sleazy category. Had he been trying to warn me? I wanted to believe it.

Then I remembered something about my last die, about the gift. At the very end, just before I was jerked back to life, I'd felt this knowledge, this strange understanding entering my mind—not a thought, exactly, but something like a memory. I had that "oh yeah" feeling of recalling something long forgotten, like seeing a photo of yourself in the dress that had been your favorite, and what you remember is not just the dress but that feeling of wanting to wear nothing else, how that dress had seemed essential to who you were. That was what this knowledge was like, this weird and sudden comprehension that came to me, like slipping into a long loved and long forgotten dress.

My body had been dissolving—not dissolving, but separating, expanding, dispersing. I could feel something essential seeping out of me, and while it was zooming away from me, it still was me. I was becoming a distillation of what I had been, minus the body, minus the neurotic whatnot and the not-neurotic whatnot, minus the self. I was entering the landscape while this feeling was entering me.

It did not feel like I was being extinguished. It felt like a return to a place I had loved but been forced— by living my life—to forget. I want to say it felt peaceful, but the word is inadequate, calling to mind the spaces between emergencies rather than that splendid music of the soul.

The 7 labors of death were the giving up of identity, which permitted you to receive the gift. And the gift was . . . life without metaphor. The body was just 1 of the metaphors we embraced, and the gift permitted us to relinquish even the embrace. We returned to something essential and pure and *alive*. But these words, too, were metaphors for the inexpressible.

It was hard to hang onto the inexpressible. Like trying to recall a dream right after you woke: you felt it there and felt it slipping away at the same time. Besides, now for some reason, there was a song going through my head, and I couldn't concentrate. It was the Velma rOOst cover of some somebody's old hit, "Big Girls Don't Cry." She would sing it while getting her skin stapled to a sheet of plywood. I started to laugh, but then realized that I was crying, tears dripping down my nose.

So I turned to *you*. You had heard the story unfold. I had kept you up to date. What could *you* do for me? Were you just there to observe? Were you the sensation that led people to believe in God? I should pay more attention to you, I knew, but I was not in a position to meditate on your existence. Why didn't you say something? What were you waiting for? I wanted to believe that you were part of the gift, but how could I know? Were *you* the inexpressible? Were *you* life without metaphor?

I slept roughly an hour, according to Stamen's illuminated watch, which was shining in my face when I woke. Long enough to dream the story Mother told me, to see the cook, who in my dream looked very much like Blu Fen, and long enough to see my father, who whispered into my mother's ear and, as can happen in dreams, it became my ear. He whispered, "He's a partial owner of death."

It woke me, the dream, my father's sweet voice speaking Charles' ominous words. If Mother and Father had turned in the cook, forcing him to become a Radabout, wouldn't that have been essentially the same thing Blu Fen had done to me? Forcing the die on me so that I would once again become a dying artist?

But my parents had decided against it. And Blu Fen had raped me, besides. I was no longer dinGy. Whether I'd been willing to sex him wasn't the issue. He *raped* me.

I went back over my conversation with him. Something about his explanation had not set well with me, and though I couldn't get to the heart of it, I did understand that he was responsible for many deaths. But the same could be said of Mother or—as she pointed out—of me. I made dying popular, and many had died while dying. Which made me—what, mathematically guilty?

I heard my name whispered from across the room.

Blu Fen was awake, gesturing for me to come to him. He looked something like a Greek god, lying there in his tunic, gesturing with 1 arm.

I started crawling to him across the floor before I even thought whether I should. The crawling made me angry—made me feel the anger that had been roiling inside me. He was making me crawl, I thought. As I came near, he pulled his tunic over his head, revealing his naked, hairless—beautiful—self.

The decision came to me while I was on all fours and furious.

I ran my hand up his legs to his cock. He smiled at me and started to speak, but I put a finger to my lips and motioned to the sleeping others. He nodded. I lifted my tunic above my thighs and crawled on top of him, inching my way up his legs playfully, until I was right on top of him, but he was not yet inside me. He moaned softly, and I leaned toward him, but just before I fell against him I grabbed the Accu and jerked it between us.

I flapped the levers down.

With the 1st jolt his entire body jerked and rose off the floor. He gave a strangled scream.

Someone in the room shouted. Sounds of people shuffling about followed. The lights came on just as I pressed the levers again. Blu Fen again heaved up and down, his head thudding against the floor.

He was burning inside.

In moments, he would be dead. Permanently dead.

He managed to focus on my face for just a moment, his luminous green eyes finding mine, and his eyes were full of love.

"You rot in hell," I said. As I said it, I felt *you* leave

me. My life was now, once again, entirely in my hands.

Ananias screamed something and grabbed my shoulders, but then he slumped to the floor. Stamen and Frankly stared from their foam pads. Qigley jerked nervously in his sleep, this ruckus, no doubt, being incorporated into his hellish dreams.

Beside me stood Jimy. He had knocked Ananias unconscious.

The door flew open. Mother appeared in the doorway holding a black revolver. Her face was pink, her hair mussed from sleep, but she assessed the situation with her usual aplomb.

"You should hurry down the front stairs," she said to me. "I may have a dress that would fit you, but you don't have time to change. When An wakes, I won't be able to control him. He is going to wake, isn't he, Mr. Schmidt?"

"He wakes before long," Jimy said.

Mother stepped to my side and kissed my cheek. "Go away, sweetheart," she said, hugging me a final time, a tender hug, and I realized that she did not expect to ever see me again. I glanced back at the 2 bodies on the floor, Ananias' crumpled form and Blu Fen's beautiful, naked, dead body.

"We are hurrying," Jimy said, taking my arm.

As Mother ushered me out the door, she slipped the pistol into my hand. What weight it had, what solemn, awful weight.

PART

3

11

I sat on the hump between 2 yammering Nowists, hurtling through rain-besotted Pennsylvania, contemplating my future as a murderer, wearing nothing but a sheet.

Welcome to my life.

We were in Jimy's car, an old Plymouth Rock—a dinosaur on wheels. Fat as a sedan, but with only a front seat, so it had that sawed-off-and-sewn-back-together look. I insisted on picking the radio station because I wanted to hear something old and sentimental, and because I was sick of their conversation: "I am in love many times with the wrong women," Frankly was saying, grabbing my bare knee as he spoke.

I responded by elbowing him in the gut *hard*.

"Ooaagh, you hurt me!" he said.

"No kidding?" I said, and glared. "Keep your hands off me!" Screaming in a car was a particularly rich effect, so I added another line: "And shut up!"

He sulked silently. I found a station playing a Blind Smoking Wilkins cut from his turn of the century disc,

Dark Hearts in Heels. His voice shouted sentimental lyrics over the windshield wipers' slap and splash.

We were on a backwoods back road, flying down an unmarked 2-lane, the asphalt shimmering, car shimmying, yours truly simmering. I had never been so furious. My life was completely gone, my future now utterly in the past.

But I didn't regret killing Blu Fen. I was furious that the Banjos and the Big Boys and Blu Fen and the dies all had taken just enough out of me to leave me with nothing—except this fury, which was sufficient to do in Blu Fen, and might be enough to keep me going until I could reinvent myself. As I thought about it, I understood the deep truth of it. This was what I now had to do: reinvent Lydia Melmoth.

It started with rage.

"You lay your hands on me again, and I'll tear your ears off!" I screamed at Frankly, who already hugged the door handle. "And the same goes for you, you ape!" Jimy flinched and the car fishtailed briefly on the wet pavement.

It was true that neither Frankly nor Jimy particularly deserved my wrath, but they were the only ones handy. If this thing had a backseat, I'd crawl there and fume myself to sleep.

Stamen had decided to stay with Mother. "It was self-defense," he had said, hugging me before I left. "And don't worry about the body. I'll find a manner of disposing of it that casts no shadow on you." It occurred to me that through all of this muck Stamen was the only 1 who had behaved decently. Everything he had done had been to protect either Mother or me. Meanwhile, he had lost everything he valued.

Suddenly I was in tears. Stamen's life was ruined. Charles and Arlene were dead. Blu Fen, who loved me, was dead. Jimy was out of a job. I was on the run from the law, and Frankly was still short.

I had every right to cry, so I really let go—convulsive, mucus-saturated bawling. The boys were far too scared to put an arm around me, so there was not even that tiny comfort. The rain, as we drove, turned to sleet and then to an ugly brown snow.

At an all-night gas station in Faraday, Pennsylvania, Jimy produced a wad of bills from somewhere among the wires under the dashboard—loot he had embezzled from Fen. "FenDough," he said, smiling at me, hoping this would make me happy. "FenBucks. FenLoot from my FenLarceny."

"I need coffee," I said. I shoved Frankly to make him move. He tumbled forward out of the Rock and onto the snowy pavement. His tunic rode up his back so that his white, hairless buttocks glistened in the snowlight. It was all I could do not to kick him while he was down.

"You are a *zer0*," he snapped at me, covering himself quickly and clambering to his feet. In Frankly's obsessed worldview, there was little worse you can call a person than a *zer0*—1 who was completely obscure. But the truth of it hit me—I had been absolutely obscure, even to myself; I had no idea who I was, am, or would become. I had been a selfzer0 ziphead. A *cabeza de nada* self-knowledgewise. No wonder I had been able to make it through the 7 labors of death; I had given up my identity before I was ever dead.

I stomped past the simpering Frankly without apologizing, truths of various sorts falling upon me like the rat-colored snow.

Here was another verity: a sheet provided little warmth. A cold draft shot up my legs and goose-pimpled me all over. Luckily, the Gas-R-Us shop was heated. A heavyset black man sat on a stool watching me shake the snow from my hair. He held a home-made shotgun against his leg, barrel up, pointed toward the ceiling. He glared at me and said, "I don't want any trouble."

If I hadn't already been freezing from the walk in, I would have felt a chill from his words. Was there already some kind of news about us? "What are you talking about?" I said.

"I saw you push your boy against the concrete," he said. "Whatever it is wrong with you, I want it kept to yourself." He cocked the trigger back in case I thought he was just being cute.

I pointed angrily to Frankly, who now approached the door. "That's no boy of mine. That's a talentless Nowist who thinks I'm going to give in and sleep with him if he keeps sniffing around me long enough. You know what it's like to sleep with a Nowist? For the rest of your life, he's saying, 'I am fucking her with great relish' like you're a goddamn hot dog!"

This speech proved incoherent enough for the man to switch loyalties. He barked as Frankly entered, shaking the shotgun in 1 meaty hand. "You try anything with that poor woman while you're in my place, and I'll blow you to kingdom come."

Frankly plopped down on his butt against the tile floor like he'd been shot. "I am doing nothing," he said, and raised his arms.

"Get up," the man yelled at him, "or you'll be Nowing in hell."

"You am pathetic, Frankly," I said, and headed for the coffee machine. "You am been pathetic since you am born."

Frankly smiled meekly at the man with the gun and climbed to his feet. "We are friends," he said. "She's a little testy at the moment."

The man just snorted.

When we left Gas-R-Us, we all 3 wore red Gas-R-Us T-shirts and Penn State sweatpants and socks. I had a huge sack of Hooch Crumbcake, diet Cokes, Raisinettes, and Cheetos. I was ravenous, and it seemed to be contagious, Jimy and Frankly joining me in the feeding frenzy while we passed through little nameless towns, 1 swelling of lights after another. We meandered through the long night, squiggling north of the interstate and then south, dipping through Barstow and Bleecker, St. Olaf and Volshtap. "What the fuck do people do in these towns?" I said, my mouth full of Cheetos, my fingers fluorescent from handling them. The streets were vacant, shops boarded up. Only streetlights and 24-hour gas stations showed life.

"Milk cows," Frankly said, hoping we were friends again.

"These once are mining towns," Jimy said seriously, his tone only slightly undercut by the Raisinette that flew out. "Now they have some little farming. Nothing else."

"I think the farms are closed down because of the groundwater," Frankly said.

"Yes," Jimy said, "but they still farm for themselves and for the locals. It's not legal to sell the meat, but they can barter."

According to the Rock's digital clock, it was 2:15 in the A.M., but it seemed much later. No sooner did the lights of Volshtap disappear completely behind us than the car lost traction on the snow-covered road, slip-slid into the other lane, and began spinning.

I was thrown into Frankly; his diet Coke trickled down my neck and chest. The headlights illuminated a dense wall of gray trees, then the black and barren road, another embankment of trees, the snow-covered road. Suddenly we were no longer spinning, but speeding backward, my head falling against the padded dash—and then I was thrown against Jimy, as we began to spin again.

The rear wheels caught the muddy shoulder and sent us flying off the road, through a mesh fence, and into the woods, where we came to rest against a huge gray tree trunk.

"Mother of God," Jimy said, his voice a coarse whisper.

Frankly climbed up from the floorboard, where he'd been thrown. "Are you okay, Lyddie?" he said, then he saw the tree that had stopped us and gasped.

"I'm alive," I say. "We're all alive."

"I am peeing," Frankly said, and scrambled out the door.

The cold air that tumbled in set off a new fear in me. We could still die. We could freeze out here.

"That is almost killing us," Jimy said. Frankly's soft splash of urine into snow punctuated the sentence. "I don't know what happens. We are just driving along—"

"See if the car will start," I said.

Jimy nodded, breathed into his hands, shifted into Park, turned over the ignition. A whirring, straining noise began, but then the engine thundered. Frankly was immediately at the door. Already snow framed the windshield.

Jimy shifted into reverse, but nothing happened. "We can't just drive out," Jimy said. "We are pushing."

"We don't have shoes," Frankly said. He had already removed his soaked socks and rubbed his reddened feet.

"We don't have a choice," I said. "Get out."

Frankly moaned but obeyed, pulling on the socks once more.

The frigid air made me immediately cough, but the car engine still idled, and I hopped up on the warm hood.

"Here it is," Jimy said from the rear of the car. "Flat tire. That's why we are spinning."

For once Nowism made sense to me, because I still felt like I was whirling, and I couldn't believe it was ever going to stop.

My socks were the driest, so they were the inside pair, followed by Jimy's, and then Frankly's. Jimy put them all on and loosened the lug nuts. Immediately after, he scampered onto the hood and gave the socks to me. I put the jack in place, but when I tried to raise the car, it rolled backward.

"There's no level ground," I said.

"Come back up here," Jimy said. "We make a plan."

Frankly slipped on the socks, the engine purred along, snow coated our skin. Frankly said, "We jack it up again." He pointed to the car's tracks through the snow, the long slope down to the road. "We jack it up and it falls again and again until we are close to the road. Then we change the tire."

"That'll take forever," I said.

"Sit in the car," Frankly said. "Then your weight is pulling us down the hill."

Jimy said, "We do this until we think of something better." He hopped off the hood, scooped me into his arms, and carried me inside the Rock. The whirring heater provided a searing pleasure. I turned on the wipers to clear away the snow.

Frankly moved the jack to the front of the car and took 2 turns jacking it up and letting it fall. We moved maybe a yard backward each time. Jimy went next while Frankly climbed in and stuck his feet over the heater vents. Softly, he said, "I am afraid we die here."

The car plunged to the snow again, rolling back another yard or 2. The next time Jimy had it jacked up, he changed the tire, which raised our expectations, but when it fell, we rolled backward only an extra foot or so.

When it was my turn, I looked around back 1st. Snow had mounded up behind, blocking us. I tried to shovel some away using the jack stand. The base of the stand disappeared into the mound, and I had to go to my knees to dig it out. I used my arms to clear a path beneath 1 of the tires. Frankly and Jimy appeared in their bare feet to see why I had disappeared. They dropped to their knees and dug away at the other side of the mound.

A cold wind rattled the bare branches above us. When we had cleared a path, we all climbed back into the car. "Give me my tunic," I told Frankly. I slipped it on over the other clothing, then took the wet T-shirt and sweatpants off. "Put these beneath the rear wheels," I said to Jimy, and handed him the clothes. "Make a little path with our clothes."

In another few minutes, the snow was carpeted with ugly apparel, and I had the front end jacked up. Jimy was behind the wheel, ready to throw it into reverse. My feet and legs ached from the cold. My ears were stinging. I gave the hood a shove. The jack flew out, just missing my head. The Rock rolled back, caught the clothing, picked up speed, rolling down to the shoulder, bouncing onto the road, spinning in a wide arc before stopping.

I ran down in the car tracks. The engine had died, but the headlights dimmed and brightened as the car came to life again.

Back in our togas, back in the dark, back in the artificial heat of the car, back on the road—alive—but anger still swam in my chest like an aimless fish. I could almost feel the flutter of its tail. The night was endless, the road endless, the dark utterly endless. How did people go on? I wondered. How did they continue to make lives for themselves?

My head was heavy with fatigue and confusion, and I let it rest against the seat, slumping, then sliding against Jimy's shoulder, finally settling into his lap. He glanced down at me, his brown eyes reflecting the reflections of the windshield. Frankly stared at me, too, as I pulled my bent legs into his lap.

With my eyes shut, the dark became the darkness of death, which made me shudder and shift. Me, the queen of death. Death was my dominion. Qigley might have died as many times as I had, but he had killed no 1. The rumbling vibration of the car felt, for a moment, like Blu Fen's stunned body, rattling beneath the Accu, beneath my body.

I missed *you*. Why had you abandoned me? Or were you still there but no longer letting me be aware of you? I felt like a jilted lover, like music still playing though the orchestra hall had long since emptied.

A little after 3:30 in the morning, I took the wheel. We had just driven through 2 burnt-out factory towns, nothing more than mounds of brick, and into farmland, barren for the winter, where the roads and weather slowed us to a skulk. The scenery more than anything else seemed to have worn Jimy out.

Frankly, too short to reach the Rock's pedals, wanted to know where we were going.

"That way," I said, pointing into the dark.

Jimy wanted us to head to Denver. He might know some people there, he told us.

"We *might* know some people in any goddamn city," I said, but Denver was as close to a plan as any of us could come up with. I had taken charge: reading the map we had bought at the Gas-R-Us, divining our way west by 1 backroad and then another, controlling the radio, the heater, the junk food, and now the steering wheel. We were making lousy time on these winding roads in this crummy weather, but I shifted into gear and we were moving.

"If we're going all the way to Denver," Frankly said. "We need a motel for the night. I'm tired."

"We're all tired," I shot back. "That doesn't mean I'm going to fuck you."

"Calm down," Jimy said.

"I don't know you," Frankly said. His head spouted out of the tunic hugely like a tulip on a short stem. "Since we leave Filly, you are a different person."

"Yeah, well, I *are* no longer the pushover. I *are* no longer the victim. I *are* no longer the deadhead flake who lets other people choose when and whether she dies or screws."

"You are no longer a friend, either," Frankly said sadly. "I do none of that to you."

Jimy said, "We drive until morning and we get a newspaper. We need to concentrate on our situation now. We don't know whether the Cops are after us."

"I just want to keep moving," I said. "You can sleep in here. You can both sleep."

Jimy let his head rest against the passenger window, while Frankly balled up in the middle. Me, I held my breath and stared out the windshield. I knew I was acting weird, rude, angry. I could see myself doing it, but I was helpless to stop. I could see myself in the driver's window, my faint reflection cast over the grim landscape—a woman who had not bathed, and whose eyes flared with a frightening intensity, like 1 who was crazy or gifted or both.

Frankly and Jimy grew quiet, still. They might have been asleep. Or merely cowering.

Something in the simple movement down the snow-lined highway soothed me. The flutter in my chest, the bubbling anger remained, but I was satisfied for the moment with the grind of rubber on wet asphalt. Nothing appeared on the road with us but the snow that glittered in the Rock's headlights.

Jimy shifted in his seat and glanced over at me. "When I am a boy," he said softly.

"I'm sick to death of Nowing," I said, surprised at the sudden renewed intensity of my anger.

He didn't acknowledge the complaint, didn't change expression. "When I am a boy, my grandmother takes me to AdventurePark in Colorado, and I shake hands with Wonder Woman, Bosco the FatBoy, the Cisco Kid. It is October and it begins to snow. This is the 1st time I ever see snow, and I think it is something they do in the park, like the lava on Ballard Peak. No, my grandma tells me, God does the snow. Not Bosco the Fatboy."

I waited for a long time to see if there was a point to this recollection. "That park went broke," I said. "I knew the Rag who dumped their account because they couldn't keep a minimum balance. Shitty management, she said, and constant trouble from the locals. Place went belly up."

"This discontent of yours," he said. "It isn't Blu Fen or your mother or Ananias who makes it. It isn't just that you are being raped—"

"Oh, goody, we have a philosopher in the car. You ever been raped?"

"It has to do with your place in the history. You are not alive in this moment. You are not permitting yourself to live in the Now."

"Fuck Nowism, Jimy."

"If you are in the now, then you are seeing the beauty of the snow, the spareness of the winter fields, you are feeling the warmth of the heater along with the coldness of the windshield against your cheek."

"You're the 1 slumping against the window. Why

do you have such a long face if everything is so hunky-dory?"

Jimy moved his free shoulder in what might have been a shrug. "I am sad but not discontent."

Jimy had finished talking. The road lay ahead of us, straight and flat, ice creeping in from the shoulders. The sky was dark, starless, and without end. The air had grown thick with snow and the quiet swish of tires on the fresh fall. I felt, for the moment, alone and almost at peace, as if my mother and brother did not exist, as if I were not on the run from the law and my old life, as if I were truly a free agent zooming through the cold and dark. As if nothing were holding me to the earth, nothing holding me to my life, or to any way of life, but the spinning tires— as if the possibilities for how to live were as limitless as the sky.

Then I spotted a figure in the road ahead. A child. Facing the car. In my lane.

I slowed and shifted lanes without braking. The child, a red-faced girl in a blue overcoat, panicked and ran in front of me. I hit the brake, then, and we slid down the road, taking up both lanes. The headlights shone out over the desolate fields, and the girl vanished in the oncoming dark. The car slid forward and I waited for the impact, the thud that would mean I had killed her.

As soon as the car finally stopped—still, miraculously, on the road—I leapt out the door and ran back through the snow. Jimy and Frankly called my name. "There's a child!" I screamed, and slipped on the ice, tumbling into the ditch that bordered the road.

Jimy reached me, helped me climb out. Frankly huffed his way there, too. The Rock sat cockeyed on the shoulder, headlights aimed askew into the fields, lighting Frankly indirectly and from behind, so that his comic figure was shrouded with illumination, a glow that made the snow he kicked up sparkle.

"There's a child," I said, coming back to the world. "I don't think I hit her, but I don't know how I missed her." Jimy helped me up, while Frankly stooped over, hands on his knees to catch his breath. "Help me look," I said, and felt tears freezing against my cheek.

We fanned across the road, calling and trotting through the snow, our teeth chattering, our bare feet freezing, the world absolute in its silence.

"Here's where you start to brake," Jimy said, pointing to the veer of tracks.

"She has to be here somewhere," I said.

"I get the car." Jimy began running back down the road.

Frankly had finally caught his breath. "You're covered with snow," he said, and dusted my bare legs. "There's no 1 out here. There isn't a house or trailer or another car."

"There's a child," I insisted.

"There are no tracks," he said.

Behind us, the Rock's engine revved. Jimy drove slowly, nosing back and forth across the road, the lights covering the snow-covered asphalt, then stretching into the snow-laden fields. As the car approached, I tried to picture the girl again. I had seen her clearly, but there were no footprints except our own.

"Come on, Frankly," I said. "There's no girl." He

took my hand, led me to the Rock. To Jimy, I just said, "Let's go." He executed a careful U-turn.

It was *you*, wasn't it?

We drove only a few miles before the Rock began to lose power.

"I floor it and nothing happens," Jimy said. Even as he spoke the car slowed more. The speedometer read 15 miles per hour. He craned his head around to look out the back window. "Is there a trail of fluid? I think we are losing transmission fluid."

"Can you fix it?" Frankly asked.

"Not out here," he said.

Already we had slowed to 5 miles an hour.

"Block the road when you stop," I said. "We may have to force someone to give us a ride."

Jimy somberly nodded. "We aren't seeing another car for more than an hour."

"Hush," I said, but I was no longer angry. It felt weird to think that we could die from the cold, from *nature*. I checked the glove box. The pistol Mother gave me lay nestled between the map and the left-over crumbcake. Even if a car did come by, it might not want to stop. We might need persuasion.

We sat in the idling Rock, heater on high. Jimy had the car turned sideways on the road, blocking both lanes. "So," I said, "you want to tell me again about how beautiful this all is?"

Jimy glared at me. "I am alive in a dying car on a snow-covered road in the deep of a winter night. You are partly here, but partly in that blank room watching Blu Fen's insides burn, and partly in some arena preparing to die, and partly in some state of temporary death, and partly in your high school clique showing off, and partly in your crib." He paused to wipe fog from his window. "Which of us, do you think, is best prepared to deal with the events of this evening?"

"Oh, *eat me*, Jimy. Do you understand that old American saying? It is in the present tense, after all."

"My head," Frankly interjected, "is of absolutely normal proportions. I prove this now by sticking it inside the glove box. I ask you, does a grotesquely large head fit in the glove box of an American-made car? Of course not."

Jimy said, "Leave the glove box alone."

"Oh, let him stick his head in there if he wants," I said. "He's a depressionist practicing his trade."

"Leave the glove box alone," Jimy said.

"This is censorship!" I said. "Who decided you were in charge—"

He cut me off by pointing. In the distance, a pair of headlights momentarily appeared on the winding road. Jimy flipped open the glove box and removed the pistol. "Here's the plan," he said, and like it or not, I listened.

We killed the engine, turned on the headlights. I stepped out into the cold air, the tunic lashing my bare legs. Frankly and Jimy ducked down onto the floorboard. I wedged the barrel of the pistol between a front tire and its rounded fender. The jutting handle of the gun was hidden from the approaching car.

The headlights stopped 100 yards up the road. I

waved my arms, lifting them high so that the tunic rode up my legs. The car edged forward a few dozen feet. "Help me!" I tried to sound pathetic and alone. The car advanced slowly. A Toyota Spandrel, silver in this light, laden with snow.

It stopped again, now just a few feet away. The window on the driver's side lowered, but I couldn't see a face. A man's voice called out. "What's going on?"

"I'm freezing," I said. "That's what's going on."

He dimmed his lights. "Who are you?"

"My name's Lydia, and my car won't go."

"What's wrong with it?"

"It won't go. It'll start but it won't go."

A noise from the car—maybe a snort—then a long silence.

"I'm turning blue out here," I said.

Again the voice from the car: "Why are you wearing a sheet?"

"I was at a party."

Silence.

"I can't feel my feet," I said. "My nose is going to fall off my face."

"How do we know we can trust you?"

"Why don't you wait till I pass out from the cold, and then you can be certain I'm up to nothing."

Silence.

"Look," I said, raising my arms. The tunic fluttered. "Nothing up my sleeves."

"How can we be sure?"

I was prepared for this. I lifted the tunic over my head and stood naked before the car. He turned on his brights. I did a 360, exposing every part of my freezing self.

The car door opened, and I slipped the tunic back over my head. "Come on," said the man. "Get in."

As I pulled the tunic down, I pretended to stumble on the ice, catching myself on the hood of the Rock. I grabbed the pistol and slipped it inside my tunic, the freezing metal pressing between my bare stomach and my crossed arms as I ran to the car.

I leapt into the open rear door, onto a plush seat, dark blue and otherwise empty. I closed the door behind me, bending low and rubbing my feet while the pistol slipped down onto the seat between my legs.

The driver turned and filled the space between the bucket seats, a big, bland-looking man with a broad face. He introduced himself, Eric Mee. In the passenger seat was a young woman, Gretchen Mosier. They were a handsome, well-dressed couple, in their late twenties. If they hadn't been out in the middle of nowhere, I would have said they were coming home from a date.

Gretchen took a coat from her lap and passed it to me. She said, "Why don't we ever get invited to parties like that?"

Eric gently laughed. "We should throw 1."

Beneath the coat, I fingered the pistol.

Eric shifted the car into reverse and backed up slowly. "If your engine runs, then your friends should be all right until we can send help."

"Friends?" I said.

Gretchen smiled. "We saw where the car slid on the road a few miles back."

Eric added, "It's rare to see footprints of bare feet in the snow. There have to be at least 2 other people in that car—1 man and 1 child."

Gretchen lifted a crystal glass into the space between the bucket seats. "Brandy?" she said.

"Where are we going?"

"We don't blame you," Gretchen said, gesturing more insistently with the brandy until I took it. "Most people wouldn't stop for a man, and you certainly wouldn't want to expose your child to this weather."

I drank quickly, which sent a shot of heat all the way to my knees. I handed the glass back to her before raising the pistol. "I hate to do this," I said, directing the barrel against the back of Eric's head, "but you know how it is."

"Holy fuck," Gretchen said. "Where did you have that hidden?"

"Is that loaded?" Eric asked. "Because if it's loaded, it could go off accidentally, and then where would we be?"

"Well," I said, "you'd be dead, and Gretchen and I would have a mess on our hands, now wouldn't we?" Without meaning to, I had started that mock-sophisticated tough-talking that criminal types did on TV.

"Yuck," said Gretchen. "Go along with her. I don't want to have to mop up your brains and eyes and things." She snorted out a little inappropriate laugh. The car stopped its backward motion, and they both stared at me. They were neither particularly frightened nor surprised.

"Let's go and get my friends, shall we?" I said. What were mobster women called? Mauls? Mills? Mobbies? "Nice little vehicle you've got here."

"It only has 5 thousand miles on it," Gretchen said.

The car slowly retraced its tracks. Eric said, "We have some money at our house. You're welcome to it. We've been robbed a few times. We don't begrudge an honest robbery, but please don't feel that you have to use any force."

"We like to get along with people," Gretchen said. "We're not gun phobic, or anything."

I almost said, *Stow the talk*, but some small remaining human element within me resisted. "We don't want to hurt anybody," I said. "We just need a lift."

"Any way we can be of assistance," Eric said. He sounded almost cheerful.

Jimy and Eric shoved the Rock off the road, and then we were gone. I drove, Jimy beside me with the pistol, Frankly in the back between the happy couple.

"The 1st time we were robbed," Gretchen said, "was right after our wedding. I was still in my *dress*, and these 2 nice men blew out our front tires with rifles."

"They were good shots," Eric put in.

"We became very close," Gretchen said. "We still get postcards."

"What the fuck is with you 2?" I said. "Aren't you the least bit worried about being kidnapped by 3 loonies wearing nothing but sheets."

"Oh, yeah," Eric said, remembering something. "You have a rific bod. Thanks for the look-see."

"Ditto," Frankly said.

"Maybe we should let them in on our little secret," Gretchen said, smiling at Eric.

Jimy flinched and caught my eye. "What is your secret?" he asked them.

Eric said, "Should I tell them or you? You go ahead."

"Okie-dokie," Gretchen said. "When Lydia took off her clothes, we decided it was safe—"

"Silly old us," Eric put in.

Gretchen laughed. "We *thought* we were safe, anyway. So we *spawned*."

"You are spawning right now?" Frankly said.

"Yeah, and it's rific," Gretchen said. "You want to spawn with us?"

"You are carrying drugs?" Frankly said. "You could get us arrested."

Gretchen smiled beatifically. "You know what they say, 'To spawn is to wish everybody was spawning.'"

"Is that what they say?" I said. "Who says that?"

"I think it's a beautiful saying," Eric said. He leaned across Frankly to kiss Gretchen.

I had never done it, but if I were into any drugs, it would be spawning. Usually it came in 1 of those throat-spray cannons, and you shot it in your mouth. Within a minute or 2, everything in the wide world was splendid, and you became so expansive yourself that you rivaled the world's splendors.

It was illegal, of course. Wealthy whozits had given away fortunes while stoked on the stuff. Frankly must have been furious. Depressionists tended to hate spawners. However, I could see all 3 in the rearview mirror, and Frankly didn't seem to mind them. I asked, "How long does the stuff last?"

"Hours," Eric said.

"But let's don't talk about coming down," Gretchen said. "It's so sad."

"We drive around to save on phone bills," Eric explained. "Once a single canister cost us 3 thousand dollars in long distance."

Gretchen laughed. "My old biology teacher lives in

Egypt. It's a lot safer driving, anyway. 1 time Eric tried to hug an electric heater—he was that happy to come in out of the cold. 2nd degree burns all over."

"I love inanimate objects," he confessed. "You guys from Ohio?"

"Are we in Ohio?" I said, which made them laugh until they cried.

"You have a rific sense of humor," Gretchen said. "It's so lucky we met you."

"It's so nice of you to drive," Eric added. "You're life-savers."

"You got it," I said, then looked to Jimy and mouthed "Shoot them."

From the back I heard Frankly saying, "I change places with you. You 2 go ahead. Cuddle."

"Then we'd be leaving you out," 1 of them said. Did it matter which? Evil words entered my head, and for the next 100 miles I muttered things like *mawkish mongrels* and *smarm maggots*. "I love you all so much," Gretchen said, apropos of, trust me, zip.

We dropped off the Boobsie twins at the bus station in Delfina, Indiana. It was late afternoon, and we were waiting until the bus was about to leave before putting them on it. They were zooming down from a major spawn and could barely stay awake. "Get your fucking hair out of my face," Eric told his sweetie.

We had bought clothes and shoes at a Walmart back in some little Ohio town. The 3 of us were wearing DuckWear, which Frankly had picked out. He had got the sizes right, so it was true that he had some talents, but I was wearing a light green Velma rOOst Polo that made my skin look avocadoish, while

Jimy was in a pale yellow Zim T (Zim the PseudoMystic Oriental Pathologist) that seemed to give him jaundice. Frankly, of course, looked spiffy in a steel gray LeeHarveyO with a big buttondown collar to make his head look smaller. He hated not to be the best dressed of any group.

The bus finally arrived, streaked gray from exhaust, and with brown splotches from the snow. People with animals got on 1st. Eric and Gretchen followed. Jimy and I led them over, while Frankly sneaked around the parking lot looking for a new license plate for the Spandrel.

"When am my going to get my car back?" Eric whispered at the door to the bus. Gretchen had already boarded and was stumbling to her seat.

Jimy answered. "Just keep quiet about us, and I am sending you a postcard with the whereabouts."

"Yeah, well," Eric said. "I'll do that, I guess. But if I don't get the card soon, I'll rat on your asses." He stepped up and paused once more. "Tell that fucking dwarf he couldn't depress an environmentalist, will you?"

On that note, we separated.

"I like them better spawning," I said. "But just barely."

"They are telling the bus driver all about us within the hour," Jimy said. "We are making time now."

It was a fascinating notion, to make (create, build, erect, invent) time. We could make life—and even death—but when we "made time" all we were really ever talking about was hurrying.

Frankly had found Colorado plates in the lot, and in a matter of seconds we were on the road. 10 minutes out of town, Frankly began tossing other license plates from the window. "I put our plates on a Continental, then put its plates on a Buick, then take a bunch of other plates to confuse people." He whirled them out the window 1 at a time. They spun like boomerangs and landed in the snow, sending up little brown puffs.

"Now what?" he said.

Jimy and I looked at each other, but neither of us answered.

"We drive to Denver," Frankly said, answering for himself. "We ditch this car and . . . and . . . "

"And we vanish," I said. We would disappear and make some time for us to figure out the remainder of our lives.

12

We arrived in Colorado the day the state legalized cannibalism. Chic restaurants were charging a small fortune for a 6-ounce human steak, and the ludicrously wealthy or hopelessly fashionable paid for the thrill of breaking yet another taboo. In every little town we passed through lines of people waiting to sell body parts. A healthy leg could bring 20 thousand dollars. The radio reported drive-by assassinations of people in line, and the Colorado legislature had already passed an emergency bill to outlaw the sale of meat from people killed while in a cash-for-meat line. "Just to ensure that the killings really are random," some local DJ said over the air, "and not inspired by relatives hoping to make a killing from the killing."

"This is so sick," I said, staring at a line that wrapped around the block—mostly middle-aged people, but some looked to be in their twenties. "How is it possible that there are this many people desperate for money?"

"They are coming from all over the country for the

past few weeks," Jimy said. "20 grand solves a lot of family problems."

"And you get a free prosthetic leg," Frankly added.

"It's sick," I insisted. The local legislator who introduced the law argued that it would keep kids off drugs. "This will provide donors with the money to get out of the ghetto and go to college," he had said over the radio, "and provide them with the kind of physical challenge they need to have meaning in their lives."

I flicked the radio off. "Who would eat human flesh?"

"It's stinG," Frankly said. "You don't really know the true greatness of meat until you eat of the flesh."

"That sounds like a commercial," I said.

"I read it right here." Frankly was poring over yesterday's *Denver Post*, which he had taken from a gas station john. The ad took up half a page. "Don't resist what's genuinely stinG," he went on, "unless you are ready for the grave."

I found myself imagining Frizzhead's voice in my head, saying even the human body had become a commodity, but that was hardly anything new. This was just the latest version.

On page 6 in the newspaper, Frankly found the article he had been looking for: "Industrialist HarveL Blu Fenester Found Dead in Filadelfia Park." Frankly showed me the headline.

The article said his body was found by the Spiritual Elitist Jogging Group at 7:00 A.M. the morning after I killed him. The article said he had been shot in the head, which baffled Jimy, but Frankly and I both understood. "Your brother protects you," Frankly said. "The poor bastard. He carries the body there and then blammo!"

"Shut up, Frankly," I said, and my voice cracked. Poor Stamen. Was there nothing he wouldn't do for me? Was there nothing I wouldn't force him to do? The article said there were no suspects.

"They are soon suspecting me," Jimy said. "My employer is murdered and I disappear. Either they suspect me, or they think they are finding my body, too."

Frankly said, "Why do you disappear? Why do you come with us?"

This was the 1st time I had considered the question. All along I had been thinking that he had to be on the run, too.

Jimy shrugged, waited just long enough that I thought he wasn't going to answer. It occurred to me that maybe he was along in order to be with me. That maybe he cared for me. Maybe, even, he was in love with me.

Finally, he said, "I have some trouble in my past. Blu Fen and I make an arrangement. I work for him for a period of time as his bodyguard, and then he establishes for me a new identity. If he dies, then I am failing as a bodyguard and the info he has about me comes out. It is coming out now, I imagine."

So I was wrong. And I was an egomaniac.

"We are getting today's paper as soon as possible," Jimy said. "We need to know what the authorities are doing and if they implicate us."

He said this, but didn't stop in FtCollins, and soon after we were in the Denver Air Tunnel.

"What is this?" Frankly said. Jimy launched into a scientific explanation. Basically it was just a bunch of faucets that spewed clean air up against the blanket of smog, creating a tunnel—a Colorado techno student's idea for how to deal with the return of heavy smog following the Collapse. People liked it, but the energy that it took to filter the air and spurt it upward accounted for a big percentage of the pollution, and only a fraction of the city had been tunneled, making the other parts—the poor parts of town—5 times as polluted. The untunneled sections were just called "the dark." Only during the night did the city become democratically dark all over.

The tunnel *was* cool-looking, a big arch of clarity you drove through with the roiling black sky pressing in on the sides. Occasionally I saw headlights out in the dark sweeping across somebody's invisible driveway, otherwise I wouldn't have known people lived out there. Frankly pointed to the 1st bright intersection—a whole tunneled neighborhood. "StinG," he said.

We stopped a few miles later in a neighborhood that looked like a downtown, but the tunnels only went so high, and I couldn't tell how tall the buildings were. It probably couldn't have been downtown, though, because we found a parking space.

Frankly emerged from a grocery with today's newspaper, fingering a spot. He liked to be the 1st in the know. Climbing into the car, he said, "Stamen protects us."

A photo on page 3 showed Qigley, dressed in black, looking at a coffin being lowered into the ground. Behind him, his head partially cropped out of the photo, stood my bony brother. Qigley had hired him to replace Blu Fen:

Stamen Melmoth, the brother of Qigley's greatest competitor Lydia Melmoth, has agreed to become Qigley's new manager. "My sister has

retired from dying," Stamen announced, "and
so I see no conflict of interest."

"I wish they hadn't cut off his head," I said. "He
needs all the fame he can get to stay clear of the Big
Boys."

"He knows what he's doing," Frankly said. "He
isn't going to do this unless he knows he can get away
with it. Does it say when the next die is scheduled?"

Jimy impatiently yanked the paper from us. "What
about Blu Fen's death?"

The article said the Cops had a couple of leads
based on anonymous tips, and noted that an assassination attempt against Blu Fen had taken place the
night before. Charles and Arlene's full names were
listed, "thought to be members of the Banjo terrorist organization," the paper said. The very last sentence of the story said that Blu Fen's bodyguard was
missing.

"Those anonymous calls," Jimy said, "that's what
Blu Fen promises for me if he dies. Someone is tipping off the police that I am his bodyguard for 3
years, and that I am now gone."

"What did he have on you?" I asked.

Jimy shook his head. "Nothing I am telling you
about," he said stiffly. "The past is now, and now is
the past." He paused a moment, then added, "Jimy
Schmidt is a dead man."

We ate at Burger King, taking turns in the bath-
rooms, washing up. Jimy was shaken, which worried
me, but Frankly was barely able to contain his glee.
Already he could see himself opening for Qigley, his

big round head in the spotlight. I should have been happy, too. Stamen had managed to keep the fact of my killing Blu Fen out of the paper and away from the Cops. Maybe I wasn't a fugitive—at least, not from the law. Stamen must believe that his fame as Qigley's manager would keep him out of the slammer, too. But now what? Did I go back to NeYork and my apartment? Would the Big Boys leave me alone? Would the Banjos quit harassing me?

Jimy said, "Christ rises from the dead, right?"

Frankly and I looked up from our food dumbly.

Jimy went on, staring at us very intently. "Lazarus rises from the dead, no?"

"You worry that Blu Fen is alive again?" Frankly said.

"Lydia Melmoth rises from the dead, this much I know," Jimy said. "This I am witnessing."

The way he looked at me was conveying some inscrutable something, which I felt I ought to catch. I nodded as if I had a clue. "What, exactly, are you getting at?" I said.

He smiled. "Precedent," he said. "I am explaining to you after I wash myself." He pulled his big self from the table and ambled toward the john.

"He's freaking out," Frankly said.

I didn't say anything, just ate my Whopper.

Frankly waved 1 of his fries philosophically. "We can't really help Jimy. But you and I are free to go back to NeYork. I am famous soon, and you are my wife soon, so we are both safe." He finished gesturing with the fry and ate it. "I am proposing to you. Marry me, Lyddie."

I choked down the bite of ground beef and took a sip of diet Coke. While Frankly had talked about us as a couple and about our coupling, he had never before formally proposed. I knew I needed to handle my rejection of him with some sensitivity. "I'm not going to marry you, Frankly. But thanks a bunch for asking."

"We are good for each other for a long time." He was punctuating with another French fry. "In another year I am teeming with dough and fame."

"Frankly, I don't give a damn."

"Movie allusion," he said. "StinG." He smiled, and for a moment I recalled that we had, in fact, been friends a long time. "Marry me," he said, and I knew that he was sincere.

"What's taking Jimy so long?" I said. "What is that awful Muzak song? Why do these places never put enough salt on their fries? Are we supposed to be health conscious while we eat these grease-bound potato sticks?"

Frankly sighed. "'The Ballad of Joe Hill,'" he said, and pointed to the pink speakers above our heads. "The song." He wagged his big head sadly. "It plays in the elevator in our apartment building. That's where you hear it before." He sighed loudly. "I hate Muzak."

The syrupy emotional whatnot distracted us, and it took a while for us to realize that Jimy was not coming back. Frankly checked the toilet just to be certain. "He leaves us a note." Written on a paper towel, the note contained just 2 sentences.

Dear F & L,
You are better off without me. You will be in my
thoughts.
—J

"Hey," Frankly says. "That's the future tense." His stubby finger covered Jimy's parting words.

"Yeah," I said, and what I felt was like another little death.

If it was true that we were better off without Jimy, it was hard to believe we were better off without the car and his money. "This is definitely where we are parking before we eat," Frankly said of a space now filled by a waffle-top pickup.

"Oh, hell," I said, "betrayed and abandoned."

This pissed Frankly off, and he started walking. I was supposed to say, "Not entirely abandoned, of course," or some other apologetic drivel, but I was too depressed to mollify him.

"Why isn't it snowing here?" I said.

"The tunnels blow it all into the dark," Frankly said.

"So what do we do now?"

The sidewalk was busy with business types, along with a surprising number of hippies, and a few MountainFins—those oppressively healthy types who wear khaki shorts in the dead of winter.

"It's obvious," Frankly said, flattening himself against a marble wall to give a bandanna-headed hippie plenty of room to pass. "We call your brother."

"If it's obviously the thing to do, why does the idea give me the willies?"

Frankly paused a beat, as if to consider my question seriously. "Because you think maybe you are wanted for murder. Or you think that you are on the Big Boys' graylist. Or you think maybe your brother is sooner or later getting nailed despite being Qigley's manager, and you are doing the same if you are returning. Or—"

"Enough, already. I'm convinced. I'm not calling."

"I am convincing you of the opposite."

"That's what you think. Besides, what number would we call?"

"He gives us a number tomorrow, I bet. In the paper. This is why Jimy leaves us. He knows we are safe. He puts us in jeopardy by staying with us. We are going back."

Up ahead a crowd gathered around a woman standing on some sort of platform. As we drew closer, I saw that she was holding a gun to her head. "Christ!" I said. "Jimy took the gun, too!"

The woman wore a gray, 3-piece business dress and spoke through tears. ". . . 24 years," she was saying, "and without even the standard 2 weeks notice, they let me go."

"So shoot yourself already," an onlooker yelled.

A female MountainFin called out, "The Rockies are an hour's drive from here. With a single hike—if you're in any kind of shape at all—"

A man in butt-shaped glasses cut her off. "The whole problem with this country is permissiveness," he said. "Why on earth should we permit this woman to disrupt our day?"

Frankly steered us into a crosswalk and across the street. "All of these worries are groundless."

"Whose worries?" I wanted to know. "That poor woman is considering killing herself. Are you telling me her worries are groundless? She's been fired after 24 years."

Frankly nodded. "Her employers can keep her retirement money in this state as long as she is working less than 25 years. But I'm not talking about her. I'm talking about you. Your worries are groundless. The future is waiting for us." He threw his arm out as if this street embodied more of our future than our next few steps. The tunnel effect did make for a pretty, glistening sort of light, but the dark was there, too, crowding in at the edges.

"Stamen passed Silk-Level information," I said. "You think being a muckity-muck's manager is going to get him out of that?"

"Not just any muckity-muck. Qigley's die gets a 79.3 rating. That's higher than the Superbowl."

"Fine. Maybe Qigley could get away with it, but his manager—"

Frankly turned, cutting me off. He raised 1 hand of stubby fingers. "I make a deal with you," he said. "If your brother's photo isn't in tomorrow's papers, you win, and we stay under. But if his photo is there, I win, and we go home."

"You're that confident that—"

"Not me." He shook his too-big head. "Your brother. He's betting his life on it."

We spent the day at the Denver Museum of Contemporary Art. The big exhibit was a mock-up of a doctor's waiting room. After standing in line 2 hours, we were permitted in. It was amazingly like a doctor's waiting room—a foam pad couch covered in stain-resistant material, a plastic rack of old magazines, framed warnings from the surgeon general, a pile of grimy plastic toys off in 1 corner, giant dispensers of condoms and Alchoquaffers on the walls, and an unmanned loan table from a local bank.

"I wish we could spend the night here," I said, and Frankly nodded. There were several funny touches—the trash basket was full of used tissues but also an out-of-date library card, expired Greenpeace membership card, and several old receipts, as if somebody had cleaned out his wallet while waiting. Loose aspirin and change filled the cracks between the couch's cushions. The artist was part of the new Radical Reality movement. They tried to make you really *see* things that you looked at all the time. It occurred to me that the tunnels, putting part of the city in brilliant light by letting the remainder fall into incredible darkness, could also be an exhibition of the Radically Real.

"Have you considered tonight?" I asked Frankly. "Where are we going to stay tonight?"

"I think someone is following us." He whispered this while sniffing plastic roses.

"We've been in line 2 hours; there are plenty of people following us."

He whispered again. "That woman in the yellow dress. Don't look! You see her?"

"How can I see her if I don't look?" I pretended to be eyeing a 3-month old *New Yorker,* but stared over the top of the centerfold at the woman. She was tall and slender, maybe 30, with a pretty but puckered face, wearing glasses with triangular lenses. She had a sea otter hairdo. Ordinary, in other words. "What about her?" I said softly.

Frankly ran his fingers over the mock-wood counter of the receptionist's booth. "I am seeing her before." He drummed his fingers casually. "She is in the Burger King."

I turned so cavalierly that I felt suddenly conspicuously inconspicuous. However, the woman was paying no attention to us. "I think you're nuts. How could you remember, anyway? She has no distinguishing characteristics."

"She looks like my mother."

"Oh." I glanced at her again. No way his head could have traversed those hips. "Why would someone follow us all this way . . ." I stopped because I didn't want to finish the sentence—none of the answers would be pleasant. "I think you're getting paranoid. Let me correct that: you've been paranoid your whole life, and it's starting to show again."

"Even paranoids have enemies," he whispered with great hissing authority. "She is following us!" He took my hand, guiding me toward the exit—a door labeled DOCTOR—and we passed through, out to the museum's lobby.

"We were only there 5 minutes," I said. "We wait 2 hours and then spend 5 minutes in the doctor's office."

"Just like real life," Frankly said. He herded me through great glass doors that took us outside. The sunlight surprised me—maybe because I usually saw a doctor in the early evening, after work. Which made me think it was a pretty good piece of art. I would have told Frankly about this, but he was tugging me into traffic. I dodged an angry taxi and cut between a motorcycle and a city tube bus. As soon as we were across the street, he said, "In here," and I went with him into a little corner store called "Noot's Apothecary & Tunes Shop."

"Watch those doors," Frankly said, pointing to the museum where we just exited.

Before I could come up with a sardonic wisecrack, the woman in yellow emerged. "Oh, shit," I said. "Damn, damn, damn."

From behind us came a male, teenage voice. "Can I assist you stapes?"

"Hide us," Frankly said.

"Stapes?" I said.

The boy had an O-cut that made a perfect halo of white hair on his pink scalp. His eyes opened so wide I thought his eyeballs might slip out of their sockets and bonk to the floor.

"Lydia M!" he said, touching my shoulder with 1 finger. "Magnifico!" He shook my hand in a jittery flurry. "I just caught your flick last night." Then he said, "Follow my treads."

I tried not to consider that "my flick" was the porno-die film Blu Fen had distributed, and glanced out the window at the yellow-robed woman. She was crossing the street against traffic, heading our way. "Frankly," I hissed. "She's coming this way. She must have helpers."

"She's a Big Boy," Frankly said. "Who else has people telling her to cross the street?"

Halo-head guided us through the store, which was a maze of ceiling-high counters filled with various drugs and music discs—some of them packaged together with recommendations for which songs to listen to as you came on to the drug. Near the rear exit, he kicked a rug to the side and lifted a trapdoor. "Trails, Stapes!" he said, which, I gathered, was his way of wishing us well in our travels.

The stairs lit as our feet alighted upon them. We were in a narrow staircase that led to who knew where. "This may have been an error," I said as the trapdoor closed over us. I felt more confident about the assertion when the steps ended in water. "We're in the fucking sewer," I said. "I always knew we'd end up here."

Frankly remained focused. "Wade," he commanded, stepping in himself. "We are escaping." He took my hand and tugged me into the murk.

The water reached my knees, Frankly's thighs, but I could barely keep up with him. I had never seen him so *directed*, as if he actually knew what he was doing.

"This is no sewer," he said. "I smell nothing."

He was right, of course. If this had been a real sewer the odor would have given him a seizure. What the hell was this? "Drinking water?" I said. He shrugged, tugging me along, his pants and my skirt soaked, but our DuckWear shirts shedding splashes off our backs as advertised. The lighting was dim at best and fluorescent, which Frankly usually commented on because it made him look greenish, which he hated. "I have a frog complex," he had told me once.

Ahead was an intersection, more brightly lit, the canal crossing something else. "I know what this is," I said. As I said it I heard the whir of fans. "We're in the tunnel fabs. This is how they make the tunnels of fresh air above—with a tunnel of clean water below and—" I quit; the whir had become becoming deafening. We paused at the brilliantly lighted intersection. Our canal fed the main channel with water purified by reverse osmosis—I had read about the process. I looked to Frankly and mouthed, "What now?"

He pointed to the continuation of the canal across the tunnel channel. We quickly passed through the light, into the dimness, running until we were distant enough from the whir to talk. "We look for another set of stairs," he said. "They are lighting only if we set foot on them."

"Right," I said, wondering again about his sudden

leadership. While we groped forward, I noticed that his lips were moving. I leaned in to hear. "I am famous. I am famous." He was chanting it, Nowing his way past this escapade, right into his opening performance for Qigley. All his dreams were about to come true, and their proximity had him acting like a general, a midget-with-a-mission—a hero.

The stairs we finally stumbled across—literally, but the DuckWear came through, and my chest and back remained dry—led us to a door that opened into another store, a liquor store, judging by the array of bottles. No sooner had we rushed past the befuddled clerk and out into the street, than we realized we had to head for the dark. Our clothes were soaked, which made us conspicuous—and incredibly cold. "Let's go to a clothing store," I said, but Frankly only glared at me. We had left all the money in the car.

We held hands and rushed to make a light, crossing the street with a gaggle of young business types. We were halfway across the street before I realized that the woman in yellow was among them. "Welcome to Denver," she said. "The tunnel fabs have a built-in monitoring system, which means the Cops will be here swarming the area, so no time to gab." She spritzed me in the face with a spray bottle.

"That stinks," I said, and the world went black.

13

ou are almost dying," Frankly said, his voice tender and hushed. I came to in a semi-dark room, Frankly standing over my cot. He touched his chest with both hands. "I'm out all of five minutes, but they cannot revive you for a long time." He took my hand again. I realized he'd been holding it, stroking it while I was under.

"I've got the instinct to die," I said, sitting up, the room tipping as I rose, my head throbbing. I grabbed Frankly's shoulders to steady myself. He stood beside the cot, and for once he towered above me.

The walls of the room appeared pink in the dim light. A long poster showed various dinosaurs and listed their names: Apotosaurus, Brachiasaurus, Tyrannosaurus Rex, Pterodactyl, Triceratops, Woolly Melmoth—make that *Mammoth*. A 2nd poster showed types of another extinct species, the whales: Sperm, Killer, Humpback, Blue, Right, Nar. A Eugene the Eunuch nightlight cast a dim, smiling glow. The single window was dark.

"How long was I unconscious?" Pressing my

temples, I felt a residual coldness in my fingers that scared me.

"About an hour," Frankly said.

"Longer than that. It's dark out," I said, pointing to the window.

Frankly rolled his eyes. "Are you dinGy?"

"Oh," I said, "I get it." We were out of the tunnel system.

"Who are these clowns who've kidnapped us?" I asked.

"Do you die just then?" Frankly asked. "I mean, do you go all the way? Does this count? If it counts, you are the sole record-holder again."

"I didn't die. I guess I came close." There was no other furniture in the room, just our cots. Two mobiles hung from the ceiling: a cardboard solar system, the planets drooping unevenly about a two-dimensional sun, one of the planets evidently missing; and a jungle scene, the big predatory cats circling antelope, zebra, giraffe, and at the center a gaggle of monkeys. Most of the cats featured, as well as the antelope, were extinct.

Frankly sat beside me on the cot. "It's not the Big Boys. They have real holding cells. Big Boys won't keep us in a child's room." He sighed and let his head fall into my lap.

"Have you noticed that all the pictures in here are of extinct things?" I said. "Are they trying to tell us something?"

"Nowists don't believe in extinction."

"That must be comforting."

"More comforting than psychology. 'Get in touch with your inner child,' or 'Speak to the earth parent,' or 'We all need to dance to our Core Music.' Nowism refutes psychology. It says that who you are is who you are. Don't blame your parents, your upbringing, your culture. Once you are accepting the Now, you're in control."

"Well, if you're in control, kindly get us out of here."

"Don't take me literally." He pointed to the jungle mobile. "Zebras are not extinct. Monkeys are not extinct. You are just feeling depressed." He waited a second before continuing. "Ironic, don't you think? Here I am, practically a famous depressionist, trying to talk you out of depression?"

"You're not that good at it," I said, although it was not entirely true. I was grateful that he was with me. "Who do you think our captors are?"

"Banjos," he said. "Renegades."

"Shit," I said. "That's depressing. That's very depressing."

Frankly shrugged. "I'm a professional."

Although I had not died, I must have gone right to the border—a partial death, like being a little bit pregnant. It had been close enough that the dream I had was something like a death. Different in some ways, but weird in similar ways.

I suddenly had found myself in a temporary hospital—a bare lumber erection with rooms separated by fluttering white sheets. Now and then the flap of sheets revealed the outside, a flash of a green, placid river bordered on the opposite side by lush trees alive with the movement of the wind.

I was one of the doctors, wearing a white surgeon's-smock. The place was full of dying children, each in a bare white cot, silent and sleeping, bloody bandages heaped in every corner. I had no idea what I was supposed to do, but I felt a desperate sense of urgency and rushed from chamber to chamber. I had forgotten something, and there would be awful consequences.

In one room, I found a man wearing a smock identical to mine. He smiled when I stepped through the sheets. His teeth were translucent. It was the ghost of Blu Fen.

"You're a hallucination," I said.

He shrugged blithely, then knelt beside the cot of a dying boy.

I said, "You're like this boy—the figment of a second-rate mind."

Blu Fen's ghost shook his bald head. "Spirit," he said.

"You're a spirit?" I knelt beside him and touched the bloody bandage that encircled the boy's skull. "Is that what you're saying?"

Blu Fen's ghost nodded.

"Am I supposed to be terrified of you? Are you planning to terrorize me?" I lifted the dying boy's hand, felt the delicate joints in the fingers. "This child holds more terror for me than you."

"Death suits me," Blu Fen's ghost said.

Upon hearing this, I leaned in close and studied his face. "I regret executing you," I said. "You deserved it, but I know you loved me."

The ghost shrugged. "It was good for the revolution."

Tears bubbled from my eyes. "May I embrace you?"

"I have no substance." He sneezed, then wiped his nose on his shirt sleeve. "This place is dreary." His eyes darted to the dying boy, returned to me. "Death suits me," he said again.

"What is it like?" I asked. "What can you tell me?"

"7 flights of stairs," he said, "7 deathly sins. Hard climbing. Distractions."

"And at the end of the climb?"

Blu Fen's ghost looked up, as if he were studying the place in question. "A promise. A reconfiguration."

I shook my head. "I don't understand."

The ghost inhaled deeply, although he was not breathing. "I'm only guessing," he said. "If I accept the gift, I cannot help you."

"You're here to help me?"

"The revolution," he said.

"What revolution?"

The boy in the bed gasped, throwing his head back, revealing his bruised neck, a row of stitches—as if his head had been severed and sewed back on. His chest lifted from the cot, blood flew from his nostrils. Blu Fen's ghost crawled on top of him. He disappeared into the boy. The heaving stopped. The boy rose, stood beside me. "Now," the boy said, offering me a hand so that I would stand beside him, "I will tell you what you are doing wrong."

I scrutinized this face. "Oh, Blu Fen, I'll have to execute you again, won't I?"

The boy stared at me unblinking. A gap in the tent revealed the river, the wall of trees. He answered, "Throughout eternity."

The dream ended. Dying ruined your dreams, but this dream was different. This dream was touched by death, as if there were some overlap, a little space of no-man's-land that ran smack through the middle of my mind.

Understanding this, I understood something more, that *you* existed in that nether region, neither alive nor dead, as if these were inadequate terms. *You* disappeared when I killed Blu Fen, but I've glimpsed you again at least once, on the frozen road. If you had been a living thing out on that road, I would have killed you with the car. Not alive, not dead. Where are you? What's going on?

When the door finally opened, a young woman wearing a purple silk pantsuit and carrying a designer Uzi stepped in. She looked like she could be a lingerie model during her working hours. The woman in yellow followed, dragging a kitchen chair. More women and men entered, each with a chair, which they positioned around our cots. Ms. Uzi passed her weapon to a man wearing a beret, fetched her own chair, then accepted the automatic pistol back from him. There were a dozen or so altogether. If not for the Uzi, it might have been a PTA meeting or a library social or a high-class closed-court dating party.

"You gave us a scare," said the woman in yellow, staring at me blandly through the triangular lenses of her specs.

"You look like his mother," I said, pointing to Frankly. Not exactly a snappy retort, but she could tell it was not flattering.

She gave a little birdlike, single-shoulder shrug. "I don't know his mother." Her eyes grew large then and glanced away before zer0ing in on me again. "But I know yours."

"Yeah, I bet," I said, cringing inwardly at my lousy dialogue.

"Behave," the lingerie model said to me. She cradled the Uzi in a funny way that made me think she used to twirl a baton.

The woman in yellow continued. "And then there's *my* mother." She glanced around at the others and was rewarded with misty-eyed smiles. "My mother started this organization."

Frankly jumped in then. "Your mother is Jeanie Eastman?"

"Who's she?" I said.

The woman in yellow offered the half-shrug again—her little gesture, the hallmark of her personality. "A banjo picker. A pretty good one, too. Until the death of my father, and then . . . and then she became a hero." She smiled nicely, but it was too practiced, her brows rising just above her glasses. "My mother inspired the Banjos, and now *your* mother is ruining the organization."

"How's that?" I said.

"By letting sentiment interfere with our goals."

I began to get the drift. It wasn't pretty. "You mean, like letting her daughter live?" I said.

"No, she had every reason to let you live. You're valuable to us. After all, if you're dead, you can't die." She looked at Frankly. "The shrimp, on the other hand, is nothing but a liability."

"I don't own a gun," Frankly said. "I am not in the NRA."

The woman in yellow nodded. "How sweet. But on the other hand, you know way, way too much about us. You've seen way, way too many of us. All of these people here, for example, are duals. You could finger us all."

Frankly said, "I like your glasses."

This surprised her. "They were on sale. Strictly ornamental."

"Well," I said, "right now, we're both alive, so I guess you have some use for us, Ms. Eastman."

She smiled. "Call me Barbie. You, Ms. Melmoth, or may I be so bold as to call you Lydia?"

"Help yourself," I said.

"Thank you. You, Lydia, could finger us all, too, of course, but you can bring us some dough. There's a phone auction going on right now. As we speak. The Big Boys have made an offer. The Ontological Museum made an offer, but they withdrew it. They thought you were dead. They're only interested in your body. Alive, you don't have any value for them."

Another one of them spoke up now. A man in a velvet T-shirt. These people were all dressed for an art opening. "They wanted to stuff you for their display." His voice was nasal and wealthy sounding. "Personally, I'm rather happy they've withdrawn."

"We're trying to reach Qigley," Barbie said. She looked at the ceiling and scratched her neck languorously, which made me think she was nervous and trying to hide it by acting nonchalant. "I suspect Qigley would make a bid for you. But he's hard to get ahold of." She pursed her lips, as if thoughtful, and I thought, *She's out of her league*. Hope welled up in my chest. I wanted to see her shrug again. Keep up the affectations, sweetheart.

She continued, "There are a few other groups putting in bids. Some scientist, who wants to study you. He thinks there's an enzyme, or something like that, in your brain which permits you to die so often. But right now, the highest bidder is Human Zoo, Inc. They'd like the shrimp, too. They've offered a guarantee that neither of you will be able to talk to the gawkers." She glanced at Frankly. "That's all that's keeping you alive," she said, but it wasn't true, I could tell. They didn't want to kill us. They were more talk than action.

"Human Zoo?" I said. "I gather I'm supposed to ask what that is."

Again, her little coy shrug. "Some freak bought an island in the Caribbean. He's converting a prison there into a zoo full of people—mainly outlaws, people who couldn't return to the States anyway. A big tourist trap. You'd be one of the main attractions, while your friend would be a smaller attraction—so to speak." Her cronies chuckled grimly, but it was all playacting. Like a snob hill drama club doing *On the Waterfront*.

"What about my mother?" I said. "Wouldn't she—"

"I wish I could sell her, too," Barbie said. This was the first thing she had said with any conviction. Quickly, she composed herself. "I'm not one of your mother's fans. We—" she looked around at the others "— we're . . . well, I guess you could call us a splinter group, although we expect this deal to catapult us to the top of the organization. Your mother's on her way out, her way down. There could well be a grenade winging its way to her right now. We already took care of your other pal. Seen the papers? HarveL Blu Fen is dead, Ms Melmoth."

"*You* killed him?" I said.

"Members of our group. They died in the process. We thought they had failed at first, but it's official, Mr. Fenester is dead."

"Why did you want Blu Fen dead?" I asked.

"He supports your mother. That was the main reason."

Frankly spoke up then. "How do you find us?"

Barbie looked to the others, evidently deciding it was all right to tell. "We had an inside source with Blu Fen. Someone on his staff, I guess. He fed us information occasionally. We don't know who he was. He left taped messages. A few days back, he called to say that Fen was vulnerable. Told us how to get through Fen's techno shields, so that our partners—"

"Charles and Arlene," I said.

"I see you've read the paper. The informant permitted Charles and Arlene to kill Fen, then he sent another message yesterday, saying we should hunt down Fen's bodyguard. No explanation. We thought he would be protecting your mother. Imagine our surprise at finding you 2."

"But how?" Frankly persisted.

"The bodyguard had a bug on him. In his skin or something. 1 of Fen's hi-tech devices. It permitted us to track him—and you—all the way to Denver. I grew up in Denver. Awfully nice of you to lead me back here."

"I'm hungry," I said suddenly. "I'm thirsty. I'd like to eat and drink. Are you all going to starve us? Is this a Nazi branch of the Banjos?"

Surprised and unsettled, Barbie hesitated a moment too long before smiling. "As I recall, you like burgers. No onions, plenty of mustard. Oh, and fries." She stood and grabbed the back of her chair. "We'll have you food and drink soon."

They left as they entered, the Uzi trained on us the whole time.

Frankly, at last, was extraordinarily depressed and not at all happy about it. The window was barred and the glass was filthy; I could see little through the murk except the occasional flashlight or candle. "How can people breathe out there?" I said, but I already knew the answer. It didn't kill you—at least, not immediately. You just went ahead and lived. You kept a bottle of oxygen in the house for emergencies. You carried goggles for the days your eyes couldn't take it. You survived.

"None of Barbie's gang live in the dark," I said. "I'd bet this is the house of one of their maids."

Frankly joined me at the window. "They don't want to get their hands dirty with us, but they are selling us to people who are getting their hands dirty all the time."

"I wish I knew how to tell them to reach Qigley," I said. The informant who had left messages for Barbie Eastman was undoubtedly Blu Fen himself. He arranged for Charles and Arlene to get into his walled yard, so that I could witness his execution of them. He wanted me to believe that they were trying to kill me. He was the deliveryman for the grim reaper. The later message Fen must have set up before his death, a way to insure that Jimy would pay for having failed to protect his boss.

There was noise at the door, and then it opened. I tried to catch a glimpse of the room beyond, but the door was shrouded with sheets. The woman who brought us our burgers was maybe 20 and thin with a square jaw and gray eyes. She wore green lipstick and smiled goofily, like she had been smoking pot. "I was told to let you know that there's a new bidder," she announced happily, as if what was being sold was something besides our souls.

"Qigley?" I said hopefully.

"Nuh-uh. I wish we could reach him. Can you

imagine? Talking to the Q?" She waved her hand at her neck as if to cool her overheating passion. Her green lips parted prettily.

"So who's made the offer?"

"Raza/Razon has outbid Human Zoo, but the Big Boys still hold the floor, so they have the option of topping it by ten percent." She continued smiling in that mindlessly good-natured sort of way. How did this girl get to be a terrorist? "The good news is that they want the both of you, get this, *alive and unharmed!*" She clapped her hands together in glee.

"Are you like a Banjo cheerleader or something?" I said.

She frowned. "I tried out, but I can't do a cartwheel." Suddenly, she laughed. "Got ya." This was her exit line. She left without saying good-bye.

"So?" I looked at Frankly. "Who the hell is Raza/Razon?"

He put his pointer finger within an inch of his thumb. "I am this close to being the most famous depressionist in America."

"Chill, Frankly. Focus on our current dilemma." The burgers were steaming, and I thought, A clue! The house was somewhere near a Burger King! Which meant it could be anywhere, absolutely anywhere in the whole fucking world, and also meant I was getting deplorably desperate.

With a little coaxing, Frankly told me what he knew about Raza/Razon, a coalition of Chicano and Radical Hispanics best known for blowing up La Platino Bridge in San Diego after the city council refused to rename it *El* Platino Bridge. "I can't see them outbidding anybody," he said, munching. "They don't have any pub in years." It seemed to bother him that we might be purchased by an obscure terrorist group rather than a popular 1.

"What the hell would they want with us?" I said.

He shook his head. "Nothing good."

They had brought us more food than we could eat. It occurred to me during my 2nd sack of fries that the food could be poisoned or something, but it was too late to worry. The whole room smelled of grease. "Frankly, we need a plan. At least an idea."

Suddenly he began hopping. "You know what I just remember?"

"What?" I said. "What?"

"Denver is the city where that woman knits a car sweater for her Buick. A huge hand-knit car sweater."

"Really?" I said. "You think she was one of our captors? Did you recognize her from the photo in the paper?"

"No," he said. "It's just this funny thing I remember."

"*Focus*, Frankly! We're about to be sold like cattle! What good does a woman knitting a sweater for a car do us?"

He scowled and crossed his arms, hopping again. The term "hopping mad" came to mind. "You say you want an idea, and I give you 1. Maybe 1 idea leads to another."

"Great. Fine. What is car sweaters going to lead you to?"

"This is also the city that 1st has the Poetry Channel. I love that channel when it is new. And *The Catalogue of Dead Ideas* is published here. I get some of my best ideas for routines from that."

He was sort of smiling while he rambled, giving me all he knew about Denver. My thoughts were more pedestrian: if we broke the window and screamed, would that help us escape, or get us bound and gagged? If we could figure out a way to blow a fuse by tinkering with the Eugene the Eunuch night-light, would that gain us anything or just make the dark darker? If we threw ourselves at the door, would it give way? And if it did, would that permit us to escape or merely speed up our already imminent deaths?

"And there is a depressionist from here who calls himself Dickless . . ." Frankly continued, entertaining himself, keeping dark thoughts from his mind. "The weatherwoman here coins the term 'drismal,'" he went on. "This is the biggest city in the first state to legalize cannibalism." This 1 stopped him.

"So?"

"So they can get 20 grand for each of our legs. That's 80 grand, and we're legless."

"You can only sell 1 leg," I began, but I quit. Clearly we wouldn't be butchered in the legal market. It might brighten Frankly's outlook a little if I pointed out that his legs were too short to get the full price, but he could take it the wrong way. Finally, I said, "You wanna hear my dream?"

Contrary to myth, nighttime in the dark was distinguishable from day. The air outside was nothing but gloom, and there was no indication of a sky, just a pressing blackness. It could have been 8:30, it could have been as late as 3:00. Frankly slept, while I still tried to figure my options, still tried to figure a way out.

The door abruptly opened. Barbie Eastman, no longer in yellow, no longer wearing glasses, entered.

"I didn't expect to find you up," she said. A short Hispanic man followed her in. He was wearing a black skintight bodysuit—the Cosa Muerte suit, complete with black tie erupting from the shirt below the collar bone, and a black jacket with narrow lapels. Evidently Raza/Razon had prevailed in the auction.

"Lydia Melmoth," Barbie began, *"quiero presentarle a Tico Escuela*, your new owner."

Tico smiled, and light from the nightlight glinted off a silver tooth. "I'm no you owner," he said in a mock accent. "Raza/Razon no owns peoples." He extended his hand and I shook it. He was perspiring. When he spoke again, the fake voice was gone. "We have great respect for your talent, and we wish to employ you—and your friend—in our organization. Raza/Razon is dedicated to human equality and social justice. *Nuestra casa es su casa.*"

Barbie giggled. "Well, well, well." She gave me a look of pure malice, but she talked to Tico. "You can see that she's in fine health. And Shorty is sleeping peacefully. So tell your boss to get the money together."

"I have no boss," Tico said, smiling at me. "We do, indeed, wish to take these fine people from you." He turned to Barbie and assumed a look of consternation and regret. "However, we have decided not to pay you." He lifted his arms apologetically. "Let's do this without violence, shall we?" He put his arm around her shoulders. "We have word that you do not have the support of the Banjo organization. You're an offshoot, a little potato eye, a tiny wart on the Banjo's buttocks."

"I can have you blown away right now," Barbie said, and Frankly rolled off his cot and onto the floor.

"The little one is not sleeping," Tico said, smiling at me. He dropped the smile, eyed Barbie evilly. "Without the support of the Banjos, you provide no reason for us to actually pay you. In fact, if we did, we'd simply send a disguised group back to steal it away from you—killing you all in the process. There are, what, 15 of you altogether?"

Barbie said nothing now, but shoved his arm from her shoulders.

"Yes, 15," Tico continued, winking at me as if we had planned this together. "On the other hand, if we offer you no money but pretend that we have paid you, then you not only survive but you get a lot of credit among the Banjos, credit you can use in your bid to oust Señora Melmoth from the position you covet."

"No deal," Barbie said.

Tico knocked on the door, and it opened. "Oh, I assure you, we will have a deal." He held the door for her. To me, he said, "I'll see you again soon." Then the door swung shut.

"Get on the floor," Frankly hissed at me. "You don't want to catch a stray bullet."

I dropped to my knees, as if I already had been shot, or as if to pray. Then I flattened myself against the floor and rolled under the cot next to Frankly. The cots provided only the illusion of protection, but at the moment it was all we had.

Back when I was a Junior Rag, I had gone out with this college student, a tall dark boy with a physics scholarship and a bad temper. He was only 22, and when he wasn't buried in a textbook, he thought almost exclusively with his Mr. Roger—that's what he called it. I'd do something radical, like suggest that we go out to eat and see a movie rather than just grapple on his futon all evening, and he'd say, "Mr. Roger won't be pleased."

Okay, he was an idiot. This story wasn't meant to illustrate my miserable luck with romance. 1 day I told him I wanted to read rather than sex, and he put his fist through the wall. Right through the drywall and into a bunch of fiberglass insulation.

"Frankly," I whispered. We were both still lying beneath the cots. "Let's try breaking out."

"The bars on the windows won't budge," he said.

"Let's go through the walls," I said. The cots were held up at either end by metal tubes. I yanked mine from the canvas, which caused the cot to fall on my face, but in another minute I was on my knees poking at the wall. "This is just drywall."

"There's an outside wall," Frankly pointed out, but he was quickly beside me. We had a splotch of insulation exposed before you could say, *Hollow gesture*.

"Uh-oh," I said, "fudge insulation. This stuff is bad for your skin." It looked more like divinity candy than fudge, and it never really hardened; already it was glubbing out onto the floor. "Yuck," I said, "but that probably means the outer wall is just plywood."

"Or cardboard," Frankly said. "They are shooting in fudge to make the walls seem solid."

I shoved a tube through the fudge until it hit the outer wall. "Here," I said. "I'll hold the tube and you kick it through the wall."

Frankly assented. His 1st kick knocked the tube through the wall and my hands into the insulation. "We can get out," I said.

"You first," said Mr. Gallantry.

The fudge already made a thick puddle on the floor by the opening. "Give me your shirt—and no stalling. Just hand it over."

Frankly, with obvious regret, removed his steel gray LeeHarveyO and handed it to me. His chest was so white it seemed to glow in the dark. I wrapped the shirt around my shoes and ankles, then I punched with my feet at the wall. My feet oozed through the fudge and right through the cardboard wall to the knee.

"We're on the 2nd floor," Frankly reminded me.

"We're also dead meat up here—maybe literally. A bunch of steaks waiting to be carved. Give me a push."

Frankly positioned his hands upon my shoulders, leaning forward like a runner in starting blocks. Just before he started pushing, we heard the door lock turning.

"Christ," I said. I barely got it out before I went plunging through the fudge and cardboard, and then through the air, Frankly still holding onto my shoulders, flying out into the dark.

14

We fell into the hands of Raza/Razon—almost literally. Tico stood on the lawn bickering with Barbie when we came flying out, fudge insulation streaming behind us. Tico popped Barbie in the snoot, then he and 1 of his thugs had us in the backseat of a Cadillac before we could catch our breath.

The car rocketed forward, hurtling around a corner. "Now they *have* to accept our terms," Tico said, laughing. He ended up in the backseat between Frankly and me. "You're quite resourceful," he said.

I was still scrambling to sit up. We were around another corner before I was settled. The car cut through the dark streets, stereophonic salsa music humping out of hidden speakers.

Tico said, "They following us?"

I looked through the back window, but he'd been talking to the driver, a big lug wearing a baseball cap who shook his head laconically. Beside the lug sat a smaller, gray-haired fellow, but I couldn't see either face.

"Barbie Eastman is too ambitious for her own

good," Tico said. "She'll take over the Banjos at some point—I hope she doesn't kill your mother to do it. But once she's in charge, she'll mess it up. She'll ruin the organization." He lifted himself up to glance in the rearview mirror. "We're lucky she didn't have time to call our bluff. At least, she hasn't yet." He chuckled. "Otherwise, you 2 would have wound up with the Big Boys, and I would be *muy* dead."

Call me cautious, but I didn't know how to respond to this. Was I supposed to be happy that I had been passed from 1 terrorist group to another?

"So what are you saying?" I ventured.

The gray-headed 1 in the front spoke without facing us. "He isn't saying anything yet." The voice belonged to a woman and sounded familiar, as if it came from 1 of my nightmares, or 1 of my dies.

Frankly, on the other side of Tico, still bare-chested, slumped down in his seat, as he almost never did because it made him shorter. "Are these windows bullet proof?" he asked.

"No," Tico said, and even the lugs in the front involuntarily slouched. Tico put his hand over his heart. "I have to remain quiet for a few miles, as it is possible, although unlikely, that they have some sort of sophisticated monitoring device planted on you. Unlikely because Barbie isn't a believer in technology. She's more a blood and social club sort of leader."

We rode through the dark, turning at almost every intersection, winding our way across Denver.

"What does Raza/Razon want with us?" I said.

Tico laughed. "Well, we'd better not discuss that just yet, just in case Barbie is listening. The less she knows the—"

"Aw, fuck," said the gray-haired woman. She poked a finger at the rearview mirror. A big black car fishtailed onto the street behind us.

I turned to look out the rear window, but Tico pushed my head down. "Don't get yourself shot," he said, ducking down with me. The Cadillac accelerated noisily. I was thrown on top of the cowering Frankly. Tico bounced off me in a polite way, eager not to damage his goods, I imagined.

"Raza/Razon has been, well, *dormant* for several years now," Tico said, settling on the floorboard beside me. The woman in the front seat screeched something to the driver, and we quicked around another corner, the tires squealing, salsa music bouncing along in the background, Frankly whimpering like a dog left out in the cold. "We couldn't really have overcome Barbie Eastman's group with physical force," Tico went on. "Although most of her group are dilettantes, society twits, and general all-around assholes." His head was thrown momentarily against my knee. Gunshots sounded, but I couldn't tell whether we were being shot at or just driving by a shooting.

I stuck my lips next to Frankly's ear. "Are you all right?"

"I am peeing," he said. Then added, "Any second now."

"Hold it," I said, "or the smell will make you puke, which will make me puke, and it could get ugly."

Tico wiped fudge insulation from his eyebrow, then he started in again. "Eastman's people outnumber us, and they have a lot better weapons than we have. If our driver weren't so busy at the moment, I'd have him show you our weapon."

"You've got just 1 gun?"

"And even that is a recent acquisition," he said. "A gift. We certainly couldn't have paid the exorbitant sum we promised Barbie. We had to rely on cunning, although, in truth it wasn't all that ingenious. If you 2 hadn't busted through the wall, we would have failed." The woman in the front laughed—a cackle—and yelled something at the driver. "In truth, we're broke," Tico continued. "Even this car is rented, and we'll have to scrub to get this insulation off or lose our deposit. This suit—" he spread his arm to display his Cosa Muerte suit "—to purchase it, we had to borrow money from enemies of Ms. Barbie Eastman, supporters of your mother."

"So you're Banjos?" I said.

"I'm not," Tico said. "I'm not even a member of Raza/Razon, to tell the truth. But she is." He pointed to the woman on the passenger side of the front seat, although from my angle on the floorboard I couldn't see anybody. "No, I—and my friend driving—we are, well, *fakes*. I, at least, used to be a member of Raza/Razon way back when."

The car suddenly hit a rough surface, fishtailing and then magic-fingering us so that our voices vibrated like those of cartoon ducks. "I don't get it," I said. "You're not terrorists?"

"Only to 7th graders," he said. "I teach school." The car suddenly braked, sliding, then rocked to a stop, the engine dying, even the salsa music hushed. We were thrown against the seat back, then into each other. The woman in the front was cackling again. She said, "No way they're coming in here, the cowardly fucks."

Tico raised his head cautiously, looked around,

smiled. "The barrio never looked so good," he said, "So awful, and yet so good." To me and Frankly, he said, "You 2 stay down. This isn't a good place to be an Anglo." To the gray-haired woman, he said, "Trade with me. I don't want trouble. People know me here."

He climbed into the front seat, and she came rolling down into the back, her face suddenly inches from mine. "Good to see you, Melmoth," she said. "Remember me?" Her face erupted into a smile.

It was the mad bomber, the protector of public education, the most wanted underground figure in America—my old bud—Madeleine Bruce.

"How did . . . Who . . . What are you doing here?" I said.

"Your buddies called me in when the word got out that you were held by that Barbie shit. Gonzales and I go way back. I'm the 1 hooked him up with Blu Fen, so I owe him for that fucking mistake. Besides, I always had a soft spot for you after that die in Filly."

"Who is Gonzales?" I asked politely, just in case not knowing him could get me killed.

She gave me a funny look, then raised up enough to slap the driver on the shoulder. "Gonzales, this woman doesn't know who you are."

The car's engine turned over immediately. The back of the driver's head appeared, then turned to face us. He took off his baseball cap as he turned.

Jimy Schmidt.

I threw my arms around him—not a good thing to do, evidently, as the others pushed me back to the floorboards. "We're in the Zone," Tico said. "No Anglos permitted. Keep down."

Frankly whispered, "Who is it?"

"It's Jimy," I said.

"Tell him I am peeing. Soon. Fear goes right to my bladder." The car began moving and Frankly added, "I am famous. I am famous."

Jimy, a.k.a. Gonzales, and I chopped vegetables for spaghetti. I was wearing a dress and underwear borrowed from Tico's wife, who was petite. She and Tico sat at the kitchen table with Madeleine Bruce and yapped with us, while Frankly listened on a stool, cradling a telephone receiver near enough to hear when he was no longer on hold; he was reserving a flight to NeYork, wearing a striped shirt borrowed from 1 of Tico's kids. We were all drinking beer; their children played in the next room. If we had been a painting, we would have been either a retro familyValues pic, or a New Wave wanted poster.

Jimy and I sliced carrots. We had found and removed the monitoring device that had been planted in him, a tiny sliver of metal inserted into the calluses of his heel. "Fen thought of everything," he said, and went on to explain his life. "I got into some trouble, and I needed a new identity," he said. "I had put Madeleine up once when she was hiding out in Denver. I got ahold of her and she arranged a deal with Blu Fen."

"You don't Now." Frankly started to say more, but spoke into the phone instead—he had finally got a flight agent.

"Chicanos don't Now," Tico explained.

Jimy nodded. "Our history is—"

"Skip the lecture," Madeleine said. "You think this group needs a Politico lesson?"

Tico laughed at this. "Go on, Gonzales, explain please what the fuck you've been doing these past few years."

"I became an indentured servant," Jimy said. "It didn't suit me." Blu Fen, Jimy explained, operated something like a protection racket, using his association with the underground to come up with names which he threatened to sell to the Big Boys.

"Playing both sides against the middle," Madeleine said. "The prick. Far as I'm concerned," she said to me, "you're a fucking hero for killing the prick." She shook her head. "He screwed me over once a long time ago. Screwed me over in a big way. But other times, he behaved decently. He was a hard fuck to understand. Very complicated. I hate those complicated types. Can't trust the shits."

"You prefer us simple ethnic types," Tico said.

"Hush," his wife said. Her name was Ursula Dominguez, and her panties were carving up my thighs. "No bickering tonight."

"Blu Fen," Jimy said, "had a larger plan that merely the acquisition of power and wealth. He wished to free all of the people in the world."

"So he claimed," Madelaine said.

"He was sincere," Jimy said. "But he had decided that the only real freedom lay in the process of revolution, not in the product. His working both sides against the middle was an ethical decision."

Madeleine sneered and guzzled her beer. She told me that Denver's dark had become an underground haven for all the obvious reasons. "You'll find you know a lot of people round here," she said to me. "Not that you want to see them. You need someplace even more obscure than here. You don't go to the dark to hide from other Subs. You too, Gonzales. Your picture's gonna be in the paper any day now. Count on it. Fen will nail you. Siberia, maybe. Fucking Antarctica. Blu Fen was connected in more ways than you can hump." She paused for a second, as if picturing something. "Mr. Fen is the son of a bitch who orchestrated the InfoTechno Collapse. Screwed millions of people with the megaVirus and those fucking Blue Laws—hardly any of the stuff they confiscated was porn. Made things we'd become accustomed to suddenly only for the elite. 'Backwards Progress,' he called it. When you can't control what the masses can make—like software programs, computer networking—you take back the techno progress that made it happen, then parcel it out for big bucks. That fucker. Had most of us convinced it was going to create a revolution. Instead, he made the industrialists rich all over again. He sandbagged us."

"No, he merely redefined the nature of revolution," Jimy insisted. "Blu Fen was despicable, but he remained true to his peculiar vision. The process of revolution has become an integral part of our culture, the constant upheaval and ongoing terrorism—it all fits in his peculiar vision."

"I think I met his ghost," I said.

The room became inordinately quiet. The tinny telephone voice of Frankly's travel agent filled the room. "How can you be in NeYork if you're calling from Denver?"

Frankly, his eyes still on me, said, "I am there soon." The agent confirmed his flight, which would leave in a few hours.

Jimy slid the sliced carrots into a cast-iron pot. "When did you meet this ghost?"

Frankly spoke before I could answer. "When they take you. When you almost die. But you tell me it is a dream."

"It was a dream," I said, "and it wasn't." I told them about the circumstances and the dream. Frankly had hung up by the time I finished. "I was close enough to death for him to speak to me. That's what I think."

"You'll excuse me," Tico said seriously, "but that's an odd thing to believe."

"I buy it," Madeleine said. "Nobody knows more about death than this girl. If you say he was a ghost and not just a dream, then he was a fucking ghost."

Jimy washed the celery, handed me a knife. "Chop with me," he said.

"Blu Fen," Madeleine said, "has haunted *me* for decades already, long before he died." She began telling about the bombing of Coutant Academy, all those many years ago. She said it was meant to be symbolic, not murderous. "Terrorism is the poor grub's way of making every person responsible for the way things are. We were saying, 'Look, so you got dough and you can afford fancy private schools while most kids are sent to hen houses? Well, you better work to make the public schools better or your kids ain't gonna be safe.'" She sneered emphatically. "But, hell, I just wanted to knock over a few walls. Fen, that fucking Fen, wanted *blood*. He had a goddamn nose for it." She shook her gray head. "I'm not apologizing for anything. I knew the risks. You all got a public school education, didn't you?"

We all nodded.

"Those kids of yours." She glared at Tico and Ursula. "They going to public school?"

"You know that they are," Tico said. "Ursula and I teach at those schools."

"Yeah," Madeleine said, "well, it had to be done. For every child who died, a million now can read—2 million, 3 million, 10 million. I didn't want any of them to be killed, but Fen forced the issue. That was his great talent. He pushed things right to the goddamn limit, and a couple yards beyond."

"What does the ghost mean about the 7 sins?" Frankly asked.

"I don't know," I said.

"The 7 deadly sins," Tico began, but Jimy interrupted.

"Did he say *deadly* sins?"

We had finished the celery, and I took my beer to the kitchen table. "*Deathly* sins. 7 flights of stairs, 7 deathly sins."

"We're all going to find out eventually," Ursula said. "I don't care to know in advance."

"I know what the worst sins are," Madeleine said, "and there are only 2 of them: doing nothing, and doing too little."

The room became silent once more.

"I wonder if death is political," Madeleine said. She finished her beer and rose from the table. "I mean, the afterlife—if there is such a thing as an afterlife. Is it political, Melmoth?" Her eyes had the hardness of chrome. "Or do people just sit around strumming their lyres—jacking off? The way I see it, anything you do, if it isn't political, it's jacking off."

"I haven't seen any lyres," I said.

"You sound just like Blu Fen," Jimy said to Madelaine. "Without politics and upheaval—revolution, in other words—life, or even death, isn't worth the time."

Ursula said, "The hottest places in hell are reserved for those who, in times of great moral crises, maintain their neutrality."

Jimy smiled at her. "I'm impressed."

She shrugged. "I'm teaching Dante next week."

"My mother said something like that to me once," I said.

"Blu Fen was not neutral," Jimy said.

"You got that much right," Madelaine said.

"Not at all neutral," Jimy said. "He simply took up both sides."

When the time came, I kissed Frankly good-bye. "I am expecting your call everyday," he said to me, and I got a little teary. He tugged at my dress to make me lean close. He whispered in my ear, "I am loving you since the beginning of time." But he ruined it by sticking his tongue in my ear. "You are calling me," he said as I jerked away. Then he and Tico departed for the airport. Just like that—the door closed and Frankly was gone.

Madeleine left soon after. "You ever die again, let me know," she said. "I saw your Fen film. 1st rate. You got a talent like nobody who ever lived."

The children shook my hand comically before being ushered to bed. While we waited for Tico to return from the airport, Ursula told Jimy and me about her life. She and Tico both taught in a middle school in the dark, and I silently took back anything I ever had said against middle school teachers. Schools in the dark had bad reputations for violence, and she said that the stories we had heard were mostly true. "But there are kids we can save," she said, "so we keep doing it." She and Tico had been married 6 years, had lived in the dark all that time.

When Tico safely returned, she took his hand and they went to the same room where their children slept. They had brought out a foam pad for the floor and sheets for the couch. "I don't mind the floor," Jimy said, but he knew and I knew that we were going to sleep together. We had both known this since before dinner when we stood side-by-side at the counter chopping vegetables, our hips touching. I waited until he was beneath the sheets, and then I joined him.

"I'm afraid to go to sleep," I said.

"We don't have to sleep," he said.

I kissed him. He kissed me. We made love on the foam pad on the floor of the living room of the Dominguez house in the dark of Denver during the long night of the beginning of my freedom.

As for the lovemaking, there were a few mechanical glitches, but that other angle—that human, tender, something-like-love angle—cooked on all its burners.

Then we slept. I slept and did not dream.

EPILOGUE

Q: Where do you end up after becoming a fugitive from both the law and the lawless, from both death and life?

A: Plittbottom, New Mexico.

I share a house with Jimy, a house made of mud. I don't speak much Spanish and virtually nobody here speaks English—the town is only nominally a part of the US, and officially speaking, it isn't inhabitable— but it isn't a bad place to live. The average temperature here shot up 20 years ago and continues nudging its way higher annually. It gets to be 140 degrees in the summer, hits 95 even in the dead of winter. The water from the Rio Grande glows, has a gassy noxious haze. Drinking the groundwater will make your eyes turn to silicone and fall like jelly to the sidewalk—if there were sidewalks. There are other troubling things, as well—incandescent scorpions, tarantulas the size of a microwave oven, mutant coyotes who'll wear your lungs like jewelry.

But Jimy has family here, a cousin named Eugenio, who has a huge reverse osmosis system in his backyard that provides clean water for the town. It's built out of old aquariums and water bottles. As for the heat, you learn to sleep during the daylight. Nights cool off.

I've only been here a couple of months. The summer is still distant enough to sound exotic.

Eugenio's wife, Steam, is Mexican but from L/A, and doesn't know much Spanish herself. If she were an animal, she'd be a cheetah—all muscle and sinew, very quick, and spotty (she has eczema). She's my best friend here.

"You can't breathe in L/A," she begins if you ask why she left civilization to live in Plittbottom, but eventually she'll tell you the truth. "I had some little trouble with my landlord, so I shot him in the groin, which was the nature of our trouble, if you catch my drift. I was looking at 5 to 10 years in prison because the little *pito* died. I hadn't intended to kill the louse, just castrate him. Anyway, no 1 had ever seen him come on to me, and there was the fact that I was 6 months behind in rent, so my alibi stunk, and my court-appointed lawyer told me that my best strategy was to lose myself somewhere nobody cares about while he set up delays and motions and confusion, but that *raton* didn't really bother, so now I'm a fugitive from justice."

We have that much in common.

I hear from Stamen now and again. Frankly (who he now manages) got him in touch with Tico, who got him in touch with Eugenio. Stamen has worked out a method whereby he can safely call us. There's always traffic in the background, so I assume he's at a pay phone. Don't ask me for more details because I don't know them. I've just come to trust my brother.

Qigley is dying for the 9th and semifinal time tonight. By tomorrow, the only death he'll have to look forward to is the ultimate 1, the final exit, the long walk across the desert that probably ends up someplace like here.

Stamen is taking Qigley off the dying circuit. As soon as he's recovered from the record-breaking die, he'll be earning his money the old-fashioned way: schmoozing for it. He's scheduled for a cubicle in the newRetro *Hollywood Squares*, and he'll make an appearance at Yankee Stadium for the 3rd annual Dying Artists Old-Timers Performance, where people lie around with their eyes closed and pretend to be defunct.

The Q's final die will earn him a fat 20 million. Stamen's share will purchase a portion of his freedom. Not that money alone can do the trick, but it isn't going to hurt. He has already managed to have some of Blu Fen's assets confiscated, claiming that Fen had been gouging and embezzling from Qigley (all true, apparently). As soon as he got the money, Stamen donated much of it to various established politicians. Then he took another, rather drastic, step to ensure his safety—he became a Mole. The Big Boys rarely pursue Moles, in part because they seem to believe that the surgically altered don't have the gumption to cause trouble, and partly from a kind of phobic distaste for dealing with them. It's similar to the old strategy of crooks and Politicos claiming to be "Born Again," knowing that they'd be largely left alone after that.

Stamen secretly donated a bundle to the Banjos, as well, so they let him be, too. He even manages to stay in contact with Mother and passes on to me info about her. He's done 1 other thing: he yanked Fen's porno-die film from distribution and destroyed the prints. He's a good brother.

Mother lives somewhere in the Midwest. Ananias stays with her when he can. He's still a dual and has kept his job in Cleveland, but he sneaks out to see her. "They live as man and wife," Stamen tells me, which is as close as he can come to saying that they're lovers. Every time we talk, I say, "So are Mom and An still shacking up?" just to make him squirm. I have to do it—he's my big brother, after all. If I really wanted to get to him, I'd ask about his surgery, where they moved his crucial parts. But I can't quite put Stamen through that. On the other hand, I can't help myself from imagining possibilities, recalling every little twitch he's ever made.

Mother's still in control of the Banjos, thanks in part to the bungled kidnapping of Frankly and me. Barbie Eastman claimed Raza/Razon had paid off, but Madeleine Bruce took a photograph of the hole in the wall and the oozing fudge insulation, and sent it circulating in Banjo circles with a description of the botched auction, including details about how 3 people carrying just 1 gun (the pistol Mother had given me) pretended to be Raza/Razon and stole the merchandise without firing a shot. The splinter group broke into little slivers.

Then there's me, Lydia Melmoth. Jimy and I live together, and we're lovers, although neither of us is certain we're in love. Not that we don't care for each other, but we don't want to pretend that this is anything other than what it seems—a couple of retreads patching things together after major blowouts. Maybe it's more than that. I'm not ruling out miracles.

Jimy's a kind man and a sweet lover, but I'm afraid my feelings stem from that old falling-for-the-guy-who-helps-save-your-life deal, which probably happens a lot more to me than to other people. We have something here, but I'm still a holdout for love. The big L. I still want the whole deep-pawing, heart-palpitating, nobody-on-the-planet-but-him-or-her thing. Although some part of me thinks that the desire to love and be loved is anachronistic, that it makes me like those weird bearded people who drive horse-pulled wagons, have no electricity, and are religious. It's like being a woolly mammoth in a herd of elephants. Or a hippie in a flock of Nowists.

Stamen says I can't come back to civilization yet—eventually, but not yet. I'm a more emotional figure than he, he tells me, and it's not safe for me to surface—unless I want to die again. "No way," I tell him, although some part of me feels otherwise. Some part of me wants the fame, the money, and —yes —the death, the shift into darkness, into the unknown. I find myself longing even for the terror.

I do dying well, and don't we all desire to do that which we do well? Isn't it the least acknowledged shaper of our lives? If I'd had a talent for baton twirling as a kid, I'd probably never have gotten into dying. I'd likely have an IQ in double figures, married to some Texas hosiery tycoon, and be happy as a goose. All right, I'm exaggerating. Trying to look on the bright side again.

Whenever I watch baseball on TV, I look at the batter and think, if that guy hadn't had the misfortune of being able to hit a pitched ball, maybe he would have found some other, more useful talent so that he could have made something meaningful of his life. Meanwhile, Jimy, in the seat next to me, actually flinches with each pitch as he mentally swings. Apples and oranges, he and I, but we're not bad for the moment.

Tonight we're going to Eugenio's (he has a satellite dish) to watch the Q die, and, more important, to watch Frankly finally get his chance at fame. Stamen tells me he's been working hard to get ready. "His preparation has been quite impressive," Stamen said, "but he won't let me see any of the material." A long pause followed. "However, I gather that some of his performance—much of it—will be about you."

"Delicately put," I said. "I know it will be. Don't worry about me. I can handle it. Once you've faced death 7 or 8 times, you should be able to face a pint-sized depressionist, right?"

"I hope so," my brother says. "That is my sincere hope."

Yesterday, I heard on the news that someone took a shot at President Stumpy Gallion outside the French Embassy. The President was uninjured, but 1 of his secret service men took a bullet in the thigh. The assassin was caught and confessed on national television: an antiabortioner who decided to kill Gallion when he heard a rumor that the vice president was a closet anti. It was the 50th assassination attempt by a right-to-life advocate this calendar year. 31 have been successful. Mother, if she can survive, will have more ammunition (so to speak) for the Banjo argument.

Here in Plittbottom, Jimy has been weaving a hammock out of old clothes. If it were finished, I'd lie in it right now and try to make sense of everything. Lying in clothing worn smooth by other bodies *should* help a person think, shouldn't it?

In my life I've only made 2 real decisions that have had consequences: I decided to die, and I decided not to die. Everything else has been haphazard and happenstance. Now I find myself in the middle of an uninhabitable desert living with a retired gunman, trying to stay sane.

Plittbottom isn't exactly a tourist spot. We don't get many guests, but I have had 1 visitor: Blu Fen's ghost. Jimy and I were walking by the river, and I saw him on the other side. He was dragging along the bloody carcass of a sheep. He called out, "To do your work, you've got to come over here—just for a little visit. Nothing too permanent." He threw the dead sheep into the river. The splash made Jimy turn.

"Can you see him?" I said.

"Sure," Jimy said. "Ugly dog." The dead sheep had become a live dog, and Blu Fen's ghost had disappeared. The dog swam across the river, and then trotted right up to us. It was hairless and pink with a lopsided head.

"Keep it away from me," I said.

Jimy yelled at it, and the dog ran off.

"That was a hound of hell," I said.

Jimy nodded. "Yeah, ugly old dog."

I've been visited, too, by the gift. It comes in my dreams. I make it to the point where I feel my body pulling away from me, scattering, joining the landscape. I hear the music, too, but when I wake it escapes me. The landscape, though, I remember well. Nothing fancy, a grassy field, but it's the *way* I see it—as if it were alive, as if it were somehow speaking to me and I just need to figure out how to

listen. Like if I could photograph it, it might be a picture that, if examined properly, would suddenly
became a map. And if you were clever, you could follow the directions on the map and discover some
treasure. But the treasure is already presenting itself
to you while you look; the gift permits you to find the
treasure, which is the gift.

Maybe I'm nuts. I know that's a legitimate possibility, but I dream the sensation of feeling myself dis-
perse, of feeling myself spread out and away from
myself, and it seems that I'm entering the world as a
part of the world, that I am the substance of gift, that
I am the recipient and the donor, that the living
world and my living body are the same, are separate,
and are not separate.

The fear I have is of annihilation, but the prospect
is of another kind of existence.

Steam doesn't like to speak to me about the gift.
"Your eyes poke out funny when you talk about that
crazy stuff," she says.

"So you really know the Q?" Steam says, making iced
tea in the kitchen while Jimy and Eugenio clomp
around outside messing with the wind generator.

I say, "Why are we in here doing 'women's work'
while they're out there doing 'man's work'? Isn't it
possible here, where the culture has virtually no pull,
that at least the 4 of us could have fair and equal
partnerships?"

Steam gives me a funny look. "It's 100 degrees out
there. Let the boys sweat their nuts off. Why should
we settle for equal?" She stirs the tea with a wooden
spoon. Ice is difficult to acquire here, and the single

chunk in the pitcher is all any of us could come up with. "So like I'm saying," she goes on, "it's hard for me to believe you know the Q. This Frankly, too? That little depressing tree stump, you know him, too? You're not just talking big, are you? There's 1 thing I can't stand is somebody talking big about knowing some runt who's on national television when she don't even know him."

"I know him, all right." I'm tempted to reveal all of Frankly's secrets, starting with the fact that he proposed to me in a Burger King in Denver. However, I have just enough pride and dignity to hold back. Besides, he'll probably talk all about us on the air, and it'll be more impressive coming from him. I'm torn between feeling an invasion of privacy on the 1 hand, and the glory of 2nd-hand fame on the other.

"You ever root-a-toot with Shortstuff?" Steam asks me.

I glare at her.

Steam and Eugenio's house is made of adobe, like virtually all the other places in town, except for the shacks, which are made of scrap wood, cardboard, and garbage. Their place is among the nicest in town. Eugenio is the only source of drinking water for 90 miles, and he doesn't charge anything for a fair-sized ration. People take care of him.

We settle in at air time, although we all know there will be interminable filler, and we're right. The host is Dick Rogerz, former President of the United States and late-night game show host.

"I voted for him," Steam says, aiming her glass of tea at the television.

The die is taking place at the coliseum in DC,

and a selective pan of the audience shows a lot of
government uppity-ups. Of course, *he* is there. The
congressman, now senator, who got dying legalized,
and who, when he was just a congressional aide,
won my piddling heart. No, he's saying, he never
expected this kind of popularity for dying, and then
he adds, "I never thought anyone would break Lydia
Melmoth's record either. I always believed that she
was the best." I might get a tear or 2 right then, but
he's got his arm around this bimbo who does face
wax commercials. Besides, Steam is pounding on my
shoulders.

"You got your name on national television!" she
says.

Eugenio is amazed, as well.

Jimy says, "Lydia is famous. She is a subtext in the
whole show tonight."

The words are no sooner out of his mouth than my
face appears on the screen. Dick Rogerz is interview-
ing me. I'm baffled for all of a second before I realize
they're using tape from the old interview with Dick
spliced in. Steam by now is in tears, her voice squeaking from the thrill. Eugenio is yammering, too, about
my knowing the former President. I can barely make
out what I'm saying.

"Death is different everytime," I say to a national
audience. "Sometimes it slips over you like a sweater,
sometimes it slips inside you like a virus."

"Why," Dick Rogerz wants to know, "are you so
good at it? Why do you have no gray rot whatsoever?"

"Oh," I say, "I get a little eye twitch now and
again. But . . ." The camera flashes to Dick and back
to me. I've changed position in the chair, and it's
clear to me that they've spliced in something from

late in the interview, as I'm slouching now and weary-looking. "I never really knew my father," I say. "He died when I was 2."

Dick Rogerz nods with what looks like real compassion. "And does your dead father . . . does he help you get back from the dead?"

In the next shot I'm smiling and chipper—the beginning of the taping. "Oh, definitely," I say.

Close up of former President Rogerz: "I'd say that we have definite evidence of life after death. This is a remarkable breakthrough in the history of human study."

Immediately the screen cuts away to a commercial for the Afterlife Hot Line. "Would you like to make contact with the dead? Call our hot line and your dead loved ones are suddenly within reach. Over 50 mediums waiting for your call." A middle-aged black woman is shown on the phone, "Harold, honey, is that you dear?" An old gruff-looking man in overalls: "Earnest? I wanna know what you did with my part of the inheritance. Say what? Invested it where?" A teenage girl with a butterfly phone, "Hey, Dad, you don't know how much I—"

"Mute!" I yell. "Mute the damn box!"

"So what if they change your words," Steam says. "You're on TV in prime time! You got nothing to complain about. I'd change places with you in a minute. Here, change places with me." She makes me switch chairs. "Now we'll see if *I* get to talk to Dick Rogerz."

Before Eugenio can put in his equally exuberant 2 cents, Jimy cuts him off. "Lyddie has mixed feelings about the dying," he says. "This is a spiritual issue for her."

Steam leaps up and pats me on the back. "I understand," she says.

But do I? I mean, is Jimy right? Is this a spiritual issue for me? For that matter, is Dick Rogerz right—has my dead father helped me die and live to die again?

My mother and father—while he was alive—were always politically committed. Mother has always had a cause to fight for, to live for. I was shocked when she became a Banjo, but maybe I shouldn't have been. Me, on the other hand, I don't know what I live for. For dying? For fame? For love? For money? Why do we live? Why do we bother going on?

Then this occurs to me: Stamen arranged for my mock interview to be on the air. He's working to make it possible for me to return, and another shot of national publicity could do it.

Steam shakes me out of my funk. "There's your runt!"

Frankly stands in the spotlight. He's wearing a new steel-gray tall suit, and a stinG cubist haircut that draws attention away from the size of his head.

"Whoo," Steam says, "a head that big oughta be on Mount Rushmore."

So haircuts can't work wonders. Nonetheless, he looks good for who and what he is. He smiles at the audience, which I've never seen him do before in any of his routines—he's a depressionist after all. Maybe he can't help smiling. He finally has all he's ever dreamed of—a huge throng of people, the largest television audience of the year. Or maybe the smile is just part of the routine.

The camera zooms in. His eyes are calm, serious. He begins, "The greatest writer of the 20th century, William Faulkner, speaks about the obligation of the artist to go to any lengths to achieve his art. He says, 'An artist has to be willing to do anything to get it right. He has to be willing to sell his grandmother to get it right. "The Ode on a Grecian Urn" is worth any number of little old ladies.'"

"What's he up to?" I say.

Frankly looks sadly into the camera. "A number of years ago, I fall in love with a woman who is an artist—a Dying Artist. Lydia Melmoth, a woman willing to face the blank, black face of death to get her art right. During this past year, I discover something new about her—" he pauses, and I'm literally holding my breath "—that she is also a terrorist."

"Oh, my God," I say. "Don't, Frankly. Please don't."

"The story begins with a man in disguise delivering a message. 'Danger everywhere,' the message claims, and little do we know how accurate it is, as the delivery man turns out to be a Banjo spy, a *dual*, which means he lives in both our world and in the subterranean world of secret organizations." Frankly pauses, stares directly into the camera. "Now I am telling you something that even the Big Boys don't know."

I can't help myself, I yell at the television. "Don't do it, Frankly!"

"His name is Ananias Long. He is a black man. He lives in Cleveland, at the corner of Skoyles Street and Flook Avenue." Suddenly, behind Frankly, a huge video screen comes to life, showing an ordinary house on an ordinary Cleveland Street, wind shaking the light from an ordinary streetlamp.

"He's going to do it," I say. "He's going to nail all of us."

Jimy is already on the floor on his knees. "I hope Ananias is watching and runs away," he says. "Otherwise, he's a dead man." Suddenly he leaps to his feet. "I've got to warn Tico."

Frankly uses everybody's name. Including Jimy's ("also known as Gonzales," he says), Blu Fen's, Tico's, Ursula's, Barbie Eastman's, Madeleine Bruce's. He's done a lot of research, so he's able to name people who had worked with Mother or Ananias or Barbie Eastman. He includes addresses, even some social security numbers. He tells 1 of the largest television audiences in history that Lydia Melmoth was fired as a Junior Rag for stupidity, that she stole a hippie van, that she made a scene at Foombah's, that she murdered Blu Fen.

"Some of you out there are probably questioning my motives," Frankly says somberly, "especially those of you who side with the Banjos—and for that matter, I'm not saying that I don't side with them—but I am providing these names and addresses in order to get at the heart of my depression, so that I can convey it to you: my deep-seated inability to commit to anything or anyone beyond my career." He pauses, choked up, eyes reddening; the camera zooms in closer. "I know it costs me the 1 person I am ever loving." He means me, of course, the person he fingered a minute ago as a murderer. "Art is worth any number of ladies," he says. "Tonight those ladies are no longer hypothetical."

"Wow," says Steam. "That little guy is incredible!"

Near the end of the routine, the video screen lights up behind Frankly once again. While he talks,

the screen shows Cops arriving at Ananais' house.
The screen divides as a 2nd location is flooded with
Cops. The screen continues to divide while Frankly
wraps up his routine. He stares earnestly into the
camera and says, "I just find out this afternoon that
Lydia Melmoth is in hiding with Jimy Schmidt in
Plittbottom, New Mexico, down at the habitable edge
of the desert."

"Oh," I say sadly. "Oh, Frankly."

"Art," Frankly goes on, "has always been a polite
form of terrorism."

We pack what little we have in a matter of minutes.
Eugenio gives us a couple of bottles of water and the
keys to his 4 wheel drive—an ancient reddish Jeep.
We're heading for Arizona. Jimy thinks we can make
it to Tucson if we travel off-road. Then we'll lose ourselves in the city. That's the nature of the underground, you lose yourself.

Steam has run over from the house to tell us about
a late news report. Barbie Eastman's body was discovered in the women's room of a bar in the Denver
dark. Bullet through the heart.

"A Big Boy hit," Jimy says. "It means they aren't
going to bother with arrests."

"Any other deaths?" I say.

"A few," Steam says, "but nobody halfway famous."

It hasn't escaped my notice that the 1 person
Frankly left out of the story was Stamen. Not a word
about his having passed Silk-Level information, or
that I got sucked into all of it in order to protect him.
Stamen is Frankly's manager, and Frankly is protecting him. There's no contradiction. He made it clear

that the only thing that's ever motivated him has been blind ambition.

Frankly took the leap and made it to the other side; his routine was so spectacular it overshadowed Qigley's record die. All of us watching at Eugenio's were in tears by the end—for different reasons, of course, but nonetheless, it was 1 hell of a show. Maybe, to achieve greatness, you have to be willing to sacrifice those about you. He also managed to put in a plug for his novel, which, no doubt, will be more of the same. Maybe greatness isn't all it's cracked up to be.

Surrounded by the black sky, the full moon shines round and white—white like the negative of a pupil and iris. Jimy and I climb into the Jeep. Steam stands beside the vehicle waving before Jimy has even started engine. We still have the gun that Mother gave me. We may need it, and we don't have the luxury of scruples. I check the glove box to make sure it's there.

"Are you sure we want to take that?" Jimy asks.

"Do we have a choice?"

He looks up at the moon for so long I stare up there, too. On another night I might think it beautiful.

"Let's go," I say.

The Jeep rides rough, and there are no doors; dust flies up in our faces. We're out of town in a matter of seconds. The only bridge over the Rio Grande within 100 miles is made of old train ties. Once across, we'll leave the road and make the Big Boys search the desert for us.

The crossing must be executed with care. The bridge is narrow and only the paths for the tires are solid—a foot to either side and you dump yourself into the river. Jimy backs up twice to be certain he has lined up the tires properly. He edges the Jeep up onto the ties.

The water below is an unreal shade of green. I know it's flowing, but it looks like it's churning. Before we're halfway across, I see, standing on the other side, Blu Fen's ghost. He's posing before a tall saguaro cactus, wearing some kind of khaki uniform, and he's smiling.

"Oh, shit," I say. I tug on Jimy's arm. "Do you see someone over there, just across the river?"

Jimy brakes. We stop halfway across and stare. "Nobody."

The ghost sticks out his thumb. I know he's going to get in whether we stop for him or not.

The Jeep crawls farther out onto the ties. I take the pistol from the glove box. Jimy, ever alert, stops again.

"What are you doing?" he asks.

"Shooting at spirits," I say.

"Oh," he says.

I fire without aiming. Blu Fen doesn't take the hint, doesn't even quit smiling. I take aim and blast out 4 more shots. The final 1 hits him, but just passes through. He seems to be laughing.

"You nail anything?" Jimy asks.

"Yes and no," I say. I toss the pistol into the river. It flies out a ways, makes a splash, and disappears.

Jimy throws the Jeep into reverse. "What are *you* doing?" I say.

"Backing up," he says. "Carefully." He brakes again to look at me. "We'll try to make Oklahoma City instead of Tucson."

"He'll follow us," I say.

"He can join the crowd."

The Jeep edges backward. The bridge creaks. Blu Fen's ghost calls something out. I turn my head to listen.

"What's he saying?" Jimy asks.

"It's hard to make out," I say, which is true, but also a lie. Jimy backs the Jeep off the bridge and begins to turn us around. The sand is soft, and he has to be careful.

Blu Fen said, "I've spoken with your father." Or maybe he said, "I love you." When a spirit talks, it isn't the sound of the words that matter, and so he could have been saying either thing.

"Wait a second." I jump out of the Jeep and run back to the bridge. I have to step up on the ties to see Blu Fen. The moon is white and high and brilliant, and he is beautiful standing there in its light. What is behind him, though, is not a saguaro; they don't grow out here. Standing behind Blu Fen is the 3-headed dog, its long necks perfectly still, its 3 sets of eyes steady and dispassionate.

I have the strongest urge to yell, "Nanny nanny boo boo." Maybe, after all, that's the relationship between the living and the dead, like that of children and adults. Or maybe I just feel like being a brat. I decide not to risk offending the dead.

Jimy has the Jeep turned around. All I really know about death is precisely what I know about the future: it can't be predicted, and the more you think you know, the less prepared you are for the surprises.

I look again at Fen and his partner, but I say nothing. I turn to walk back, but Blu Fen is there, on the bridge, standing between me and the Jeep, and already, just in turning, I've stepped into him—literally *into* him—so that the world is filtered now by his body, which is not a body but something I perceive as a body. Looking through him, I see a completely different landscape, although it is the same place. Everything is alive. A simple rock at the base of the bridge pulses with life, with internal movement, with all the hubbub of activity it takes to remain outwardly still. And there's more. Because while I look at the rock, I also see the parts of it that are not-rock, the larger shapes that surround and issue from the rock—as if this rock in the desert were a pebble tossed into a pond, and what I am seeing is both the rock and the ripples the rock has made and the arc the rock traveled when thrown, all of which are really part of the rock itself. The landscape is alive and moving, and everything moves by staying still, by not wasting energy on physical movement, so that larger movements are possible, larger movements like aging, like comprehending, like dying. Or maybe it's like looking at woman and seeing in her both the child that she was and the corpse she will become—all at once. Which permits me to see that *you* are here, too: the woman I was and will be, the ignorant and knowing, the living and dead, the past and future of me, the observer who is not me, but who is necessary for me to exist. You hear my words, words I discover by telling them to you, which permits you to imagine me, and me to imagine you. All the worlds, living and dead, are thus united.

Then I step through Blu Fen's body, and the world blinks back to its usual forms—all deceits, I understand now, all lies of perception, though I can't exactly explain how or why.

Blu Fen—gone from the bridge, wholly invisible—

speaks to me. "We are alive, and we are dead," he says, "but a few of us more so than others."

"Give me a break," I say, but I stop myself from going on and ask, "Are you a threat to me?"

"'Threat' is a Breethie word."

I say, "What did I just see?"

His voice, from inside my head, says, "The truly blind cannot imagine light, the genuinely color-blind cannot conceive of color, the authentic Breethie cannot articulate scope."

"Articulate scope?" I say.

"A scream is as much made up of the quiet before it and the quiet after it, as of the vocal gymnastics," Blu Fen says, and suddenly the desert is rocked by a scream.

Jimy jumps at the sound, hitting the horn, which sticks.

"So much for the quiet after," I say during the blare.

"You know what I mean," Blu Fen says.

The horn finally dies. Jimy sticks his head out the window. "Come on, Lyddie," he says. "It's going to rain. Listen to that thunder."

"Coming," I say.

Blu Fen says, "You'll be hearing from me. Always and not always a scream. Pleasurable sounds soothe us because they are not screams, and so they embody the scream in their power to soothe."

"For all I know, you're just a sign of gray rot," I say. "Some little neurological disorder that makes me hear undergraduate pseudo-philosophical whatnot played out in my deteriorating head."

He laughs. "The tadpole leaves the water to become a frog. Breethies leave their lives to become

The Life. But you're of The Life and still living your life. A Breethie with the gift, a walking contradiction, a cosmic paradox. You were born to be a pilgrim. I tried to tell you that while I was alive."

"You raped me."

"It was an act of love. As was your killing me." Then he says, "Your skin is alive. The air you breathe is alive. The soles of your feet have souls."

Finally he sizzles out of my head.

At the base of the bridge I pick up the rock that I'd focused on—nothing special, just a plain gray rock about the size of a candy bar. I stick it in my pocket—a vision is a vision, even if it is an incomprehensible mess.

"Made your peace?" Jimy asks when I climb back in beside him.

"No," I say. "I'm more confused than ever. How about you?"

He gives me a sweet sort of look, and I picture how his face might appear if I still had that strange perceptual filter, but all my living imagination can come up with is a valentine—a clichéd image, but still I get the picture: Jimy loves me. He really loves me.

He shifts into gear. We plow across the pliant ground until our wheels find the ruts in the road and we pick up speed. I love him, too, I realize now. I love Jimy. I've got what I thought all along I wanted—someone to love, someone who loves me. I've had it for a while without knowing it.

Thunder rolls above us, sounding this time nothing at all like a scream. We drive off into what remains of our lives, the eternal now of terror and loss and friendship and love, the long scream that is preceded by quiet and followed by death, the endless rounds of little deaths and big ones. *You* travel with me. I can feel you with me.

"I love the smell of rain in the desert," I say. I inhale deeply, breathing it all in, holding it inside as long as I can.

$1,000.00

FOR YOUR THOUGHTS

Let us know what you think. Just answer these seven questions and you could win $1,000! For completing and returning this survey, you'll be entered into a drawing to win a $1,000 prize.

OFFICIAL RULES: *No additional purchase necessary.* Complete the HarperPaperbacks questionnaire—be sure to include your name and address—and mail it, with first-class postage, to HarperPaperbacks, Survey Sweeps, 10 E. 53rd Street, New York, NY 10022. Entries must be received no later than midnight, October 4, 1995. One winner will be chosen at random from the completed readership surveys received by HarperPaperbacks. A random drawing will take place in the offices of HarperPaperbacks on or about October 16, 1995. The odds of winning are determined by the number of entries received. If you are the winner, you will be notified by certified mail how to collect the $1,000 and will be required to sign an affidavit of eligibility within 21 days of notification. A $1,000 money order will be given to the *sole winner* only—to be sent by registered mail. Payment of any taxes imposed on the prize winner will be the sole responsibility of the winner. All federal, state, and local laws apply. Void where prohibited by law. The prize is not transferable. **No photocopied entries.**

Entrants are responsible for mailing the completed readership survey to HarperPaperbacks, Survey Sweeps, at 10 E. 53rd Street, New York, NY 10022. If you wish to send a survey without entering the sweepstakes drawing, simply leave the name/address section blank. Surveys without name and address will not be entered in the sweepstakes drawing. HarperPaperbacks is not responsible for lost or misdirected mail. Photocopied submissions will be disqualified. Entrants must be at least 18 years of age and U.S. citizens. All information supplied is subject to verification. Employees, and their immediate family, of HarperCollins*Publishers* are not eligible. For winner information, send a stamped, self-addressed №10 envelope by November 10, 1995 to HarperPaperbacks, Sweeps Winners, 10 E. 53rd Street, New York, NY 10022.